Fitzgerald's Wood

David Nwokedi was born in Nigeria in 1965 to a Nigerian father and a British mother. He grew up in Newhaven and Brighton. Married with two children, he lives in Brighton and is a senior social worker. He is currently working on a second novel.

Fitzgerald's Wood

David Nwokedi

JONATHAN CAPE
LONDON

Published by Jonathan Cape 2005

2 4 6 8 10 9 7 5 3 1

Copyright © David Nwokedi 2005

David Nwokedi has asserted his right under the Copyright, Designs and Patents Act 1988 to be identified as the author of this work

'The Streets of London' by Ralph McTell © 1970 Westminster Music Limited. of Suite 2.07, Plaza 535 Kings Road, London SW10 0SZ International Copyright Secured. All Rights Reserved. Used by Permission.

First published in Great Britain in 2005 by
Jonathan Cape
Random House, 20 Vauxhall Bridge Road,
London SW1V 2SA

Random House Australia (Pty) Limited
20 Alfred Street, Milsons Point, Sydney,
New South Wales 2061, Australia

Random House New Zealand Limited
18 Poland Road, Glenfield,
Auckland 10, New Zealand

Random House South Africa (Pty) Limited
Endulini, 5A Jubilee Road, Parktown 2193, South Africa

The Random House Group Limited Reg. No. 954009
www.randomhouse.co.uk

A CIP catalogue record for this book is available from the British Library

ISBN 0-2240-7343-5

Papers used by Random House are natural, recyclable products made from wood grown in sustainable forests; the manufacturing processes conform to the environmental regulations of the country of origin

Typeset by Palimpsest Book Production Limited,
Polmont, Stirlingshire
Printed and bound in Great Britain by
Mackays of Chatham plc, Chatham, Kent

For Jill, Keita and Asher
with love always

O Life, a road to life art thou, not Life. And there is no man makes his dwelling on the road, but walks there and those who fare along the road have their dwelling in the Fatherland.

Saint Columbanus

Do not neglect to show hospitality to strangers, for by this some have entertained angels without knowing it.

Hebrews 13: 2

Contents

I

St Roderick's

It is fair to say I really came to know my father, and become more like him, on the day he was killed by a lorry.

He was a big man, my father, thick and solid. He was like an old oak bookshelf, even though he wasn't actually very old when he died; he was only thirty-six, and I was thirteen. Because my father was so big it seemed strangely right that it should be a lorry that killed him. He had been out shopping at the timberyard at the end of Drummond Street. It was a fairly typical spring day; the sun was in the sky, a slight chill was in the air and birds were singing. Spring was my father's favourite season; no one would have guessed that death too was in the air. Whenever he shopped for his wood my father always bought it from the timberyard. He was a carpenter. He would buy large amounts of wood – long planks, short planks, blocks, shelving, mouldings, whatever and would bring them home and store them in the shed at the bottom of the garden until the time was right for him to create something. The shed was made out of wood that my father had bought from the timberyard. It was also full of wood that my father had 'rescued' from skips as he passed by. 'It's worse than a murder,' he'd say, 'to throw wood into a skip, or to throw it anywhere for that matter.'

The lorry that killed my father had been delivering groceries to the store next door to the timberyard. My father never shopped at the store, he left all the food shopping to my mother. She said, 'If I left it to your father to buy the food we'd be eating boiled wood shavings for tea and toasted plywood for breakfast.'

The lorry had not been going fast at all, about thirty miles an hour or so, when it hit my father who had stepped out into the road without looking. The lorry would have been driving up Drummond Street aiming to loop back round, turning in the cul-de-sac just off the road, to pull up outside the grocery store. Most of its load, I later heard, was milk and rice. I think that would have made my father smile, his favourite pudding was rice pudding with a spoonful of plum jam in the middle; my mother often made it on a Sunday (unless it was too hot and then she would open a tin of peaches and my father would have most of the juice).

My father was part English and part Nigerian. His skin was pale brown with the occasional freckle, mainly around his nose. He had tight brown curls and misty blue eyes. His English mother, my grandmother, was part Irish, 'Only a little part,' my father had told me, 'but part enough,' and my father had inherited his blue eyes from her. I got my name from her – Fitzgerald, an Irish name meaning son of Gerald. I wasn't a son of Gerald but my great-grandfather's name was Fitzgerald and he had been a son of Gerald, an Irish Gerald, and that's where my little part of Irishness came from.

My father always wore grey clothes; loose, baggy clothes that made his body appear even bigger than it actually was, which was very big, or so it seemed to me. My father chewed tobacco, never smoked it, just chewed it, rolling it around in his mouth and leaving little specks between his front teeth. It was a strange habit, but one that was just right for my father. When he'd finished chewing he would spit out the ball of tobacco into a little stained cup he kept next to the breadbin in the kitchen. 'Where's me spittin' cup?' he'd often say when he'd chewed the life out of his baccy ball. Like most things in our house, our kitchen was small, very small and the spittin' cup was never far from my father's giant hands wherever he was in the kitchen. He simply had to move his arm a little and the cup would be in his hand. As a consequence of his baccy balls, my father always smelled of tobacco, a strong smell and one that somehow comforted me. There were always pieces of sawdust in my father's hair, on his clothes and in his pockets. My father loved wood. It was more than a passion for him; he was, my mother often said, *addicted* to wood. A wood addict. He smelled of wood too; cedar, pine, mahogany, each had it's own distinctive smell and sometimes the combined woody odours would overpower the smell of tobacco. Usually however, the smells would merge together like the confluence of two rivers.

The third thing that people noticed about my father, after his tight brown curls and misty blue eyes, were his giant hands (although perhaps some actually noticed them first). My father's hands were so big and firm that people would sometimes say that they were not hands at all but oars; huge wooden oars. Maybe, they said, he had carved them from a fine piece of wood when he was in his mother's womb. Or maybe, they said, his Maker had deliberately given him wooden oars for hands because He knew how difficult my father would find it to swim later in life (my father was never very confident in the sea). Either way people always commented on how much my father's hands resembled oars. Some would even wonder how, with such heavy hands, he managed to use them so well. But he did. He used them to shape and produce wonderous wooden creations, anything from chairs to pianos, which he would then sell across our town. On occasion he would even receive orders for some of his creations from London and as far away as Scotland. I have been blessed with large hands because of my father. 'You can get more done with large hands, son,' my father would often say. Like my father, I too am quite big, but my eyes are brown. My hair is not as tight as my father's, the curls are looser and they are a darker brown, an altogether earthier colour, like my skin, which is also darker than my father's. My father once told me that my skin was the colour of afrormosia wood whereas his, he said, was much nearer in shade to European beech.

Mrs Freemantle, who lived nearby, saw my father getting killed by the lorry. She told me later that he died with a piece of wood in his hands (three foot of 1½ x 4 inches of fine teak), and that she was sure his eyes had been shut when the lorry struck. She said he'd seemed almost to be floating in the air when the lorry crashed into him. Mrs Freemantle also said that the ambulanceman had told her that he wouldn't have suffered; he died instantly, his neck clean broken. The wood, however, had stayed intact. The police constable at the scene of the death gave the unbroken piece of wood to Mrs Freemantle who solemnly agreed to deliver it to our house.

When the police constable, a slightly built man with narrow eyes and cracked lips, came to our house, my mother answered the door. She began to cry even before he could begin to impart his grim news. My mother was like that, she had a sense when grim news was about to be imparted. Sometimes my mother would know days, even weeks, in advance if grim news was in the air. I can remember when my father was made redundant from his job at the waxworks museum – Brady's Waxworks Well (which, I was told, was the oldest surviving waxworks museum in southern England; a gaudy, surreal affair, where all of the famous dummies were set out to look as if they inhabited some strange underworld at the bottom of a well) – my mother cried for a week before my father even had an inkling that he was about to lose his job.

As the constable was delivering his grim news, Mrs Freemantle arrived wearing a floral-print dress and matching headscarf; in her hands she clutched the unbroken piece of wood my father had been holding when he was killed by the lorry. My mother invited Mrs Freemantle and the constable into the house and offered them both a cup of tea and some of the carrot cake that she had made the day before.

Whilst my mother prepared the tea, the constable continued to deliver his grim news, raising his voice slightly in order for my mother to be able to hear from the kitchen. He stood throughout, holding his long arms uncomfortably by his side. Occasionally he would fold them across his chest but as that made speaking more difficult he would quickly unfold them and let them hang loosely by his side again. I noticed that he had beautiful long fingers and perfectly manicured fingernails. I also noticed that his left thumb seemed to be double-jointed and every now and then he would click it out of place and for a few seconds it would jut out at a bewildering angle. Mrs Freemantle began to cry. My mother, who was no longer crying but now appeared to be in a state of shock (her eyes were glazed and the colour had left her cheeks), served the tea and asked me to take the unbroken piece of wood out to my father's shed. She rubbed my cheek as she spoke, gazed into my eyes and made a soft cooing sound. I held the piece of wood tightly and obediently carried it out to the shed. The shed stood forlornly at the bottom of the garden; it seemed to know that its owner would not be returning and it looked cold and empty. I couldn't bear to go in (not then) so I eased the door open, leaned my arm around and placed the unbroken piece of wood carefully up against the shed wall. I turned and hurried back to the house.

When I returned to the front room, the constable had finished delivering his grim news and was swallowing the last milky dregs of his tea, his narrow eyes darting from side to side as he drank. He spoke between mouthfuls of warm tea, licking off the milky droplets from his cracked lips before each sentence. Mrs Freemantle was clutching her cup and saucer, which were balanced on her floral-printed knees, and was wiping tears from her eyes with a balled handkerchief. Her knees trembled slightly and the odd splash of tea dampened her lap. My mother excused herself while she went upstairs to get ready to go to the hospital. I sat down and fiddled with a piece of wood shaving I had found on my seat. The shaving seemed heavier than usual and the more I fiddled with it the more I thought of my father. I felt close to tears but they didn't come.

There are two things I don't recall my father ever doing; the first is crying, the second is eating my mother's carrot cake – even though she always asked him if he wanted a piece. 'No,' he would reply, 'I don't like carrots.' On the day my father was killed by the lorry I don't remember crying and I noticed that nobody ate any of my mother's carrot cake, except me, and that was the last piece of carrot cake I ever ate.

I went with my mother and the constable to the hospital to say goodbye to my father and, as the constable nervously pointed out, to identify the body. Mrs Freemantle went home to feed her cats – 'They've been on their own long enough,' she said, standing up and placing her cup and saucer gently on the mantelpiece, the clink of the china like a child's triangle being played in a classroom. 'They'll start to wonder where I am.'

We lived in a town called Wistful, which was about a thirty-minute drive south of London. It was situated on the banks of the River Wist which meandered down from the Great Green Hills that were to the north of the town. The Great Green Hills were green, *very* green, but they were not really that great. The River Wist was an unobtrusive river that only really came to life when it reached the English Channel where it merged with the rolling waves and the thriving schools of fish.

Wistful was a small town; a place that was noted for very little, a town that often went unnoticed. My mother told me that, in days gone by, people had often passed right through Wistful on their travels north to London or south to the sea and that, on reaching the other side of town, they would be unaware that they'd actually passed through the town, such was Wistful's anonymity. Some, my mother said, would stop a passer-by and ask, 'Can you tell me the way to Wistful?' The local would point back at the grey road and stolid houses, from whence the traveller had come, and say, 'That was it. That *was* Wistful.'

To rectify the concerns that Wistful was indeed somewhat overlooked and more often than not went completely unnoticed, the local Wistful councillors agreed, at a long and heated council meeting, to erect a landmark to catch the attention of passing travellers. During the arduous debate several ideas were discussed including painting all the houses bright colours (using all the colours of the rainbow as a template) and changing the name of the town from Wistful to 'Noticeable'. Final agreement was reached, however, on an idea submitted by a councillor called Councillor Tuwey, who, my mother said, was an artistic man with large watercolour eyes and a pencil-thin moustache. He suggested that the council commission the erection of two huge wooden arcs, a set to the north of the town and a set to the south. The arcs, he said, would be a visible reminder to travellers that Wistful existed, both as they entered and as they left the town. They would, he said, look up at the arcs and think to themselves what a great town of interest Wistful must be. The arcs, Councillor Tuwey stressed, would divert the travellers' attention from the inherent dullness of the town itself.

The arcs, which were made of wood (stained Dutch elm), were erected. On each side of the northern road that entered Wistful, a thick sculpted trunk of steam-bent wood was placed approximately thirty feet in height leaning over the street. Another enormous trunk was erected on the opposite side; the two wooden trunks crossed above the middle of the road and were hammered together with thick golden nails. A replica of the arcs was erected on the southern road that led out of Wistful (or into Wistful depending on which way you were travelling). They became known as *The Wistful Arcs*. They were painted in a bronze finish and looked quite stunning. They were built by the finest craftsmen and women in the town (my own father being part of the group, fleetingly given the name the *Arc and Craft Group*). The Arcs were erected within several months. For some weeks after they went up people in the town would stop to behold their splendour and birds of all types perched on the huge trunks, chirping and singing. The arcs dominated discussion in the town for many months more.

'Have you seen *The Wistful Arcs*?' someone would ask.

'Yes,' another would reply. 'They are truly marvellous.'

'Can any other town boast such dazzling arcs?' a wife asked her husband.

'No,' her husband replied. 'We have something to be proud of here.'

Others would pat my father on his back and acknowledge his part in their construction. 'Good job,' they'd say and his smile would be broad.

To a degree the arcs worked and travellers did retain Wistful in their memories and very few wandered through without realising they were in the town. Sadly, however, the arcs, splendid as they were, failed to conceal the innate solemnity of the town itself and in fact perhaps only served to draw attention to Wistful's pensive, inner yearnings.

My mother and I waited on two hard, brown chairs in a long, grey corridor at the hospital. The lights above our heads were dim, adding an eerie, dreamlike quality to the waiting area. The hospital was one of those 'Saint' hospitals, named after a saint who had been long forgotten and was usually unheard of save by a select few. There were two Saint hospitals in Wistful; St Bernadette's, a small, rundown hospital on the outskirts of town and the hospital we waited in which was called St Roderick's, a stark, red-brick building on the corner of Passover Crescent, about a twenty-minute walk from our house.

When I had been at primary school, my class tutor, Mrs Eugena Braithwaite, a strong, tidy, Jamaican woman with dark hairs above her top lip, one of the few other black people in Wistful, had told our class that St Roderick's was named after Saint Roderick of Leicester the Patron Saint of Unsound Minds, a man who, she said, had altruistically given his life to the helping of the so-called idiots, morons and the criminally insane in the sixteenth-century asylums. Saint Roderick had ministered to these poor unfortunates in madhouses throughout the entire Midlands for most of his adult life (which, as it turned out, was not very long).

The first time Mrs Braithwaite told us about Roderick of

Leicester the Patron Saint of Unsound Minds was three days after our Easter holiday, or the Resurrection of the Blessed One's Special Time as Mrs Braithwaite called it. I was about seven or eight at the time. Mrs Braithwaite often told us stories. She said they weren't really stories but fables.

'What I'm about to tell you children is not a story, it's more of a fable,' she said, the hairs on her top lip quivering as she spoke.

'What's a fable, Mrs Braithwaite?' Barry Saddler asked from the back of the classroom as he sat, one hand supporting his sizeable chin, the other rolling pieces of his writing book into small, neat balls of paper to use as cannon balls to flick at Lucy Hermington during our next and most boring lesson of all, Science and Nature, with the dour Mr Humber.

'A fable, young Barry Saddler,' she replied, 'is more than just a story; it's legend, it's mythical and most important of all, Barry Saddler, it has a moral in it.' At that point Barry Saddler stopped rolling his cannon balls and sat up straight; we all did. The way Mrs Braithwaite spoke the words made our hearts skip a beat. You could almost hear them all skipping together in unison. What she was about to tell us was a legend, was mythical and most important of all it had a moral in it. None of us was entirely sure what a legend was, mythical was entirely outside our mental framework and as for morals, well we knew nothing at all about morals or why one should be in Mrs Braithwaite's fable. But the stern tone of her voice told us that we should pay close attention to what she was about to say.

Once, whilst we were queuing for dinner outside the main hall, we'd had a discussion about what a moral actually was. My best friend, Michael Sawyer, thought a moral was like a cherry or a currant and you usually put them in pies and poured custard over them; I thought a moral was some kind of dwarf or an elf that lived in caves in the olden days; and Clive Barrington, who thought he knew everything and actually knew very little, said he knew exactly what a moral was. Clive Barrington said that if you were moral it meant that you only lived until you were sixty-five, seventy at the most, and then you died. But if you were immoral then you could live for ever and ever and never die. Even though I found it hard to believe that Clive Barrington might actually be right, his version sounded the most plausible. I made a silent vow to be as immoral as I could for the rest of my life so that I could live for ever.

Mrs Eugena Braithwaite wasn't everybody's favourite teacher but she most certainly was mine. She was also the only black teacher in my primary school. In fact she was the only black teacher I ever had throughout my school years. And I was the only black child in my primary school, except for Jasmine Khan who was Asian and had the longest and most beautiful hair I'd ever seen. She let me touch it once, when we were standing waiting to jump into the shallow end of the swimming pool, and it was even smoother and softer than I imagined. It felt how I imagined clouds might feel. Sadly, Jasmine only stayed at our school for two years before she and her family moved up to Manchester.

I liked the colour of Mrs Eugena Braithwaite's skin; it was dark and oily and shiny like the ebony keys on the piano that she played in assembly, 'Onward Christian Soldiers', 'Lord of the Dance' and on sunny mornings, 'Morning Has Broken'. I also liked the way Mrs Eugena Braithwaite smiled at me and squeezed my cheeks between her big, soft fingers whenever she came near me, whispering to herself, 'Sweet child, sweet lickle pickney' (which I always thought was sweet little pickle). She only ever said that to me and it wasn't until I was older that I realised why. I even liked the soft row of whiskers that sat neatly above Mrs Eugena Braithwaite's top lip. Other children would laugh at her row of fine whiskers, until they got to know her that is, and then they too would begin to appreciate and respect them and watch them with awe when she spoke to us in class. Some of us even wished our own mothers would grow fine whiskers above their top lips or hoped we would one day marry someone with fine whiskers above her top lip so that we would be able to sit and watch them while she talked to us over the breakfast table. But what I liked most about Mrs Eugena Braithwaite was her smell. I once told my father about Mrs Eugena Braithwaite's smell and he said. 'Why do you like her smell, son?'

'I don't know. Maybe it's because she smells different, different from the other teachers in my school,' I said.

'In what way, son?'

'She smells warm and . . . red.'

'Homely perhaps?'

'Yes, I think so. I don't know, maybe.'

'Does it take your fears away, son? Does it make you think of a better place?' I wasn't sure quite what my father meant but I nodded all the same. 'Somewhere just out of reach? Somewhere just over the hill?'

'Yes, I think so, Dad.'

'Try to always remember that smell, son. Never let it fade from your memory. You should never forget the important smells in life, Fitzgerald.' And my father sniffed at the air and I sniffed too.

'I won't, Dad,' I said emphasising my sniffing. 'I'll try my hardest not to.'

'Today, children,' Mrs Eugena Braithwaite had continued, 'I want to tell you something about my favourite saint; Saint Roderick of Leicester the Patron Saint of Unsound Minds. Saint Roderick of Leicester was one of the greatest men ever to live on this small and wonderful island. He is a man about whom very little is said these days, but he was a man, nonetheless, whose influence affects all of our lives today. Even you my lickle children.'

We shuffled in our seats, anxious to hear more of this mystical man and anxious to hear when Mrs Braithwaite would tell us about the moral.

'Saint Roderick of Leicester the Patron Saint of Unsound Minds was a kindly soul, y'know. He gave up the whole of his life to helping the so-called idiots, morons and criminally insane in the sixteenth-century asylums.' The authority in Mrs

11

Braithwaite's voice held us spellbound even if we weren't entirely sure what all the long words meant. Mrs Braithwaite used a lot of long words – 'No word is too long to be understood,' she'd tell us, 'and you are never too young to understand any word. Just concentrate on the words you do understand and the rest will follow.'

'Saint Roderick helped those poor people in the madhouses throughout the whole of Middle England for most of his adult life,' Mrs Braithwaite continued. 'He fought for many years. The inmates were a befuddled people and he just wanted to make their lives a lickle better.'

Barry Saddler put his arm up.

'Yes, Barry,' Mrs Braithwaite said. 'What is it?'

'What's "befuddled" mean?' Barry asked.

'Confused, Barry. Befuddled means confused,' Mrs Braithwaite said. 'Now listen to the story or you'll be fuddled too.'

We chuckled and Barry muttered, 'Fuddle di de.'

'Saint Roderick carried on trying to help the befuddled people until he died when he was only thirty-three,' Mrs Braithwaite continued. 'He was killed falling from a step-ladder whilst reaching for a weighty tome on "The Martyrs of the Faith" from the top shelf of the Abbey Library . . .' Mrs Braithwaite stopped speaking, Barry Saddler's arm was up again, she seemed to know what he was going to ask. 'It's a very big book, Barry. A tome is a weighty book with so many unnecessary pages that it could only ever bring death – from tome to tomb, "*The study of many books wearies the soul.*"'

Mrs Braithwaite paused, her eyes watering slightly, Saint Roderick's plight obviously still affecting her. We waited patiently for her to continue. A sense of great expectancy descended upon us all as we sat at our desks, open-mouthed as if waiting to receive holy bread and wine.

'Saint Roderick of Leicester was a man with a mission. He was a keeper of the light, a man on the narrow path of righteousness,' she continued, her voice rising as if she was speaking through an unseen loudhailer, or preaching from a pulpit. 'Many are called, few are chosen.'

Some of us sat on our hands to stop us from fidgeting.

'Now,' Mrs Braithwaite went on, 'Saint Roderick was born plain old Roderick Tumbrel in a lickle village near Preston in the year of our Lord 1750. Does anyone know where Preston is?'

'Oop North!' Michael Sawyer shouted trying to mimic the northern accents we had heard on telly. We all chuckled.

'That's right, Michael,' Mrs Braithwaite said. 'Preston is in the north-west of England and 1750 was a very long time ago, before even your grandparents were born. History books show that baby Roderick was born into a long line of cart-makers from the local area . . .'

We sat in total silence as Mrs Braithwaite continued with her tale. She went on to tell us that Roderick refused, at the tender age of fifteen, to go into the family cart-making business. As the Tumbrels' first-born son the expectation to continue in cart making weighed heavily on the young Roderick. Far heavier than it did on his younger brother Will Tumbrel, who never felt the immediacy of the pressure, protected as it were by being the second born. However, Mrs Braithwaite said, Will did in fact go into the cart-making business with his father without any fuss or mention of any other possible choice of his own. Will was very placid by nature and, if truth be told, entirely lacking in imagination. He firmly believed he was born to make carts. Mrs Braithwaite paused, possibly for dramatic affect, and then she continued with her fable whilst we sat still in our seats.

Sadly, Will (the brother) was killed, she informed us, after only a year as a cart-maker when he was attacked by a stray bull called Destiny as he was making a regular delivery on Crackett Lane by the Juniper cattle farm. Despite Will's sudden and tragic death and his father's ongoing battle with an ultimately fatal bowel complaint, the young Roderick remained steadfast in his refusal to take over from where Destiny had cruelly struck. The young Roderick felt he had a higher calling than that of cart-making, believing that the finger of God would soon pick him out for a greater purpose. Word soon spread around the tiny village that young Roderick Tumbrel, son of the cart-maker, was being saved by God for a greater and ultimately holier purpose than that of helping his father to make carts.

For several seasons, Mrs Braithwaite said, Roderick became known as 'Roderick the Holy' and he would be seen sitting on various hilltops in a variety of positions; prostrate, cross-legged and even squatting. He was waiting for the Lord's direction. He waited for many months on local hilltops, rarely returning home, living only on bread delivered by his mother every other morning and water from a local spring (which, centuries later, was to be bottled and sold in supermarkets across the country). The young Roderick, by now only seventeen, waited for a further two years (by which time, Mrs Braithwaite said, he had lost several pounds and grown a very long beard), until he was visited by a travelling bishop who informed Roderick that he had had a vision of him living amidst a haze of purple, wearing a robe-like garment, giving bread to a confused and bawdy group of men and women. The travelling bishop continued on his way and the young Roderick continued to wait for confirmation of the travelling bishop's vision.

Confirmation came within two weeks when the young Roderick was visited by a second travelling bishop who said that God had spoken to him to confirm the vision concerning purple hazes, dresses and confused masses. God, the bishop said, had told him that young Roderick was being called to the priesthood and that his wait was over. It is said, Mrs Braithwaite informed us knowledgeably (although no one has been able to confirm this as the only witness, the second travelling bishop, died before he reached the next town, from a gangrenous infection in his toe), that on hearing the message Roderick's face was swathed in a golden glow and that a white dove hovered above his head. Whatever the truth of the matter, young Roderick picked up his sleeping mat and returned home to inform his parents of his destiny.

On returning home from the hill behind the Lucas Farm with

his sleeping mat and his now gaunt features, Roderick was met at the door by his mother, who informed him that a bowl of hot rabbit stew and warm bread awaited him in the kitchen. The smells of stewed rabbit and warm bread made saliva trickle out of his mouth. Roderick was also met by his father, a man who didn't believe in God or visions, and who was, to say the least, wholly dismayed at the thought of his only living son becoming a priest and sternly informed him that:

'You're no son of mine, Roderick Tumbrel, and I'll be buggered if you says you ain't making carts. If it's good enough for me and good enough for your buggering grandfather and his buggering father before that to be working every buggering hour under the buggering sun making buggering carts then it'll be good enough for you, Roderick Tumbrel! You bugger!'

We giggled at this point; Mrs Braithwaite often forgot she was talking to children when she really got going and would let the occasional swear word slip out. From behind me I could hear Barry Saddler mumble under his breath, 'Bugger, bugger, bugger.' In fact I heard him repeating the words, 'Bugger, bugger, bugger,' quietly to himself over and over again in different places around the school for the next few weeks as if he'd discovered some magic formula or holy mantra. I heard his voice coming from behind a tree in the lower playground. I couldn't actually see him but I'd heard the 'buggers' coming out of the tree and knew who it was. On another occasion I'd been in the toilets having a pee. Just as my jet of wee had started to splash on to the back of the urinal, I heard the 'buggers' coming out of one the cubicles behind me. He giggled between each 'bugger': 'bugger,' giggle, 'bugger,' giggle, giggle, 'bugger,' giggle and so on. I'd also heard the 'buggers' coming out from under the prefab classroom. I knew that Barry Saddler would have been lying on his back under the prefab (he often did); he liked to be on his own sometimes and usually in confined spaces. He was saying 'Bugger, bugger, bugger,' quietly in his self-imposed exile and I knew it was him.

Mrs Braithwaite had finished her fable by informing us that

Saint Roderick had indeed defied the wishes of his father and once he had had his fill of rabbit stew and warm bread bade farewell to his weeping mother and fuming non-believing father. He disappeared for several years only to resurface in Leicester as a fully ordained priest and immediately took up his ministry in the asylums and madhouses. Ironically one of the occupational skills that Saint Roderick taught the inmates was the craft of cart-making. Some of the finest carts in the country were made by the inmates taught by Saint Roderick. Mrs Braithwaite said that, according to the history books, Saint Roderick was supposed to have been very pleased that everybody in the entire country, even the very richest, were riding around on carts made by mad people. He had said, apparently, that it was positive proof that the meek shall indeed inherit the earth.

Finally Mrs Braithwaite had leaned forward in her chair, the hairs on her top lip moving a little as if a slight breeze had passed by her. She told us that we should always use our own hands to create something good; something good for others. 'The moral is,' she said, 'always use your hands for what God made them for and not for what others want you to use them for. You can bless others with your hands or you can use them to harm others. The choice is yours.' I looked across at Clive Barrington, there had been nothing in the story about living for ever. He shrugged his shoulders. Mrs Braithwaite also told us never to let our hands be idle and to use them to make something good for the world.

We sat in silence and looked at our hands. We quietly turned them over in our laps, studying them and imagining what things we could create with them. As we looked at our hands, Mrs Braithwaite sat in her chair and hummed a tune, a tune she often played in assembly – 'He's Got the Whole World in His Hands'. As she hummed, a white pigeon landed at the window. It sat on the sill for a while and cooed, its head bobbing back and forth. Then it lifted its white wings and fluttered away. Shafts of sunlight streamed into the classroom, sprinkling our heads with light. We all looked at the sunshine and squinted, so bright was the sun.

Later I looked up Saint Roderick of Leicester the Patron Saint of Unsound Minds in our history books, but I could not find him anywhere. I did find one Saint Roderick (in *The Book of Saints*) but I don't think it was him, all it said was:

RODERICK (SAINT) M. – MARCH 13
otherwise Rudericus, q v.

It said nothing about morons, purple hazes or step-ladders or carts for that matter. I also found, under the Rs: Saint Rodingus, an Irish monk, who preached in Germany and emigrated (or was called) to the Forest of Argonne; and Saint Rogation of Carthage, who is said to have 'witnessed a good confession for Christ'. But I could find nothing about Saint Roderick of Leicester the Patron Saint of Unsound Minds. I even tried to find out about Saint Roderick at Our Gracious Lady of the Morning Dew, our local Catholic church on Gravel Street. Sadly the priest, Father Ferdinand, a portly man with little hair, thick eyebrows that appeared to live a life independent of his face and a tic in his left eye, told me to bugger off before he'd give *me* something *unsound* to think of. It was sad to see the spirit of the young Roderick Tumbrel's father alive and well in Father Ferdinand. I didn't go back to Our Gracious Lady of the Morning Dew after that and whenever I saw Father Ferdinand on the street I would look away, not wanting to see his thick eyebrows and afraid he might tell me to bugger off again.

II

Bix, Cab and *Jollof* Rice

It was further twisted irony that my father's body should be taken to St Roderick's on the corner of Passover Crescent, a hospital named after a man who had given his life to disabled and mentally ill people, as my father hated (or was afraid of, I never quite knew which) disabled and mentally ill people. He called them 'nutters' and 'weirdos' and would avoid them at all costs. He would make great haste down the road, even crossing to the other side, if anybody who even vaguely looked like they might fit this category came within a few yards of him.

My mother told me that once, when I was 'still a tiny tot in shorts', a man with Down's syndrome (or a mongol as they were referred to back in those days) had tickled my chin as I stood, sucking a gobstopper, outside Cohen the Baker's on Drummond Street. At the time, my mother and father were inside chatting to Mrs Cotterill (Cotterill the Undertaker's wife) about the Yom Kippur War in the Middle East (which, my mother told me in response to my question, 'Where's the Middle East?' was slightly nearer England than the Far East). When my father realised that the man with Down's syndrome, a short man with full cheeks and a tight belt, was tickling my chin with his soft, chubby fingers, he leapt out of the shop, grabbed a narrow piece of plywood that he'd just bought from the timberyard and left resting against the wall next to where I stood, and smashed it over the man's head. My father was arrested for 'Disorderly Conduct', but was later released without charge. The man with Down's syndrome was taken to St Roderick's with mild concussion, where he was later collected by his mother who was herself in a state of severe shock and fretfulness. She, when the bewildered nurses gave him the all-clear, hurriedly took her bruised and battered son away from the foreboding gloom of St Roderick's to the warmth and comfort of their family home in Hubble Square.

It transpired, as my mother later learned from Mrs O'Reilly, the soon-to-retire dinner-lady, as she queued for chips at Gray's Fish and Chip Plaice, that the man with Down's syndrome had only been home on one of his weekend visits away from the countryside institution he, rather unhappily, lived in. A few months after the fracas the family moved their son to a quiet and friendly seaside town in Essex, taking him away from the bleak yearnings of Wistful and from the high walls and cold soup of the institution in the countryside.

The man with Down's syndrome's mother said, on leaving our little town, Mrs O'Reilly told my mother, that they planned to look after their son in their own way and as far away from nutters and weirdos with bits of wood as was possible. 'She called your husband a mad wog,' Mrs O'Reilly reported. 'She said, "A mad wog with a piece of wood is a dangerous thing."' My mother told my father when we were eating our tea in the kitchen. He'd shaken violently and smashed his mighty hands down on the table sending flakes of sawdust flying through the air. A few minutes later he got up and stormed out to his shed. For several minutes all we could hear was the sound of things being thrown and wood being smashed and my mother held my trembling hands until the shed became quiet again. My mother looked at me and whispered, 'He's not a mad wog, Fitzgerald, and don't you ever let them make you think you are either. It kills your father when they say things like that.'

On the day that the family left, I'd seen the man with Down's syndrome looking out of the back of their car as they drove off to their seaside town. He was singing to himself and starlings circled the car as it drove down North Cross Hill. When the car reached the end of the road and disappeared from sight it started to rain. I ran home. My jacket was drenched when I reached our house and I hung it over the banister in the hall to dry.

'I saw the mongol,' I had said to my mother who was in the front room watching *Crackerjack* on our small television (it was five to five).

'What was he doing?' she asked, her head not turning from the screen.

'Singing,' I replied. 'And he had birds flying over his head.' My mother said nothing else and neither did I. I sat down next to her on the orange sofa, she touched my hair and frowned, appearing surprised at how wet it was but she didn't say anything. Nothing was ever said about my father's violent outburst. We watched *Crackerjack* together in silence and I thought about the man with Down's syndrome and the starlings and I tried to figure out why my father had been called a 'mad wog' instead of just 'mad'.

Not long after the incident, my father took me to the timber-yard. When we got there he stopped outside and pulled me close to him, wrapping his mighty arm around my shoulders. He held his freckled nose up towards the sky and breathed in huge lung-fuls of air.

'Can you smell it, son?' he asked, in between breaths.

'Can I smell what, Dad?' I said twitching my nose like a rabbit, to let him know I was trying to smell whatever it was that he wanted me to smell.

'Heaven, son,' he said. 'Can you smell heaven?'

I twitched my nose again and sniffed at the air. 'No, Dad. I can only smell woody things. I don't think I can smell heaven.'

'Sniff again, son. Let the air fill your lungs.'

I breathed in again taking in so much air that one of the buttons on my bright orange shirt popped off. It fell down the drain. My father didn't notice it.

'Can you smell it now, son?' he said, his eyes fixed firmly on the timberyard. 'Can you smell heaven?'

All I could smell was the multitude of woody fragrances, but I didn't want to disappoint my father – 'Yes, Dad,' I lied, 'I can smell heaven.'

'Some people think all you can smell, when you stand here, is wood,' he said, closing his eyes, his freckled nose still held aloft. 'But it's not. It's heaven. You can smell heaven if you stand here, just outside the timberyard.

'One day, son, I want to get away from all this and be in heaven with my wood, every day and every night. I'm sure there'll be lots of trees in heaven and no darkness. And the trees won't even cast a shadow.'

'They won't, Dad?' I said, looking up at my father as he towered above me like a huge industrial building, wondering what he could mean by getting away from all this. I noticed that he had fresh sawdust in his curly hair; a few pieces fell on to me like snow falling from the branches of a winter tree.

'Do you believe in God, Dad?' I asked, hoping more snow would fall from his head.

'Yes, I believe in God, but I believe in heaven more.'

'Will you get called a "mad wog" in heaven, Dad?'

'No, son.' A flash of pain shot across my father's face, and he clenched his fist into a ball. 'Of course I won't.'

'Will there be nutters and weirdos in heaven?'

'Probably, son, but I won't hit them with pieces of wood. Not in heaven. I won't need to.' He squeezed my body closer to his. My father didn't squeeze my body close to his often; I liked it when he did. It felt good, like being wrapped in a warm blanket or soaking in a hot bath.

I breathed in, one last time, filling my lungs with the smell of wood, of heaven. As my father breathed in, his head shook and more fresh sawdust fell from his brown curls. I turned my face heavenwards and let the flakes fall on to my upturned face. It was one of the rare times I could recall my father ever having talked of heaven and the nearest he got to talking about God.

But as I stood under the falling sawdust, I silently hoped that, if there was a God, he would love my father, perhaps even more than my father loved his wood.

The hospital corridor where my mother and I waited patiently to identify my father's body was quiet and alarmingly cold. The pungent odour of disinfectant assaulted my nose. Every so often a nurse would shuffle by in her crisp, tidy blue uniform, her face flushed with the heat of caring. Very occasionally a junior doctor would hurry past in a state of wild panic, smiling inanely at my mother and me and the other waiting few. By now the police constable, having dispatched his grim news in its ghastly entirety, had departed (although not quite so literally as my father). The police constable had had a call over his radio; he'd have to go he said, avoiding my mother's eyes. A well-known and very violent criminal had escaped from a nearby prison and all available officers were required to apprehend him before he was able to do anything else violent to add to his notoriety. Before he bade my mother and me farewell, the police constable stood uncomfortably in front of us as if unsure of exactly what to say. He appeared to choose his words carefully before he said, his voice echoing slightly in the drab corridor, 'Thank you. Thank you very much . . . for the carrot cake.'

'But you didn't have any,' my mother said.

'I know,' the police constable replied nervously, his long fingers curling at the ends. 'But thanks anyway.' With his carefully chosen words still hanging in the air he was gone, having hurriedly added that a member of the hospital staff would be with us as soon as was possible and that a WPC would arrive to accompany my mother. We watched him leave, his dark blue uniform disappearing into the fading light of Passover Crescent, like a splash of paint falling into a glass of water. We then sat together silently in the greyness of St Roderick's. As I looked at my mother's pallid face I noticed the beginnings of a tear forming in the corner of her left eye. It hung there for a few seconds like a raindrop on a leaf, then it let go and rolled slowly down her cheek.

* * *

My mother, unlike my father (as she was often quick to point out to him), was not part anything. She was, she said, wholly, one hundred per cent Anglo-Saxon (which my father always said was a contradiction in terms). Rumours were rife, however, in our family (on my mother's side) that there was some Spanish blood somewhere in our ancestry, but nothing could ever be proven. My Uncle Albie, my mother's elder brother, always claimed that his passion for Hemingway's *For Whom the Bell Tolls*, which he had read aloud to me several times before I was even old enough to understand what a book was, and his passion for authentic paella were proof positive of their Spanish ancestry. My father, however, would not concede. 'Albie,' he'd say. 'You're about as Spanish as George Formby's lamp-post.'

My father told my mother that all Anglo-Saxon people were not white but grey and that she was arguably the greyest person he had ever met. 'You don't have white skin,' he said. 'It's grey.' My mother got extremely irate when my father said this and pointed out that he was hardly qualified to comment on greyness as his favoured choice in clothing was grey, which therefore made *him* an extremely grey person. My father always replied that this did not count, as the fact that he chose to wear grey was infinitely different from being *born* grey. He would add that he could stop being grey whenever he chose to which, rather confusingly, he never did. I noticed that when my father said this he never looked convinced by his own argument and his face would droop, his jowls hanging sadly like overloaded shopping bags and his eyes would momentarily lose their sparkle. Sometimes, after my mother had left the room, he'd choke a little and I'd hear him muttering under his breath until he realised I was watching him and then he'd look away, usually out of the window.

My mother was a short, stocky woman, with sharp eyes, sandy hair (usually pulled tightly back in a bun) and ample, firm breasts. I once heard my father telling her that her breasts were like snow-covered mountains only not as cold and lovelier to touch. Another time I heard him tell her that her breasts were like ripe fruits from the greengrocer's, fruits he loved to eat; or like Belgian buns from the baker's and her nipples were like the cherries on top. My mother was attractive in a quiet, almost embarrassed way, her face neither stunning nor plain but nestling somewhere in between. She was known in our neighbourhood as 'The Whistling Woman'. This was because my mother whistled when she was happy and she whistled *and* danced when she was very happy. My mother whistled along to old jazz and big-band numbers. She would whistle, and always in tune, to Bix Beiderbecke when she was happy and to Cab Calloway's 'Minnie the Moocher' or one of his other uptempo numbers like 'Corinne, Corinna' when a happy event was on the horizon – like a wedding or Christmas or even Easter. Once, my father told me over breakfast, my mother had started whistling three whole months before Christmas, but that, he said, was unusual. Usually she started whistling about three weeks before the event.

My mother was usually a happy woman, but every so often, before the arrival of some grim news, she would stop whistling, put away her Bix Beiderbecke and Cab Calloway records and begin to clean the house from top to bottom. An uneasy silence would descend upon the house and a certain sadness would linger in every nook and cranny until the grim news had passed. Then my mother would slowly start to whistle again and Bix and Cab would be allowed out and would start to play again, enjoying their release from the darkness of the cupboard. The only time I can remember my mother being caught out by the arrival of grim news was on the day my father was killed by the lorry. On that day I remember my mother whistling along to Cab Calloway's 'St. James Infirmary' (which perhaps, with the benefit of hindsight, was a sign) only hours before the police constable had delivered his grim news. Which meant she must have been quite happy. It was not until my mother saw the police constable and his narrow eyes that she realised that grim news was on its way and for my mother that was very late indeed.

Apart from music, my mother also loved anything to do with words: crossword puzzles, magazines, letters. But most of all she loved books. It was my mother who taught me to read, long before I ever went to school. Most afternoons, when I was about three or four, if my father was in his shed or out selling some of his wooden creations, my mother would pull out her tartan shopping trolley from the cupboard under the stairs and say, 'Let's go to the library, Fitzgerald.' She would leave the trolley standing in the dark hallway and then clamber up the stairs to get her books. She'd return laden with hardbacks and I would help her load the trolley. I loved to breathe in their musty aroma and sometimes the dust on the covers would make me sneeze. As I gained more confidence with my reading I would sometimes try to read out the titles as we loaded: *Wuthering Heights*; *Of Mice and Men*; *Frankenstein*; *Catch-22*. I would always get the words wrong – Worrying Heats, Frank and Stan – and my mother would smile and get me to read it again until I got it right.

'Right, we're ready,' she would say when the trolley was loaded and we'd wander off together in the direction of the library, which was at the opposite end of Drummond Street from the timberyard. I often thought, in later life, how odd it was that my parents' great passions were situated at opposite ends of the same street; my father's timberyard at one end and my mother's library at the other. They did in fact spend a great deal of their lives walking in the opposite direction from each other. As we walked, the heavy-laden shopping trolley would trundle along behind us, creaking and groaning under the weight of its heavy load. My mother would hold my hand tightly in hers; her hands were usually a little moist and warm.

'You have lovely, soft hands,' she'd say. 'Like clotted cream or shampoo.' And whenever I ate clotted cream (which was rare in our house) or whenever I washed my hair, I would look at my hands and compare the softness.

I loved it at the library; the musty smell grew stronger at each visit and the rows of books stacked above my head seemed never-ending. I loved all the different authors' names and all the varied titles. I loved the solitude of the library and the strange way people spoke in less than a whisper. I was fascinated at how the librarians, who were usually women and who always seemed to be able to frown and smile simultaneously, could understand what the whispering customers were saying. I could barely hear them let alone understand them. Even my mother would do it; she'd lean over the counter, handing the librarian her musty books and they would whisper to each other; the librarian would nod and smile and frown. I once heard an old man with a protruding jaw and a long brown coat speak in normal, audible tones. Tones that I could hear . . .

'September is not usually as cold as this,' he said to the woman behind him in the queue and he shivered a little, tightening his brown coat around him. The woman, a wretched thing with eyes like fried eggs and hair that was greasy enough to fry the eggs in, froze; her jaw dropped. She was speechless. The librarian stamped a book and fixed a steely gaze on the old man. The volume of his voice had clearly unnerved her, as it had the whole queue. The spirit of the battlefield descended upon them as one; they were under siege. The old man in the brown coat was the enemy. His voice echoed around the walls of the library like the shots from a rifle. No one was happy. The clarity of his voice had disturbed them, it had pierced their fragile eardrums. It was out of place. It was not welcome. My mother frowned too and she held her hands over my ears. Neither she nor anyone cared that it was a particularly cold September or, if they did, they did not wish to discuss it at such volume, at least not until they were at a safe distance from the library. They shunned the man and returned to the comfort of their silent queuing and inaudible whisperings. My mother grabbed my hand and, pulling me gently, guided me away from his foul influence to the quiet refuge of a reading room.

We often sat together in one of the library's reading rooms. My mother would select a big, bright hardback, full of words and pictures, and spread it out in front of me. Then she'd hold my finger and run it beneath the words, getting me to read it out in a quiet, whispered voice. She'd hold my finger and make me repeat each word over and over until I got it right. I would read the whole book like that and when we got home she would ask me what the story had been about to make sure I'd understood.

'Wherever you go in life,' she said, 'you will always need to read. It's no use having eyes as beautiful as yours or beautiful brown skin if you can't read.' And she would gaze deeply into my eyes and stroke my brown cheeks. I could always see my reflection in her sharp eyes and I liked to smile at my reflection and watch it smile back at me. Seeing myself in my mother's eyes brought me a strong sense of safety and comfort. I liked my reflection. It always seemed happy even when I wasn't feeling happy.

My mother and father rarely argued with each other, but one thing I do remember them arguing about was cooking. My father, who never shopped or cooked (except scrambled eggs that he cooked every other Sunday and claimed were good for our bowel movements, 'They bind your motions,' he told us), would complain to my mother that she did not even attempt to cook African food. Our diet, which rarely changed unless one of us had a birthday (which in our family only happened three times a year, when we would buy a Chinese takeaway and my father would drink the sweet-and-sour sauce straight out of the pot), consisted of traditionally British food. We ate a roast with all the trimmings on Sundays, bubble and squeak on Mondays, shepherd's pie or lamb casserole on Tuesdays, something from the freezer (usually fish fingers or meat pie) on Wednesdays and Thursdays, fresh fish on Fridays (my favourite was haddock, although we could usually only afford cod) and sausage and chips (my father would also have two pickled onions or a gherkin) from Gray's Fish and Chip Plaice on Saturdays.

My father told my mother that I should eat African food in order to help me to be truly aware of where I came from or at least where part of me came from. He argued that fish fingers and bubble and squeak were depriving me of my heritage. After many years of arguments over the issue of African food, my mother eventually gave in to my father's guilt-inducing pressure and learned to cook two Nigerian dishes; *moin moin* and *jollof* rice.

Whilst my father was on the one hand extremely delighted with my mother's new-found culinary skills, I think he secretly missed the arguments with her. After that they could never find anything to argue about that would cause them both to be so animated. My father in particular seemed sad that they could find nothing else about Africa to talk about. We then had *moin moin* on Wednesdays and *jollof* rice and plantain (from my father's occasional visits to London) on Thursdays. Shortly after my mother's culinary rebirth she decided she had little further use for our oversized freezer, as she always cooked fresh vegetables, so she sold the freezer to Mr Josiah, the rag-and-bone man.

I can remember the day Mr Josiah came with his hapless son, Bobby, to take our freezer away. Mr Josiah had stood in the doorway, his frame blocking out what little light there was, Bobby standing behind him like a shrunken shadow, all ears (they stuck out) and red cheeks (they seemed to be burning). It was raining outside and Mr Josiah's huge, dirty boots left big, dark stains on our hallway carpet. They clattered clumsily into the tiny kitchen to take the freezer away. As they departed, heaving and groaning with the weight of it, Bobby's eyes darted suspiciously from side to side as if he was stealing the freezer and was afraid of being caught. What with the grimy empty gap left in our tiny kitchen, the foreboding stains on the hallway carpet and the torrents of rain outside, the house felt full of gloom following their departure. It felt like a minor death in the family, akin to the loss of a hamster or a slightly bigger pet; a rabbit perhaps, but not quite a cat and certainly not a dog.

To add to the sombre atmosphere in our house on that day, my father was bedridden with a hot-water bottle and a bottle of lemon barley water. My father often retired to his bed with a hot-water bottle and some lemon barley water. My mother would never tell me why, she would simply say, 'It's one of his "dark" periods. Your father is having a "dark" period.' And he would remain in his bed, with the curtains drawn, sometimes for several days at a time. If ever I mustered the courage to look in, all I could see was the outline of my father's huge sleeping body under the covers and I could smell a combination of sweat and lemon barley water and of course the wood. I could hear the grunting of my father's breathing and my mother was right, the room always looked and felt very 'dark'. I could almost taste the darkness. I could certainly smell it.

Immediately after Mr Josiah, his wretched son and the hefty boots left our house my mother set to work with a brush and some hot, soapy water on the stains, scrubbing until her hands were red raw and the sweat sprang from her brow. Sweat often sprang from my mother's brow – even when it appeared she had no reason to be sweating; it was a physical trait that I was to inherit when I entered the murky depths of puberty.

My mother learned to cook *moin moin* and *jollof* rice from her Dominican friend, Mrs Cuthbert. They met when they worked together for a brief period at the post office on the corner of Argyle Street. Mrs Cuthbert, my mother told me when I was older, was an exceptionally tall woman with an exceptionally small bust and an exceptionally enthusiastic interest in fly-fishing (though only an interest, she'd never actually tried it). My mother said that Mrs Cuthbert had herself learned to cook *moin moin* and *jollof* rice from her Scottish friend, Fiona.

Fiona was a red-headed Glaswegian who had worked as an historian at the British Museum in London and had been married for a short time to a Nigerian engineering student whom she met while studying at the local university, a short bus-ride away in Maybank. Fiona told Mrs Cuthbert (who later told my mother) that the students at Maybank had a saying about their university, one that was always quickly circulated to all new students upon their arrival: 'You can't bank on getting married whilst you're a student at Maybank, but you may bank on getting a good shag.'

I only ever heard the tale because I once walked in on my mother telling my grandmother the story. I had asked her later (when Grandma had gone home) what a shag was. 'It's a carpet, love,' she said looking a little embarrassed. 'Students love them. They like to lie down on them a lot.'

My mother went on to tell me that it was Fiona's Nigerian engineering-student husband's auntie, Aunt Mercy, a devout Catholic, who lived in London, who had taught Fiona to cook *moin moin* and *jollof* rice in a small, dark flat above a betting shop in Peckham. Fiona had told Mrs Cuthbert that Aunt Mercy had a shock of white hair and a penchant for spraying spittle with gay abandon whenever she spoke. She had little time for gambling, a sin she rated third only to fornication and sodomy, and would often present herself at the door of the betting shop at its busiest hour and castigate the sinful throng with carefully chosen verses from her weather-beaten King James Bible. Aunt Mercy taught Fiona to cook *moin moin* and *jollof* rice over a two-week period during the long, hot summer of '76 – a time when, my mother told me, Aunt Mercy had convinced herself that she was back home in Africa again; that's how hot it was.

What we actually sat down to eat on Wednesdays and Thursdays was a hybrid version of traditional *moin moin* and *jollof* rice due to the roundabout way in which my mother had acquired her skills. At the time I dearly wished that Mr Josiah, the rag-and-bone man, would bring us back our freezer, even if it meant he might leave his dirty, big boot stains on our hallway carpet. I dearly missed my meat pies and fish fingers.

My mother let me watch her cook *jollof* rice once and she scrawled down the recipe in my wallpaper-covered exercise book for me to learn. She didn't write the recipe for *moin moin* (she said it was too complicated). At the time it was way beyond me to learn how to cook anything, let alone *jollof* rice. I was at an age when boiling water seemed to be a miracle of modern science (which I guess it is).

***My mother's* recipe for jollof rice:**

1 tablespoon cooking oil
1 onion – chopped
thyme and curry powder to taste
3 teaspoons of chilli powder
1 bay leaf
a little salt
½ pint chicken stock
4 dessert spoons of tomato puree
10oz Uncle Ben's long-grain rice – washed
   & drained
bag of mixed vegetables (optional)
tin of corned beef (optional)

Wash and drain rice, cook for twenty minutes.
Heat oil. Gently fry onions. Add stock. Add
bay leaf. Add puree. Add thyme and curry
powder. Add chilli powder. Add salt. Reduce
heat and simmer until you have a thick paste.
Add mixed vegetables and corned beef if
you want and continue to simmer until everything is hot through. Remove from heat. Mix
into cooked rice until rice is orange in colour.
Serve and eat!

III

Hyacinth

We waited slightly longer than one would reasonably be expected to wait to identify and say goodbye to a loved one. My mother sat still on the hard, brown chair, the only movement her right hand fiddling with a loose thread on the hem of her skirt. The man to our left, overweight and pale, read his *Daily Mirror* with a practised familiarity, reading and re-reading the same sections, particularly, I noticed, the horoscopes. To our right a young man with large gold hoop earrings, starched pale blue jeans and one arm in a sling used his good arm to fiddle with his shoelaces, which I noticed did not match; one was black, the other was navy blue.

The lady opposite us, ancient and seemingly almost forgotten, unwrapped and sucked noisily on a boiled sweet almost every ten minutes with uniform precision. Every time she popped a sweet in her mouth I looked up at the clock and counted the minutes that had passed: ten, twenty, thirty, forty. The sweets came from a crumpled bag. She ate the sweets in flavour co-ordination (or so it seemed), lemon first then raspberry, then orange, then blackcurrant and strawberry always last. The lime flavour remained in the crumpled, bottomless bag (either she did not like lime or more probably, I thought, she was saving her favourite flavour for the bus ride home). Every now and then I caught a glimpse of the remains of her teeth hanging like sleeping bats from the roof of her mouth, dark and mysterious, waiting to take flight. Her face was aged, decrepit, but her eyes were gentle and warm, familiar almost.

Occasionally one of the others waiting would cough or shuffle in their seat or catch my eye in that life-threatening moment of unrehearsed embarrassment; when each of us would be unwillingly drawn into each other's souls, pondering the other's fate and purpose for being here in this dark, cold corridor on this particular day. As the bent hand on the battered wall-clock struck five, I heard the sound of someone breaking wind. The old lady looked up, a slight (possibly embarrassed) flush to her cheeks. She unwrapped a raspberry sweet and gracefully popped it into her mouth, neatly slotting it in between the ochre stumps. The colour of the sweet matched a discarded headscarf which lay abandoned on the seat to her right. I caught a fleeting smell of the fart and felt a little sick.

As we waited, a nurse swept by, pushing a trolley and breaking the uncomfortable silence with her orchestrated clatter. Her buttocks, huge and comforting, swayed in time to the noise. My eyes followed her backside as she swayed rhythmically down the corridor. She passed a porter leaning against the wall by the telephone kiosk with an unlit hand-rolled cigarette in his mouth.

'Don't you smoke that in here, Charlie darling,' the swaying nurse chimed, her rhythm undisturbed by the act of speaking.

'Be more than my job's worth, Florrie,' he replied and shuffled slowly away, the cigarette hanging limply from the corner of his mouth, and out of the door marked 'Exit to Gwennarth St.'.

As the door swung slowly on its hinges, I caught the merest glimpse of the fading light outside and the sadness of the day began to creep up on me for the first time, sending a faint chill through my entire body. I looked at my mother beside me, deep in thought, and I realised that the grim news had now begun to sink into her, into the core of her very being where grim news always hurt the most. Her lips were dry, her eyes damp. The old lady sneezed, the remains of her teeth appearing to shake visibly in her mouth. Again her cheeks flushed, showing the merest hint of embarrassment. I looked away quickly and in my mind's eye I caught a glimpse of her sixty years ago and truly in love for the very first time, younger, happier with a full set of shiny white teeth (not a bat in sight). I thought of Saint Roderick of Leicester the Patron Saint of Unsound Minds, and wondered whether his altruism would have extended to old ladies with few teeth sucking boiled sweets. I looked up at her again. She smiled at me as if knowing my thoughts. I smiled too.

'My name is Hyacinth, my dear,' she said, her stumps trembling as she spoke. I felt almost compelled to lean forward with my hands cupped to catch them in case any of them were to fall out.

'My name is Fitzgerald,' I said. 'And this is my mother,' I added, turning to my mother. My mother nodded and then returned to her thoughts, picking at the skin around her nails with her fingers.

'Pleased to meet you,' Hyacinth said, and I could not help but stare at her teeth, or lack of them. 'I was named Hyacinth after a flower, you know. My mother chose it.'

'Did she?' I said. 'What kind of flower?'

'The hyacinth of course, my dear. You find them in the Mediterranean, originally that is. Thick stalks, bell-shaped flowers. They smell nice.'

'Did your mother like flowers?' I asked.

'She loved them, she adored them,' Hyacinth said, and as she leaned forward I caught another full-frontal view of her teeth. They were horrifying, like vandalised tombstones. 'And she loved men too, my dear, more than she should have, especially dusky types; Mediterraneans.'

'Did you have a father?'

'Yes, I did, my dear, of course I did. But he wasn't dusky and my mother never told my daddy how much she liked the Mediterraneans. It was her secret. My daddy was from Suffolk; he was a very pale man, almost translucent. There wasn't anything

34

dusky about my father at all, my dear. Mother said you could almost see right through him in strong sunlight. And she was right, you could.'

'Why did your mother marry him if he was translucent and not dusky?' I said trying to picture a see-through father.

'Love, my dear,' Hyacinth said. 'It's what's inside that counts is what Mother always told us. Maybe that was because she could almost see inside my father. She knew what it was that she was loving. In many ways she would have preferred to be with a man who didn't always have to sit in the shade but love moves in mysterious ways, my dear, we can't help who we fall in love with.'

'Do you have any brothers or sisters?' I asked.

'Siblings,' Hyacinth said.

'I'm sorry?' I said.

'Siblings,' Hyacinth said. 'It's one word that means "brothers and sisters". It's easier than having to say "brothers and sisters" all the time.'

'Oh,' I said. 'Well, do you have any siblings?"

'Only Gentiana.'

'Gentiana?' I said.

'Gentiana, my sister.'

'Was she named after a flower too?'

'Yes, my dear, the Gentian. *Gentiana*. Red, yellow, white or blue showy flowers, bitter-tasting roots.'

'Was she translucent?'

'Who?'

'Genitalania.'

'*Gentiana*, my dear, it's *Gentiana*. There was no "l" in it, thank heavens. I called her Genny.'

'I'm sorry, *Gentiana*, was she translucent? Was Genny translucent?'

'No, you couldn't see through Gentiana at all. None of us inherited our father's translucence,' Hyacinth said.

'She's dead now of course.'

'Who?' I said.

'Mother,' Hyacinth said. 'She died of acute exhaustion.'

'Acute exhaustion?' I said.

'Yes, my dear, very acute if there is such a thing. As acute as acute can get. She was dancing the charleston. Mother was always dancing to something or other.'

'My mother likes dancing too,' I said and my mother looked up at the mention of her name, smiled briefly then returned to her thoughts.

'The doctor said she was too old and too frail to be dancing,' Hyacinth said, 'and that she made matters worse by not drinking anything; she danced and didn't take on any fluids. My mother hated drinking, she said it got in the way of dancing and having fun. She said that the only good thing about having a bar in a ballroom was to give you something to lean on when you needed a rest from dancing.'

'How old was your mother when she died dancing to the charleston?' I asked.

'Very old,' Hyacinth said. 'Too old.' Hyacinth looked up at the flaky ceiling and there she held her gaze for a moment or two, as if trying to conjure up an image of her mother's face. I tried to picture her mother too; graceful, ageless, alive, bopping across the dance floor in that frantic twisting motion of the charleston that I had seen on the television one Sunday afternoon. I had been watching an old black and white film with my mother (my father had been asleep upstairs after complaining of a stomachache, which I really knew to mean he was having another one of his 'dark' periods), when the two stars of the film had suddenly started dancing; kicking and jerking their knees.

'That's the charleston that is,' my mother said and first I thought she meant the name of the actor and was puzzled at her incorrect use of the definite article (which we had been learning about in school). But I knew what she meant as soon as she got up and started dancing. 'Look,' she said, pulling me up from my seat to join her, 'the charleston.' She was whistling too and she whistled along to the tune as she gyrated in front of the television, her warm hands clutching mine.

I imagined Hyacinth's mother dancing on that fateful night.

Jerking across the dance floor, dozens of eyes gazing at her perfect form; desiring her, falling in love with her and perhaps a little puzzled by her constant refusal to accept their offers of a drink. I wondered what her husband (Hyacinth's father) would have thought of it all.

The door to Gwennarth Street swung open again and Charlie ambled through in no particular hurry, his hands firmly wedged into his sagging pockets, his shirt hanging untidily over his belt. As he passed by, I noticed that he had an intensely sad look on his face, as if he knew that death was in the air. He looked as if he had seen and not been able to do anything about too many of life's troubles. He was only the porter after all. What *could* he do? He wore scuffed black shoes, shoes that reminded me of the ones I used to wear when I first started at primary school. '*Tuff*' shoes they were called. Though my mother always said they should be renamed '*Scuff*' shoes as no matter how many times she scrubbed at them with the scrubbing brush she kept in the cupboard under the sink in the kitchen and no matter how much she polished them with the black polish she kept next to the scrubbing brush in the cupboard under the sink, they still remained scuffed. I also noticed that Charlie had a mass of silver hairs protruding from his aquiline nose. I made a mental note that if ever silver hairs (or any colour hairs for that matter) began protruding from my nose, I would trim them religiously every day before leaving the house in the morning and again on returning to the house every evening. I knew I wanted nothing ever to protrude from my nose.

As Charlie and his protruding silver hairs passed me he glanced in my direction, his own sorrow catching my eyes and drawing me back into my own sadness, reminding me again of my reason for being in this cold, dark, fragile place. I caught a faint waft of tobacco lingering in the air and for the ghostliest of moments I could feel the presence of my father in the room. I could see my father's misty blue eyes; his tight brown curls, his oar-like hands. I could not only smell the baccy but I could smell his wood too. For the first time that day I began to realise that my father had gone somewhere and that he was not coming back. If I had been going to cry it would have been then, but I didn't. I looked at my mother and she looked at me. I was sure she had smelled the tobacco too. My mother moved her arm gently towards me and rested her hand on mine, her pale whiteness making my own light brown skin dance with colour.

'After she died,' Hyacinth continued, recapturing my attention, diverting me from my sorrow, her teeth trembling and shaking with the vibrations of her words, 'the first thing my daddy did was got himself pissed. Oh sorry, dear, pardon my French. He got clobbered, you know, drunk. He went down to The Swan and got absolutely slobbered. He left Genny and me at home on our own, for a few hours we 'ad no mum or dad. We was orphans, that's what Genny said we was, orphans, for a few hours.'

'Did your daddy often get clobbered?'

'Not before Mother died,' Hyacinth said. 'Me and Genny never saw him drunk before our mother died. Remember Mother loved him because he was good inside, because of what she could see, and she never drank at all, not alcohol, she never touched it. She would've hated to see him drunk. He only ever drank a sherry at Christmas when she was alive and he'd dip his little finger in it so's me and Genny could taste it. Genny first, then me. Genny was the eldest, see.'

'Why did he do it?' I asked.

'Do what?' Hyacinth asked. 'Dip his finger in the sherry?'

'No,' I said. 'Get clobbered.'

'Love,' Hyacinth said and she rubbed her chest as if she was in pain as she spoke. She was rubbing her heart. 'He got drunk all the time after Mother died because he loved her too much, because he was in pain, because he missed her. He said she danced too much and drank too little. "She should have been like me," he told me and Genny, "I never dance, not ever." He would sing though, he would hold his bottle of booze like it was Mother and he would sing to it.' Hyacinth began to hum a tune as she remembered her father. The notes squeezed out from between her stumps, causing her hum to have a little buzz to it like a wasp trying to play a tuba. '"Here in My Heart"' she said.

'Al Martino,' I said and my mother looked up.

'Number one, November 1952,' she said and pulled a tiny cuticle away from her finger – then she looked back into the folds of her lap.

'He drank for the rest of his life after Mother died,' Hyacinth said, 'and we never saw him smile again, not in a real way, my dear. I don't think it was the pneumonia that really killed Daddy. The doctor said he did well to live as long as he did. No, it was his broken heart that killed him. When someone has a heart as exposed as my daddy's was there's only so much it can take. Death's a terrible thing, my dear, a terrible thing indeed, but not as terrible as love. Gentiana always told me that there's got to be better ways of dealing with death than getting clobbered. Do you know anyone that's died, my dear?' Hyacinth looked at me. I looked at Hyacinth, her aged skin, her dazzling eyes, her suicidal teeth waiting to hurl themselves in one last despairing plunge from the roof of her mouth. Something inside me told me she knew the answer to her own morbid question. Something told me that perhaps the whole story of her father's death was just that, a story, the only purpose of which was to lead up to her final question.

'Yes', I replied, 'I do . . . *my* father.'

The man with the *Daily Mirror* rustled his horoscope pages; his sallow eyes peeking over the top of his paper, his ears straining at the mention of death. His eyes darted from mine to Hyacinth's and then back to his horoscopes and their promises perhaps of good fortune, a journey to a far-off land and a tall dark stranger on the horizon. I thought perhaps that he silently hoped that the tall dark stranger was not Death himself and that the far-off land was not a journey to the other side of the grave. Not for him anyway. He appeared to concentrate his mind on the good fortune to come and closed his eyes as if trying to blot out the sights and sounds of death.

'Oh dear,' Hyacinth spoke firmly and with surprising authority, there was only the hint of surprise in her voice, 'I'm sorry to hear that, my love. When did that happen?'

'Today,' I said, my hands beginning to dampen and shake ever so slightly. 'It happened today. That's why we're here, my mother and I, to identify and say goodbye to the body. My father.'

My mother stiffened, Hyacinth moved closer to me, I felt warm. She hurriedly unwrapped a boiled sweet and popped it into her mouth, it was an orange one. She offered the bag to me. I took an orange one too. The flavour was incredibly sweet and strong; it oozed over my tongue. The *Daily Mirror* reader's eyes fell to the floor. We all gazed for two or three minutes at one of Hyacinth's discarded sweet wrappers on the grey, stained floor. I could make out the words 'lime flavour' between the creases of the clear wrapping (it struck me as strange as I was sure Hyacinth had not eaten any of the lime sweets). I could hear the battered clock ticking loudly above my head. It was getting late and the day was drawing in. I could feel my mother's warmth next to me, bringing me small comfort. I could hear Hyacinth's breathing. I'd not noticed it before; a faint rasping, phlegmy sound. Somewhere way off down the corridor I heard a baby crying; a loud, yelping sound as if in sudden pain, followed by a mother's cooing sounds. Nobody spoke. Nobody knew what to say. I somehow felt that maybe Hyacinth should speak but she didn't.

I turned around in my seat and a woman police constable stood before us. She was a small, rotund woman with pale, blotchy white skin. She had a look of strained compassion on her face. Her uniform was tight and appeared to be a size too small. I noticed her hands, which were stubby, and her nails that had been bitten to the quick.

'I'm WPC Fordham,' she said rather too quickly, the words running together, *I'mwpcfordham*. She looked from me to my mother. 'Would you come this way please . . . to identify your husband's . . . to see your husband. I'm sorry to have to meet you on such an unhappy occasion.' WPC Fordham looked at me. 'Was the deceased your father?' she asked, her eyes rolled to the top of her head as she spoke, as if she was looking for cracks on the ceiling or spiders perhaps.

'Yes,' I replied trying to follow her rolling eyes with my own.

'I'm terribly sorry,' she said, her eyes rolling again. 'Such a bloody tragedy.' My mother winced at the mild expletive.

'Thank you,' I said to WPC Fordham. 'Yes, it was.'

My mother often winced at mild expletives and she *always* winced at strong expletives, such as the words 'cunt' and 'fuck'. They were words that we were never allowed even to think of in our house. She would allow other slightly milder expletives without even so much as a frown, some swear words she even seemed to enjoy – 'the poetic or funny ones' she called them ('twat' and 'shag' being two of her favourites); but not 'cunt' and 'fuck'. She referred to them only as the 'c' word and the 'f' word and as aberrations of the English language. Words of utter horror. 'The "c" word and the "f" word are forbidden in this house,' she once said, wincing at the mere thought of them. 'Never let them darken the light in this house.' She hated the word 'bloody' too; what joy was there, she would ask, in bringing unnecessary blood into the house?

My father never used either of the words in our house. My father wouldn't even use any of the words in his shed at the bottom of the garden when he hammered a nail into his fingers instead of the piece of wood he was holding. He did tell me once that he often thought of the words, usually when he was bored or if his fingers were chilled to the bone while he waited for a bus in the middle of winter, and he would feel tempted to use them. He also said it was all right to quote them if someone else had used them, but even then only if it was absolutely necessary. But, he told me, he had stopped even thinking of them in more recent years within earshot of my mother, as she seemed to know even when he was thinking of the words and would look at him and tut. My mother would often look at my father and tut.

On one dark occasion my best friend, Michael Sawyer, despite having been warned, recited a limerick to us all with both the 'f' and 'c' word in it.

> There was an old hag from Brazil,
> Who swallowed a dynamite pill.
> Her heart retired,
> Her bum back-fired,
> And her cunt fucked off up a hill.

When he had finished and started giggling to himself my mother lifted him, one hand holding him by the trousers, the other by his jumper and carried him down the hall. She placed him heavily on the pavement and slammed the door on his shocked face. He had not been allowed to return to our house for a full month and then only with a written apology. I'd scrutinised his letter of apology before he handed it to my mother just to make sure he had not used the 'f' or 'c' words in the letter itself.

We got up and followed WPC Fordham. I looked back at Hyacinth, I felt compelled to. She gestured with her ancient hand motioning for me to go, to follow WPC Fordham. I turned and followed obediently. We walked slowly and with solemnity down the corridor, through a pale door and into a quiet, sterile, white room. A dim light bulb hung naked from the flaking, stained ceiling. A forlorn bunch of pink tulips stood withering in a stainless steel vase. A nurse sat starched and suitably sombre on a wooden chair next to a rusting trolley, its wheels jutting out at obscene, gymnastic angles. On the trolley, I could see the shape of a considerable body under a pristine, white sheet. From the slight gap in the window above the starched and sombre nurse's head I could hear the faint throb of the evening traffic weaving its way home. WPC Fordham looked at me then at my mother, a sudden panic flashing across her face.

'I'm sorry,' she said holding my mother's arm, her hands pressing in to my mother's flesh, 'Do you want him . . . your son . . . to wait outside?'

My mother moved forward, nearer to the considerable body

under the pristine sheet. She turned slightly, trailing her left arm behind her, reaching towards mine. I clasped her warm hand, its slight moistness passing warmth through my whole body.

'No,' she said, her gaze switching from my father's body to the starched and sombre nurse. 'No, I want my son to be here to say goodbye to his father.'

WPC Fordham smiled weakly. We stepped forward. The starched and sombre nurse removed the part of the sheet covering my father's head. She flicked a strand of hair from her face and looked away, at the wall just to the right of my mother. The traffic outside increased. A horn clanked, sounding a clarion call. A loaded trolley clattered by in the corridor. A pot fell further down the corridor and I could hear a faint and mumbled curse and my mother tutted again. Life continued and at the same time it appeared to stand still.

There was no mistaking my father. His brown curls appeared tighter than ever before as if hanging on to his head in their reluctance to leave this world. My mother always said that my father's hair looked exactly the colour of mahogany and under the pale light I could see what she meant. I looked closely and could see one or two specks of sawdust nestling in his hair. My father's pale brown skin, the European beech, looked dull under the tenebrous lighting. My father's eyes were shut and I could not see his misty blue eyes. I wished I could see them, I longed to see my father's bright blue eyes just one more time, but I could not. I realised I would never see them again. There was no sign of injury to my father's sizeable head and he did not look like he was asleep, as I had been told dead people are supposed to look.

'What's a dead person look like?' I'd once asked my mother whilst I was picking at the bits from the roasting tin after a Sunday lunch.

'Like someone who's asleep, only quieter,' my mother replied as she transferred the uneaten sprouts into a bowl to use for tomorrow's bubble and squeak. I hated sprouts and every week when we had sprouts I would silently wish that my mother would stop transferring the uneaten sprouts into the bowl and would transfer them into the bin instead. She never did.

In this dim twilight world my father looked more like a waxwork dummy. Like one of his own charges from his days in the surreal world of Brady's Waxworks Well. My father was now a pale imitation of the man I had known, an almost convincing likeness. I realised as I stood in the half-light that my father had gone somewhere else. That he'd gone somewhere in a hurry, unexpectedly perhaps, and had been able to leave behind only this lifeless reminder of his real self. A good likeness but nonetheless not the real McCoy, not the man who was addicted to wood, not the man who chewed tobacco, not the man who wanted me to be proud to be an African; not the man who had oars instead of hands.

My mother's hands, still moist, clenched my own hand and her warmth continued to shoot up my arm. I knew that she too realised that my father had left us and had gone somewhere else.

'Is it him? Can you identify him?' WPC Fordham's voice broke the silence. The nurse straightened some of the starchiness from her uniform, still looking at the wall.

'Is it who?' my mother replied reaching out to touch my father's tight curls.

'Your husband, is it your husband?'

'Yes,' my mother said, her fingers playing with my father's mahogany curls. 'Yes, yes . . . it *was* him'.

IV
Wood Fairies

My father's body was cremated and his ashes came home in a small wooden casket, painted red. Ernie Devlin had made the casket. My father had met Ernie Devlin when he was out buying wood from the timberyard. Ernie was a small man with thick sideburns and tobacco-stained, crooked teeth. My father once told me that he found Ernie incredibly dull company, but their shared love of wood bridged the gap and gave them endless hours of discussion. When they stopped talking about wood, they would sit together in silence, my father chewing a baccy ball, Ernie stroking his sideburns and puffing on a hand-rolled cigarette. They had nothing else to say. Ernie painted the casket red because he thought that my father supported Liverpool Football Club and that it would be a fitting gesture. What Ernie didn't know (as their conversations had never turned to anything other than wood) is that my father had no interest at all in football. Ernie, in his grief (and grief it was) had confused my father with another friend, who was not, as yet, dead.

After my mother and I identified my father's body and said goodbye to him we had returned home to our terraced house. We walked slowly and deliberately away from St Roderick's, almost as if rehearsing the funeral march. My mother walked achingly slowly, her head bowed, her arms crossed tightly beneath her breasts, her face flushed and bereft of emotion, still grappling with the shock of the day's events. I trailed behind with my head bowed and my hands wedged tightly into my pockets. I felt cold and, if truth be told, a little sick. My mind raced, a jumble of thoughts; carrot cake, Mrs Freemantle, Hyacinth, WPC Fordham, my waxwork father. It was quite dark now, car headlights twinkling in the night. When we passed the timberyard at the end of Drummond Street my mother's pace quickened to a gallop and I hurried to keep up with her, my long legs skipping through the air. My mother didn't look up at the timberyard as she passed it but it was as if its ghostly presence screamed out at her, reminding her, taunting her with the day's grim news. A faint chill ran from the top of my neck to the bottom of my feet as I quickly glanced up at the now foreboding façade. It sat dark and lonely between the grocery store and Kenny's – Keys Kut While U Wait. The smell of freshly chopped wood was in the air.

I had spent many a day sitting in Kenny's – Keys Kut While U Wait waiting for my mother to get her keys cut by Kenny the Keycutter. Kenny had fabled hands. Legend had it in our neighbourhood that Kenny the Keycutter was really a magician and only cut keys to make money. Kenny was incredibly tall, so tall in fact that he often banged his head on the top of doorframes, as if he had forgotten how tall he was. He smoked woodbines and had dry, orange hair that reminded me of cornflakes. Kenny could do things with his hands that would leave you gasping, and all while he cut you a key. He would show you a hundred different card tricks, make your watch disappear from your arm and then pull it out again from behind your ear. Other times he could make your belt disappear and your trousers would fall down and on one occasion he made three rabbits suddenly appear from my mother's shopping trolley as she was about to leave. Some of the ladies in our street would talk about Kenny the Keycutter in hushed tones, about the things they'd like him to do to them with his hands and of what they would like him to pull out of *their* shopping trolleys. My mother though never talked about Kenny the Keycutter in hushed tones, or in any other tones for that matter, but I did always wonder why my mother seemed to need so many keys cut.

'I'm just off to Kenny the Keycutter's, love,' she would shout to my father as she wheeled her tartan shopping trolley out into the street.

'Why?' my father would shout back.

'To get some keys cut.'

'Do we need any more keys cut?'

'If you want to be able to open doors we do.'

When we arrived at our house my mother stopped outside. The house seemed smaller. She looked up at the front bedroom window with its peeling beige paint, the bedroom she had shared with my father since they had married, fifteen years before he was killed by the lorry. My mother stood staring at the window, her head tilted back, her arms hanging loosely by her side, awkwardly, as if they didn't belong to the rest of her body and she had nowhere to put them. My mother began to sway a little from side to side, a gentle rocking motion, and she began to hum to herself a song I recognised from her record collection – 'Stranger in Paradise' by Eddie Calvert; a song my mother and father would often hum to each other when they looked at old wedding photographs together. I stood behind my mother as she gazed up at the bedroom window and as she gently swayed I too began to sway and very quietly, so as not to disturb her, I also began to hum softly.

Some of our neighbours began to peek out at us from behind the curtains to watch the Whistling Woman and her son humming along to Eddie Calvert. Word had already spread that the lorry had killed my father, and you could feel a tangible sadness in the whole street. Two or three of our neighbours came out to join us in our sorrow. None of them joined in the humming but two stood next to my mother, one rubbing her shoulder the other making the appropriate cooing noises that often accompany a death. I could hear another neighbour, I think it was Miss Gossett from number nine, standing behind me reciting what I later learned was the Twenty-Third Psalm, King David's great ode to trusting in God even in the shadow of death:

> *. . . though I walk through the valley of the shadow of death, I will fear no evil: for thou art with me; thy rod and thy staff, they comfort me.*
>
> *Thou preparest a table before me in the presence of mine enemies: thou anointest my head with oil; my cup runneth over.*
>
> *Surely goodness and mercy shall follow me all the days of my life, and I will dwell in the house of the Lord forever.*

I thought of my father and hoped that wherever he was that he had passed through the valley of the shadow of death safely and that (wherever it was) he was now in paradise. But I sincerely hoped he was not a *stranger* in Paradise.

When we went into the house, the neighbours having returned to their homes, my mother turned to me and took my cheeks between her thumbs and forefingers and rubbed them, it was something my mother often did, she called it chubbing. 'Can I chub your cheeks?' she'd say as she reached out to hold my cheeks. I never minded, in fact when I was feeling anxious or afraid I would often ask my mother to chub my cheeks, which she would happily do and I would always feel better. She stood chubbing my cheeks for several minutes and told me over and over how much she loved me and how much my father had loved me too. She started to whistle too, a pitch-perfect rendition of Eddie Calvert's song. When she had stopped her chubbing and whistling, my mother asked me to go get the unbroken piece of wood my father had been carrying when the lorry hit him.

I shuffled out through the kitchen to the shed at the bottom of the garden while my mother made us a pot of tea. It was slightly damp now outside and a chill was in the air. Sparrows chirped as I walked up the garden path and snails slid slowly in the wet grass. My father's shed looked forlorn, lonely and vacant.

I eased the door open, my father never locked it. 'Who'd want to steal my bits and bobs?' he'd say. 'And if they did, good luck to 'em, there's plenty more where they've come from.'

I loved my father's shed. The first day I can really remember thinking about being African was outside my father's shed. It was the same day I passed my ten-yard swimming certificate (in truth I only actually managed nine yards but Mrs Craven, the swimming instructor, let me off the last yard and said I could make it up when I went for my twenty-five-yard test). I was seven at the time.

My father had always told me that I was part African but he never actually told me *which* part was African. When I was very young I would be confused by his references to only part of me being African. I remember sitting on a stool outside my father's shed, my hair still damp from the semi-victorious swim, every now and then my left ear popping as I hadn't dried inside properly. My father had made the stool during a particularly creative period shortly after he'd had an ingrown toenail removed at St Roderick's. At the time he'd also made two other stools and a rocking horse for Clyde, the boy at number twelve who was dying of leukaemia. My mother told me that Clyde had rocked it every day for three months until he had died. Then, after his death, his mother had put the horse outside her door. For two weeks it remained outside the door and everyone in our street placed their own floral tributes on it. The tributes became so numerous that it was soon impossible to see the rocking horse and Clyde's grieving mother had difficulty getting in and out of her front door. The fragrance from the flowers grew stronger and more alluring by the day, however, and passers-by would stop outside the house, holding their noses in the air to breathe in the heady aroma. It was an aroma that masked the smell of death. Eventually the bin men came and took the flowers and the horse away. They were thrown on the council skip, as neither Clyde's mother nor my father could bear to have the horse back in either of their houses. It was the only one of my father's finished creations that he had knowingly allowed to be thrown away.

My father also made a coffee table for the front room (which we never used as our front room was too small and we all thought it got in the way) and a pair of clogs for Hannah, my school friend, whose family was moving to go and live in the Netherlands.

'Where's the Netherlands, Dad?' I asked my father as he rolled a baccy ball and put it into his mouth.

'In the back of beyond, somewhere in the nether regions,' my father answered. The word 'nether' seeming to amuse him so much that he almost choked on his baccy ball. He coughed so violently I had to rush inside to get him a glass of water.

'What's wrong?' my mother asked, looking up from the kitchen table where she was completing a crossword.

'The nether regions are making Dad cough,' I said running back out with my full glass of water.

'Oh,' my mother said and went back to finishing her crossword.

My father would never allow me into his shed at the bottom of the garden. He said I couldn't come in in case the wood fairies got me. He would always make me sit on the stool just outside the door, which was propped open with his bruised and battered edition of *The Official Rules of Sports and Games*, a hefty volume which I never actually saw my father read or for that matter show even the remotest interest in. I was allowed to peek into the shed and I would watch as my father chiselled, sawed and planed, but I was never allowed in. Neither was my mother. He said I would be safer on the stool as wood fairies only ever came out at night and only then if all the children in the neighbourhood were asleep.

As my father sawed into a particularly stubborn piece of wood, he told me that I was African and that I should be proud of it. I was only part African, he told me, but added that there was no reason why I shouldn't be as proud to be African as someone who was wholly African. My father stopped his sawing and came over to me, his great frame towering over me like the Blackpool Tower that I had seen on a postcard that my Uncle Albie had sent us the summer before.

'Don't you ever forget you're African, son,' he said placing his huge hands on my shoulders and squeezing them, his blue eyes penetrating deep within me. As he spoke I could smell the warm aroma of baccy balls on his breath. Specks of sawdust floated through the air between us, making my nose twitch. The words *'You're African'* held me spellbound. At the time I didn't know what African was, or how I could have part of it in me. I only knew that my father had said I should be proud of it and so I would but it would have been helpful if my father had gone on to explain why. He didn't. Instead he released my shoulders and went back to his stubborn piece of wood.

Every night, before I went to sleep I would usually say the Lord's Prayer through once and then touch wood seven times (usually the wooden frame around the mirror above my bed). My mother taught me to say the Lord's Prayer (even though she didn't see herself as religious) and to touch wood (she was very superstitious) for luck and to keep in Jesus's good books.

'I don't really believe in prayer, or in Jesus, Fitzgerald,' she once told me, 'but it's better to err on the side of caution. If Jesus is the Son of God, I wouldn't want you to be in his bad books.' She also told me that saying the Lord's Prayer would help to keep the bad spirits away (and I often hoped it would keep the wood fairies away too). Once, after a particularly exciting day spent standing on the breakwater with my Grandma at Marvel's Point near her house on the coast, I was so tired I fell asleep before I got to seven and only actually touched wood six times. I woke in the morning from an undisturbed sleep and remembered my nocturnal omission. There was no sign of any bad spirits or wood fairies having visited me during the night and the house seemed perfectly normal. I could hear Bix Beiderbecke's 'Clarinet Marmalade' playing downstairs, which meant my mother was happy, so all must be well. I didn't tell my mother of my previous night's somnolent error but made sure that the next night I touched wood eight times (an extra one) just in case.

On the night that my father told me I was African, after I had said the Lord's Prayer and touched wood, I stood looking at myself in the mirror. I gazed at every part of my reflection, every nook and cranny of my brown skin, and tried to work out which part of me was African and how I could be proud of it. I wondered whether Africa was a place I could go and see; perhaps my father would take me there one weekend instead of visiting my Grandma's. I wondered if being African was like being a good swimmer and that if I tried hard I could get better at it and make my father even more proud of me, or at least the part of me that was African. From that day on my father told me very little else about Africa or of being African, except that I should be proud of it.

After I finished looking in the mirror, I folded my school uniform and put away my grey socks at the back of my top drawer. My father once said – 'Always put your socks at the back of your drawer son, then if they're smelly there's less chance your mother will notice them.' I made up my mind that the next day I would ask Mrs Sharratt, the dinner-lady, why I should be proud to be African. Mrs Sharratt knew everything, she'd once shown me how to make the fastest paper aeroplane in my class and how to store my marbles without them chipping. I was disappointed with her answer, all she said was that I was British, that I was born here and that I didn't need to worry my little head with finding out about Africa. I didn't know why her answer disappointed me at the time but it did. Somewhere deep inside I knew it just didn't feel right.

I eased the door of my father's shed open and peered inside. The smell of my father's baccy balls hit me first, followed by the overwhelming smell of wood. I almost fell backwards, such was the force of the smell. The two odours converged and seemed all the more powerful in my father's absence. I stepped inside, tripping on the battered and bruised copy of *The Official Rules of Sports and Games*. There was no sign of wood fairies. I looked even though I no longer believed in them. I remembered how my father used to say to me – 'Fitzgerald, live your life and be free. Enjoy being young. Enjoy things when the days seem long.

Create whatever you can create and never let your hands be idle. Most of all, son, don't wait for death. Let death wait for you. Always be one step ahead of the darkness.'

It puzzled me in the days following my father's death why death had not waited for him and had come to him so early. It seemed as if somehow he must have known that death was on its way. As I sifted through his wooden creations I realised he had created an awful lot and that maybe he had created just about all he was able to create. Nothing in his shed was left behind unfinished. Even the last pieces of wood he was working on, a pair of bookends for Mrs Justice from Tapestry Street, had been finished on the night before he was killed by the lorry. Later that week I stoically delivered the finished bookends to Mrs Justice on behalf of my father.

'Thank you,' she said, reaching out to grasp the bookends; she was an angular woman, all corners and edges (it was no surprise that she would want a set of bookends to keep her many books neatly ordered); she smelled of detergent. 'I'm so sorry to hear of your sad news, young man. Of the death, I mean. Please tell your mother how sorry I am.'

'I will,' I said, gazing at a crack in the pavement as I spoke. Mrs Justice took the finished bookends into her house and closed the door behind her. I stood for a few minutes longer than was comfortable outside the house, scraping my shoe backwards and forwards over the crack in the pavement. Mrs Justice had not offered me anything for the finished bookends and I had not liked to ask.

'Did she offer you anything for the bookends?' my mother asked as she loosened the lid on a jar of plum jam with a bent teaspoon when I entered the kitchen on my return home (virtually all my mother had been able to make us to eat since my father had died was plum-jam sandwiches).

'No,' I said. 'And I didn't like to ask'.

'Oh,' my mother said and she eased the lid open and dipped her finger into the jar, pulled it out again and licked off a smattering of the jam.

* * *

The only mystery surrounding my father's death was the piece of unbroken wood he had been carrying when he was hit by the lorry. My father rarely bought wood that he did not plan to use, even though my mother said his wood buying was an addiction – 'You're a wood addict,' she'd say and she would tell him that he needed a daily fix. My father would reply that it was better to be a wood addict than to listen to the music of dead jazz players. 'They're not all dead,' my mother would shout back and storm out of the room to put Bix or Cab on to the turntable.

My father once told me in secretive tones that the real reason he bought so much wood was to keep the wood fairies happy. He told me that the wood fairies understood why he needed so much wood even if my mother didn't. My father said that everything the wood fairies ever used was made of wood – their cars, their houses, their clothes – and that they even dined out on the best wood shavings money could buy. Then he winked at me and ruffled a huge oar through my tight curls.

The unbroken piece of wood was a mystery. Nobody in our street had commissioned anything from my father in the days before he was killed and nobody in the wider community came forward to ask if their commissioned piece was now finished. A man in an unironed black suit had called at our house in the twilight hours a few days after my father's death. He stood at our front door in front of my mother, short, crumpled and bland. The red glow of the sinking sun behind him illuminated one side of his featureless face.

'Was the wood for you?' my mother asked, looking him up and down. 'Did you come to collect your finished piece?'

The creased man looked perplexed and shook his head. 'No,' he said, 'I don't know anything about wood. I've come to read the gas meter.' My mother let him in. He ambled past me, clutching a clip board and a strange gadget. As I sat on the stairs at the end of the hall, I caught a full-frontal view of his face and was shocked as to just how dull it was. He glanced up at me and then quickly looked away, as if he knew what I was thinking. The beautiful rusty glow of the sun disappeared as my mother shut the door behind him.

My mother later said that my father must have bought the fatal piece because of his addiction. He must have gone down Drummond Street without any intention of buying wood. Maybe, she said, he had gone out for a 'wander and ponder', as he often called it, when he was bored or just wanted to clear his head. My mother surmised, in her grief, that it was proof positive that my father had indeed been addicted to wood. In all probability he had, she said, managed to 'wander and ponder' right past Butler's the Chemist, right past Cohen's the Baker's, past the post office and on past the grocery store next door to the timberyard. My mother said that during all that 'wandering and pondering' my father had not felt the slightest urge to buy anything, not a packet of Strepsils (even though he knew she had a sore throat), not a nutty cob, nor a packet of envelopes, not even a pint of milk. When he reached the timberyard, however, temptation must have overtaken him. My mother said that his addiction would have been unable to resist the smell of the wood; the seductive resin oozing out. He would, she said, have been able to taste the wood on his tongue, as enticing to him as a strawberry-flavoured ice cream or a rich chocolate cake to others. Even though, she said, he had nothing left that he had to make as he had created his last creation (Mrs Justice's bookends). No, my mother said, buying the fatal piece of wood was the final act of an addicted man. His final fix. How ironic that the wood had survived but he hadn't. If my father had been able to control his addiction and had 'wandered and pondered' right on past the timberyard, chewing his baccy ball and turning his freckled nose up at the woody fragrance, he would still be alive today. She said, he had been wooed by the wood, she was sure of it. Sure that that was the reason he had fallen under the wheels of the lorry. How then could she have known any different?

'Temptation is a terrible thing, Fitzgerald,' my mother said, 'But not as terrible as giving in to temptation. It is better to never let yourself be tempted at all, for then you will never know how terrible it is to give in to temptation when you are tempted. It's more terrible to have given in to temptation than to have let yourself be tempted in the first place. Don't ever let yourself be tempted into giving in to temptation.'

I made a mental note that temptation was something to be terribly confused about.

A few weeks after my father's ashes came home in the red casket, my mother invited several people around to our house. They came to discuss the fate of my father's ashes – where should be his final resting place. My mother invited all of her 'nearest and dearest' as she called them (our relatives and family friends). The only relatives who actually did come were my mother's brother and sister, Uncle Albie and Auntie Nerys. My mother's mother, my grandma, couldn't come due to a particularly bad dose of sciatica – 'Put his ashes on the mantelpiece,' she had told my mother when asked where she felt his ashes ought to go. 'Or in the cupboard under the stairs. At least he'll be warm there and he was always rummaging around in there anyway.' My mother's father, my grandfather, had disappeared at sea shortly after the Second World War had started (he wasn't fighting, he was too old for that, he had just disappeared when he was out fishing for cod), so he wouldn't be coming. I'd only ever seen his pictures (long face, full beard and seafaring eyes) and I'd been told that he and the whole crew and the small fishing boat they were on had disappeared too. None of them was ever found. Obviously I'd never known my grandfather.

All of our other distant relatives (on my mother's side) either failed to reply to my mother's letter or wrote giving their apologies and expressing their deepest sorrow. We were never very close to our distant relatives and they never contacted us, unless one of them needed something wooden to be made. They seemed to prefer being distant, both biologically and geographically. Many of them had not even made it to my father's funeral.

My father's English mother, Granna, as I called her, had died several years previously (they had not been close and I could only remember having met her a few times). I remember her as a tall woman with blue eyes, dirty white hair that resembled a small unkempt flock of sheep, heavy legs and feet that appeared to belong to someone else. My father was, like me, an only child and had never had any contact with his African relatives. In fact, Granna told him that she wasn't exactly sure who his African father was. He could have been one of two men. Both, she had said, were one-night stands (although in truth, she said, one had stayed for two nights) and both, she said, were Nigerian. This is what my Granna told my father about his father; I know because I heard her tell him when we visited her once.

'I don't know which one was your father,' she said. I was in the kitchen eating a boiled egg; they were in her living room. 'It was during the war. They were soldiers in the 81st West African Division on their way back home from fighting with the Tommies in Burma. They stopped off in barracks near Wistful for a while. Apparently a group of the 81st had got on the wrong boat and instead of going to India and back home they came to England. Silly buggers. I slept with them both in the same week; they were black; they were from Nigeria. That's all I know. I'd never made love to a black man before and two came along in one week. What was I supposed to do? I wasn't a tart you understand, but I wanted to know what it was like to make love to a coloured man. I wanted to kiss their dark skin.'

'Did you love them?' my father asked. 'Did you love either of them?'

'No,' Granna said and I could hear her shuffling her someone else's feet as if they were trying to find their real owner. 'It was sex and only sex, with both of them. I don't remember anything about them now except that one said he was a very good cook and wanted to cook me breakfast. I didn't let him. And the other wore green socks even when we were in bed together. I didn't like his smell, he smelled too overbearing; of musty uniforms and boot polish and army things. There's nothing else you need to know.'

'Were they friends?' my father asked. 'Did they know each other well?'

'Yes, I believe they did,' Granna said. 'But neither one knew I had slept with the other.'

And that was how it was. My father had no real knowledge of exactly who he was except that he was part Nigerian (or 'African' as he preferred to call it) and that his father had fought in Burma and may have been a good cook or have liked to wear green socks in bed.

'None of them told me anything about Africa and I didn't like to ask,' I heard Granna telling my father. 'All we did was have sex; neither of them were great talkers – at least they were more interested in the sex than talking if I remember rightly. There's nothing else to tell you about your father, nothing at all. The past is not important.' And when Granna said that I noticed, through the gap in the kitchen door, that my father's face quivered as if he was in pain and a darkness fell upon him. It was the same darkness that choked his bedroom during his frequent 'dark' periods and a darkness that would follow him all the days of his life, lurking behind him like an unwanted shadow.

V

Mrs Freemantle

On the day we met to decide what to do with my father's ashes I had a cold. I couldn't smell a thing my nose was so blocked.

My mother, still existing in a cloud of grief, baked a malt loaf for tea. I loved the smell of my mother's malt loaves. I could imagine the smell wafting through from our tiny kitchen into our tiny front room (even though I couldn't actually smell it). I sat on the wonky stool that my father called the 'Wonky Stool of New Cross' (New Cross being the area where he had bought it on one of his visits to London).

'Did you make it, Dad?' I asked him when he brought it home and placed it in front of the bay window, standing back to admire it with his mighty hands on his hips. The 'wonk' was plain for all to see.

'No, son,' he said ruffling his mighty hand through his curls, sawdust falling from his head like blossom from a tree, 'Do you think I would make anything as wonky as that? No son, that's the Wonky Stool of New Cross, a famous artefact.'

'What's an artefact?'

'Something made or given shape by man, such as a tool or a *wonk* of art or an object of archaeological interest.' My father often spoke as if he was quoting directly from a dictionary and in this case he was, almost. Sometimes he'd change a letter or word to shift the meaning. My father read the dictionary for pleasure; he said he preferred it to novels as they were too predictable. The dictionary, he said, was always full of surprises.

I dearly wished I could smell my mother's malt loaf, but I couldn't. When it came to eating my mother's malt loaf later on I wouldn't be able to taste it either. Uncle Albie said it tasted great.

'Great malt loaf, Paulie,' he said, licking butter from his lips. 'Tastes great.'

My father's ashes remained in Ernie Devlin's red casket on the mantelpiece above the fireplace, next to a faded black and white photograph of him when he was a small boy. He looked just like me (only bigger) when I was that age. My father was smiling in the picture, the corners of his mouth turning up only slightly but his smile was huge all the same, and his blue eyes were grey and appeared to be gazing at someone to the left of the photographer. His brown curls were grey too and the picture failed to catch their dancing vibrancy. The tops of his curls were not in the picture; even then my father was too big for all of him to fit into photographs. My father held his hands gently in his lap and appeared to be clutching something – a toy car perhaps, or a soldier. Even at that tender age, it was startlingly obvious that my fathers hands were more than hands and looked more like oars. They swamped his lap.

My mother always kept a box of household matches on the mantelpiece above the fireplace even though neither she nor my father ever lit the fire. It was a waste of time messing around with all that coal and soot and stuff, they would always say. If it was really cold my father would go to the cupboard under the stairs and pull out the rusty two-bar heater and plug it into the socket by the television. The heater took the minimalist approach to heating and would heat the air and carpet immediately in front of its two bars and no more. The rest of the room, and usually the part I was sitting in, would remain icily cold. My mother's chair was also usually too far away from the heater to feel any of its paltry benefits. My father, however, would always sit just next to the two burning bars, the orange glow illuminating his face. From a certain angle it would appear as if my father was sitting in the heater itself. Sometimes he would take off his socks and wiggle his huge toes (toes that looked like a group of brown field mice but without the whiskers) in front of the two bars. Sometimes, if my father had had a particularly active day, his huge toes would smell musty, a little like my school sandwich box if I hadn't put it in the washing-up bowl for my mother to wash up for a few days. Sometimes I quite liked the smell of my father's huge musty toes and sometimes, quite inexplicably, I didn't.

I sat alone in our tiny front room on the Wonky Stool of New Cross for what seemed like an age. In reality it was probably only about twenty minutes. Whilst we waited for the rest of the nearest and dearest to arrive to decide the fate of my father's ashes, my mother busied herself upstairs. I could hear the thumping of things being moved, being dragged across the floor and the creaking of doors being opened and shut. My mother appeared to be opening and shutting a lot of doors. There was an almost deliberate rhythm to her opening and shutting. I couldn't think why my mother needed to open and close so many doors (there weren't that many doors upstairs anyway), but perhaps she was only opening and closing two doors or the same one over and over again. I dearly wished my mother would dance or even whistle, I wished she would put on one of her big-band numbers and pull me up from the wonky stool and get me to jive. But somewhere deep inside I knew that my mother would not be dancing or even whistling for a very long time. I tried to whistle myself as the opening and shutting noises continued upstairs but all that came out was a kind of strangulated whimper like a sad dog or the end of a kettle boiling when it's turned off.

Apart from me, the Wonky Stool of New Cross, the red casket, the standard-lamp, the mantelpiece, the TV, the record-player and the telephone, the front room was empty and felt even smaller than it usually did. My mother had pulled out three other stools from my father's shed to add to the bright orange sofa and the two threadbare chairs for the nearest and dearest to sit on.

'If Mr Plucker comes . . .' my mother said to me as she picked pieces of fluff from the chairs with a roll of Sellotape, 'don't let him sit on the Wonky Stool or any of the threadbare chairs, will you.' Mr Plucker was our next-door neighbour, a man with little flesh and melancholic eyes. He was a very close friend of our family.

'Why not?' I asked

'Because with his poor hips he leans enough to one side already and you know how threadbare his clothes are, we'd lose sight of him in our chairs.'

My mother made one of her huge pots of tea and laid it on the small sideboard where she kept her best crockery, *'China dishes, earthen vessels etc., collectively,'* as my father once recited when someone had said the word on a TV quiz show. Next to the huge teapot (which was blue and white) my mother placed her best cups and saucers that were a bright red and almost matched the red of the casket that held my father's ashes. From a certain angle, if I tilted my head, the whole collection looked like the French national flag, the tricolour. If I tilted my head the other way and shook it just a little, then they looked like a psychedelic Union Jack.

The piece of unbroken wood that I had brought in from my father's shed was now resting comfortably against the bay of the window. Since my father had been killed I had taken to keeping the unbroken piece of wood in my bedroom, usually lying it on the floor beside my bed. When I woke up, in the morning, it would be the first thing I'd see. Sometimes my mother would come up to my room and gently knock on the door.

'What is it, Mum?' I'd ask, knowing what she had come to see.

'Can I come in, Fitzgerald?' she'd reply, easing the door open. 'To see the piece of wood?' Then she would quietly slip into the room and stand and stare at the unbroken piece of wood with a misty look in her eyes and her arms folded across her chest, making a strange blubbing sound from the back of her throat like a drain being cleared with a plunger.

For a few days after my father's death I rubbed the last remaining bits of his baccy balls into the wood so that I could remember his smell and think of him chewing the balls. The baccy soon ran out, however, and shortly after that the smell began to disappear. It wasn't long before it had gone completely and I struggled in vain to recall my father's smell.

'Should we bring the piece of wood to the meeting?' I asked my mother over a sullen and overcast breakfast that morning.

'Will it get in the way?' my mother replied, prising a stubborn piece of bacon rind from between her back molars (we were eating more than plum-jam sandwiches by then).

'I don't think so, it's not very big.'

'Put it over by the bay window then. But don't make a fuss over it. You know how upset Mrs Freemantle gets when she sees it.'

The first thing Mrs Freemantle did when she arrived for the meeting was to sit down heavily in a threadbare chair. To Mrs Freemantle's left, under the bay window, was the unbroken piece of wood. Mrs Freemantle burst into tears upon sight of it. My mother tenderly comforted her and hurried her into the kitchen to dab at her tears with a piece of kitchen paper.

'It's only a piece of wood,' I could hear my mother say but I knew that she too felt the same.

Mrs Freemantle lived on her own in a house full of cats (Tommy, Jasper, Colin, Suzie, Winnie and Noah), on Albion Hill. She had not always lived on her own in a house full of cats even though it appeared she always had. Mrs Freemantle, or Agnes Hermione Freemantle to give her her full name, had been married for thirty-three years to Henry. Henry Freemantle had died from a heart attack whilst watching his favourite film – *Oh What a Lovely War!* – on a summer's day in the early seventies (several years before my father died).

Mrs Freemantle would often come to our house for tea or just to chat to my mother. They got on well together, despite their vast age gap (Mrs Freemantle was in her sixties). She shared a love of crossword puzzles with my mother. They would do them together, sitting in silence in the front room, each doing her own. When they got bored they would swap the crosswords around, mumbling sentences to each other like, 'What's another name for vespers; eight letters, two across, second letter "v"?' Or, 'Four down; a state of physical or mental tiredness; nine letters, begins with "l" ends in "e"?' They rarely did crosswords when my father was about because they knew he would shout out the answers from his lexical head.

When she wasn't engrossed in a crossword, Mrs Freemantle loved to tell me about her and Henry's life together. She would tell me about how much she had liked to lie in bed for hours in the morning next to him – 'Away with the fairies,' is how Henry would describe her she would tell me. 'You sleep so soundly Aggie,' he would say, 'you must have been away with the fairies.'

Mrs Freemantle would tell me about her favourite day of the week with Henry which was Sunday, a day when she never stayed in bed. On Sundays they would go to church together. They would dress in their finest clothes. Henry in a plain navy suit and a crisp Panama hat, Mrs Freemantle in a bright floral-print dress and large gold, dangling earrings. Sometimes, Mrs Freemantle said, they would hold hands. Sometimes they would walk just close enough for their hands to touch as they walked, just to reassure themselves that the other was close by. Henry was an occasional eccentric and usually wore a bright, shiny pair of black and white spats (polished and buffed) and on the short walk to church he would smoke a long, brown Cuban cigar, holding his head back with pride to savour the smoke. He always made sure he had extinguished the cigar before he and Mrs Freemantle rounded the corner into Gravel Street where their church stood between Mrs Poetaster's (the retired midwife's house) and a run-down but much used bingo hall.

Mrs Freemantle would tell me that she and Henry always attended the late mass at their church; the Catholic church, Our

Gracious Lady of the Morning Dew. They always sat in the same seats at Our Gracious Lady; to the rear, three rows from the back, Mrs Freemantle on the inside and Henry on the aisle seat. 'I can stretch my legs from here, Aggie,' Henry would say. Mrs Freemantle would smile at him, a familiar smile, and squeeze past him into her seat. Sometimes, she told me in hushed tones, if no one was looking, Henry would pat her bottom gently with the palm of his hand, once, maybe twice. Mrs Freemantle would then take her seat, smoothing out the creases in her dress, sitting to the right of her husband and to the left of Hermann Zucker. Hermann Zucker was a piano tuner from Candle Square. Many in our neighbourhood said that Hermann Zucker was an Austrian Jew who had settled in England shortly after the war upon discovering that his entire family had been murdered in the Nazi death camps. Mrs Freemantle told me that she knew little about the true horrors of Hermann Zucker's past, or for that matter of his present, and why he now attended a Catholic church. All she did know, she said, was that Hermann Zucker always sat to her right every Sunday, said very little and smelled ever so slightly, almost mysteriously she thought, of rosemary.

Mrs Freemantle said that she would remain quite still throughout the Sunday-morning services, her head cocked to one side, except during the hymns when she would stand, rub the creases out of her dress and sing with a monotone familiarity. 'I could sing those hymns in my sleep,' she told me.

During the sermon, Mrs Freemantle said, she would rest her hand in Henry's lap and gently fiddle with his wedding band. Sometimes she would let her gaze wander up to the glorious technicolor of the stained-glass windows at either side of the pulpit. She smiled as she told me that often her eyes would fix on the icy gaze of the Blessed Virgin as she shone out over the faithful throng.

'If I gazed too long, at her blessed face, Fitzgerald,' she said, 'my bladder would go weak; it would tingle. Sometimes she made me feel like wetting myself. It was her eyes. The Blessed Virgin's eyes.'

Mrs Freemantle said she would then squeeze Henry's hand and he would squeeze hers back; she'd turn her head slightly toward him, gaining comfort from his presence. If the day was grey, and the stained-glass windows lost their colour, then Mrs Freemantle would carefully watch Father Ferdinand, the priest with the thick eyebrows, as he spoke with a firm authority. She liked to listen to his peculiar array of words; words of *damnation*, of *persecution*, of *blasphemy*, of *Heaven*, of *Hell*, of *salvation*, of *grace* and of *penance*. Words, she told me, that she only ever heard within the austere confines of Our Gracious Lady of the Morning Dew. At the time I had little idea of what the words meant, but I would nod in agreement. Sometimes, she told me, the words filled her heart and she would swoon and swirl and ascend to the unseen places, to the heavenly realms. 'When I felt like that,' she said, 'I would believe everything he ever said.' On other occasions a sense of dark foreboding would descend upon her – 'I can only say then that it would feel like a deep winter's night,' she said. 'Or the middle days of sorrow.' Mrs Freemantle would watch Father Ferdinand as he spoke, the wisps of silver grey hair on his shining head, his broad midriff, the furry black eyebrows (that appeared to live entirely independently of his face) and the ever-present tic in his left eye. Every so often Father Ferdinand seemed to catch her eye and she would let her gaze drop and try frantically to recall the words he had been saying.

Almost as quickly as it had begun, the service would be over and Mrs Freemantle and Henry would file dutifully out of Our Gracious Lady past the oak-panelled doors to shake Father Ferdinand's hands; a heavy, almost debilitating shake. 'Those hands could break the Berlin Wall with one blow,' she said. 'They were not of this world. They were not of any world.' When it came to Mrs Freemantle's narrow, feline hands, Father Ferdinand always seemed to hold her hand just a few uncomfortable seconds longer than anyone else's. Mrs Freemantle said his eyes would bore into hers, searching her soul, and just before he was about to let go, his left eye would flicker and jerk with the slightest suggestion of a wink. Then Mrs Freemantle would be free, just her and her beloved Henry and the short, blissful stroll from Gravel Street to their own mid-terraced on Albion Hill. I loved to look at Mrs Freemantle's face when she got to this part; her eyes would glow and her face would become like that of a love-struck teenager again.

Once home, she said, Henry would change out of his navy suit and exchange his black and white polished spats for his familiar pair of worn, purple slippers. Mrs Freemantle would go into the kitchen to prepare the vegetables to accompany the roasting meat that they always had on a Sunday. She and Henry would then sit down together at the kitchen table and eat in silence, pondering their own thoughts. The only noise that could be heard, she said, was the gentle clinking of cutlery on china, a sound she grew to love. They would eat slowly and deliberately, Mrs Freemantle told me, passing condiments to each other without verbal communication.

'Sometimes, Fitzgerald,' she said to me, 'even now, I sit at home, with the cats and clink a knife or a fork on my china plates; just to hear it. I can't describe how that sound makes me feel inside.'

When the meal was over, Mrs Freemantle said, Henry would lean back in his chair and sigh – 'You should have been a chef, Aggie.' Mrs Freemantle would blush and say, 'I know Henry, I know.'

Henry would then clear away the table and wash and dry the plates and cutlery in his own methodical way, glasses first, then cutlery, then plates, cooking pans last, picking at the remnants of meat in the roasting tin as he washed. Mrs Freemantle said she would sit at the kitchen table watching him, sipping from a glass of red wine or musty port.

She told me that after Henry dried the final pan he would fold the damp teacloth, hang it on its peg and take her by the hand and lead her into the front room. Henry would then go over to their ancient record player and carefully select a record from their collection (Matt Monro or Dean Martin in the colder months, Acker Bilk or Chris Barber in the summer) and there together, Henry in his worn, purple slippers and Mrs Freemantle in her floral-print dress, they would dance together, arm in arm, for the rest of the afternoon.

Whenever Mrs Freemantle got to the end of her Sunday story she would grin from ear to ear, her cheeks would flush and her feet would shuffle from left to right and back again as if her body was remembering their dance. 'I can feel his arms around me now,' she would say. 'He always had such lovely arms.' Whenever I saw Mrs Freemantle, usually on Drummond Street when she was out shopping or at home in our front room talking to my mother or doing a crossword, I would think of her and Henry and the Sundays they had spent together.

Mrs Freemantle enjoyed telling me about Henry. 'He was a grand man. He had eyes like shining jewels and hands that were softer than a baby's little cheeks. No one has ever known me like my dear, sweet Henry and no one ever will again.'

Sometimes when she talked about Henry in our front room Mrs Freemantle would jump to her feet and dance across the room, holding her aged hands out in front of her as if Henry was dancing with her. She would glide across the room, humming her favourite tunes.

'People always said my Henry looked just like Dean Martin!' she would shout as she glided past me. 'Do you know Dean Martin, Fitzgerald?'

'Yes!' I'd shout back, raising my voice to counter Mrs Freemantle's increasingly loud humming. 'I do. I've heard some of his songs. Mum plays them!'

'Dean Martin is a beautiful man! But not as beautiful as my Henry!' Sometimes Mrs Freemantle whirled close to me, humming, and grabbed my arms, twisting me around so that I was close to her, my feet clumsily trying to keep up with her practised steps.

'Dance, Fitzgerald! Dance!' she would shout and pulling me close to her chest she would hum even louder.

On occasions, if my mother was dancing that week, she would hear the commotion from wherever she was in the house (usually upstairs in the bedroom going through drawers or in the kitchen cooking) and she would scamper into the tiny front room and stand for a few moments watching me and Mrs Freemantle twirling around the room, spinning, dizzy, giggling, humming, parts of our bodies bashing into the walls. My mother would rush over to the record player, pull out a Dean Martin record from the rack and hurriedly place it on the turntable. The needle crackled as it skimmed across the vinyl, picking up fluff as it went, and then Dean Martin's distinctive, crooning voice would purr out of the speakers, joining us in our dance, singing 'Mambo Italiano', 'Sway' or 'That's Amore'. Then my mother would join us on the dancefloor, jiving, bopping, twirling around. She would grab hold of me and Mrs Freemantle and the three of us, arms clasped together, would swirl around the room together, heads held back singing, shouting along to the words. Sometimes Mrs Freemantle would suddenly shout out above the boom of the music – 'I love you Henry Freemantle! I STILL LOVE YOU!' – and we would hold her tighter still as we twirled.

Mrs Freemantle continued to attend Our Gracious Lady of the Morning Dew religiously, even after Henry's death.

'I have to go,' she told me, 'I'm a Catholic. What good is a Catholic that doesn't go to church? Deep down I'm afraid not to believe.'

She told me that going to Our Gracious Lady was never quite the same after Henry had died. She said it felt colder and more solemn after his death and the stained-glass windows never shone any more – 'Even the Blessed Virgin seemed to stop shining. Can you imagine how it felt?' And she said that even Father Ferdinand rarely looked at her after Henry was gone. It seemed, she said, that he was embarrassed or ashamed, like he struggled to cope with her as a single woman; as if he needed the security of her marriage to be able to look at her. 'He certainly didn't seem to wink any more after Henry died,' Mrs Freemantle said. 'Unless it was just that his tic was getting better.'

'I still believed after Henry died,' she said, 'but it stopped being a joy to believe, more of a duty really or a habit. My belief frightens me, Fitzgerald.'

'Do you miss Henry?' I asked. 'Even now?'

'Like a desert misses water in a drought; like Monday misses the weekend,' Mrs Freemantle replied and then she stopped talking and sat in silence for several moments, her flushed cheeks twitching slightly. I stayed quiet, not even daring to cough, and watched her as her eyes scanned the room searching her memory for a picture of her one true love.

I scanned the room too, searching for Henry's face, but I couldn't find it. All I could see was Dean Martin and I knew that that wasn't enough. I'd seen one or two pictures of Henry and it was true, he was far more handsome than Dean Martin.

VI

The Sombre Meeting

Mr Plucker didn't sit in the threadbare chair or on the Wonky Stool of New Cross when he arrived. Instead he sat on one of the good stools that my father had made. Mrs Freemantle, on her return from the kitchen, sat as far away from the unbroken piece of wood as was possible (which in our tiny front room wasn't much further away than quite close). She sat on a stool by the door ready to make a hasty retreat should the wood become too much for her to bear.

Uncle Albie and Auntie Nerys sat together on the orange sofa, which was unusual for Uncle Albie as he usually sat on his favourite (threadbare) chair by the standard lamp. The standard lamp was broken and awaiting repair in my father's shed so Uncle Albie decided that a place on the sofa was a more fitting place to sit. Uncle Albie felt that as Auntie Nerys was the only other member of the nearest and dearest who was actually a blood relative (except for me and my mother of course), sitting next to her was a small sign of family unity. Apart from Mr Plucker and Mrs Freemantle, the only other person to arrive for the meeting was Hyacinth. Hyacinth sat on one of the threadbare chairs. She was wearing a big, brown coat, which she didn't take off throughout the meeting.

Following our fateful first meeting at St Roderick's, Hyacinth had found out that my father's funeral was to be held at the Resting Place Crematorium on Holy Wood Hill, the only crematorium in Wistful (I never got to ask her how or why). It was a beautiful place with red, white and pink roses and a variety of clematis climbing the walls of the entrance. Squirrels scampered up and down the huge oak trees that lined the perimeter. Hyacinth had quietly slipped in at the back. I stood at the front of the crematorium, soberly attired in a dark grey suit, head held low listening to the minister, sallow cheeked and morose, talking in desolate tones of the tragedy of death and the sure and steadfast hope of a resurrection. I soon became aware of a loud sucking noise coming from behind me; behind us all. I looked across the pews and the heads behind me and was startled to see Hyacinth with her strands of wispy hair, her dancing eyes and her ochre stumps. She sat alone in the very last pew. She held in her hands a crumpled paper bag identical to the one she had been holding at St Roderick's. I knew what was in the bag and knew what was making the loud sucking noise. One or two people made shushing noises in Hyacinth's direction and several others tutted, most notably my mother who hadn't realised it was Hyacinth. As I gazed at Hyacinth I caught a glimpse, between the gaps in her teeth, of the boiled sweet responsible for such disruption; I think she was sucking an orange one.

On realising I had noticed her Hyacinth smiled weakly. It was a bereavement smile, a misfortune smile, a knowing smile. She reached out an arm in my direction. Even from such a distance, it felt as if she was touching me. If Hyacinth had been close enough I feel sure she would have cooed and I feel certain she would have rubbed me with her gnarled hands, on my back perhaps or my shoulders. Although I'd met Hyacinth only once, she seemed more familiar to me than someone I had known a long time.

'. . . and it shall come to pass', the sour-faced minister droned, 'that on that day WE ALL SHALL BE CHANGED! Yes my friends, the dead shall rise and they shall be clothed in raiments, in *new garments . . . garments of RIGHTEOUSNESS! And HE shall separate the wheat from the chaff, the kernel from the tare, the GODLY from the UNGODLY. And Satan, Beelzebub, that FATHER OF LIES! shall be cast into the fiery furnace. And on that day peace shall reign THROUGHOUT THE EARTH! Yes, beloved, we all shall be CHANGED!'*

Hyacinth's sucking appeared to be loudest each time the minister paused for an intake of breath. As the minister spoke of the fiery furnace I shifted uncomfortably on my pew (as did many around me) aware of the apparent incongruity of his leaden words. It struck me as somewhat insensitive that the pasty minister should talk with such religious relish of people, the ungodly, being thrown into fiery furnaces in a place that was, after all designed solely for that purpose, throwing people into fiery furnaces godly and ungodly alike, who could tell? I wondered which my father would be classified as, godly or ungodly? I knew who Satan was; we had often talked about him in assemblies at junior school and in Religious Education at my secondary school. I knew he was the Devil. I'd heard of Beelzebub too, I knew it was another name for the Devil.

As for the Father of Lies, I didn't know who the minister meant when he referred to a 'Father of Lies'. I hoped he wasn't referring to my father, whose body was quite literally about to be thrown into a fiery furnace. I was sure my father must have lied – 'We all lie,' my mother had once told me. 'It's as natural as getting wet when it rains; as natural as waking up in the morning.' But I couldn't think of any that really stood out, not any that might really affect the course of world events. I certainly couldn't think of any that might cause the minister to refer to my father as the 'Father of Lies'. The 'Father of Wood', yes, the 'Father of Baccy Balls', maybe or even the 'Father of Fitzgerald', but most definitely not the 'Father of Lies'. It had a hollow, sinister ring to it. As my father's coffin slowly edged through the doors behind the pulpit, on its way to the crematory, I glared at the minister of doom hoping he would catch my eye so that I could convey to him my anger at his choice of words.

Hyacinth was waiting for us outside the crematorium as we filed out. Despite her frailty she looked quite awesome, a knowing figure, as she stood sucking her boiled sweet; by now she was on to a lemon one and I caught a whiff of the sweet lemons each time she opened her mouth. Unfortunately I also caught sight of her distraught teeth each time as well. The air around her seemed clearer, brighter, crisper than the air around everyone else. The smell from the roses seemed stronger than I'd noticed as we had entered, overpowering almost. She smiled broadly which, despite the solemnity of the day, seemed the right thing to do. My mother, her face straining with sorrow, came over to Hyacinth. They stood opposite each other, silently, for a few moments, the sound of Hyacinth's stumps sucking on the boiled sweet appearing to be amplified by the general lack of noise and unspoken grief around them. My mother moved toward Hyacinth.

'How nice of you to come . . . Hyacinth,' she said, her voice slow and modulated despite her pain.

'It was an honour,' Hyacinth spoke, her voice ethereal. 'Fitzgerald's father seemed like such a lovely man, it was the least I could do.'

Hyacinth offered the crumpled bag of sweets to my mother who reached out and took one, a lime one. Hyacinth then turned to me and offered me the bag. I took a lime one too. I popped the sweet into my mouth and sucked. It tasted wonderful, like a real lime but without the bitterness.

'Will you come back to the house?' my mother asked, the lime sweet making her voice sound muffled – my mother was clearly struggling to keep the sweet in her mouth and talk at the same time.

'I would like to very much. Of course I will,' Hyacinth said.

Hyacinth came to our house several more times in the weeks following the cremation and she always came with a full bag of boiled sweets. She usually sat in the front room and talked to my mother on any subject under the sun but quite often about my father. It was as if Hyacinth was an old friend. Her presence seemed to go some way in filling the void left by my father's absence and helped to stem the grief. Sometimes my mother remained in the same room and conversation would be easy. Other times Hyacinth would be in the front room talking and my mother in another room altogether; in the kitchen cooking perhaps, in the hallway dusting or even upstairs sorting through her special papers for a much needed document – which, she said, are usually required following a death. 'All I ever seem to have to do', she told Hyacinth, 'since he died, is produce various documents. Documents for this, documents for that.' If they were in different rooms then conversation between my mother and Hyacinth was almost like a telephone conversation. Hyacinth, straining to raise her voice, would call from the front room. My mother would return the call, in an even louder voice, from wherever she happened to be in the house. Sometimes, if Hyacinth was called really to raise her voice, then her sweet-filled mouth could not cope with the pressure and the obligatory boiled sweet would slip from between her stumps on to the threadbare chair. It would quickly be returned on completion of Hyacinth's next sentence, complete with bits of fluff and the odd hair.

If my mother was vacuuming then conversation with Hyacinth would be held in between the pauses of the Hoover, like a transatlantic telephone conversation but with a longer time delay. What with my mother's vacuuming and Hyacinth's sweet sucking, words were often misheard or completely misunderstood leading to some quite baffling conversations.

'Isn't it shocking now, the price of bread?' Hyacinth once shouted.

'I know, Hyacinth, I know,' my mother replied, switching off the Hoover, 'and especially as he loved his rice pudding so much. I'll never get over it.'

'I'm sure you will, dear. Things will have changed by the next Budget, you'll see.'

Hyacinth had been a great comfort to my mother, always saying the right words. She usually turned up at our house when, it seemed, my mother most needed to be comforted; when her tears were ready to spill. On another occasion we had been in the front room watching the telly, my mother on the orange sofa and me on the threadbare chair. It was quite late and *The Two Ronnies* were on the telly trying to make us laugh. I could see their mouths moving on the screen but I couldn't really make out all that they were saying; their glasses seemed thicker than they usually did and big Ronnie's tie seemed to be taking on a life of its own. My mother was silent and seemed barely able to move. I could hear the ticking of the clock which was louder than the clock we had heard in St Roderick's on the day we saw my father's body and I could hear the sound of a dog barking somewhere in our street as if it was trying to warn somebody or maybe it just wanted its bone. The knock at the door startled me but my mother remained unmoved.

'That was the door,' my mother said, her mouth opening and shutting like a puppet but her body remaining still. The screen was flickering and big Ronnie was now dressed as a woman and little Ronnie was trying to chat him up.

'Shall I get it?' I said.

'Yes,' my mother said.

I went to the door and was surprised to see Hyacinth so late in the day. 'Hello, Hyacinth,' I said. 'It's late. *The Two Ronnies* are on.'

'I know,' Hyacinth said and she removed her brown coat and handed it to me. 'I was just passing.' Hyacinth slipped into the front room whilst I hung her coat over the banister. She sat down next to my mother on the orange sofa. I sat back down on the threadbare chair and picked at a thread. It wasn't too dissimilar to one of my father's tight curls. Little Ronnie was dressed as a woman now too. They were both dancing. Little Ronnie was the better dancer by far.

'Do you like *The Two Ronnies*, Pauline?' Hyacinth asked.

'Yes,' my mother said and again her mouth moved but her body was still. Her eyes remained fixed on the screen. 'It was one of his favourites you know. He loved them.' The studio audience were laughing; they sounded kind of ghostly. 'They would have him in stitches sometimes, wouldn't they Fitzgerald?'

'Yes, Mother,' I said.

'Do you want a cup of tea, Hyacinth?' my mother said, though she made no effort to get up.

'No thank you, dear. I was just passing.'

Little Ronnie was on his comfy chair now doing his bit on his own, telling a long, rambling joke. His cardigan was unnecessarily tight and he kept fiddling with his glasses. The studio audience were in stitches themselves now, every time he moved his big glasses.

'This was his very favourite part,' my mother said. 'Sometimes he would cry with laughter. Sometimes it would make his stomach ache.'

'He is a funny chap, that little Ronnie,' Hyacinth said and, as little Ronnie said something about golf and his mother-in-law, Hyacinth began to laugh. Quietly at first, almost to herself but then she couldn't hold it in and her laugh came out in huge chuckles. She moved closer to my mother and her knobbly hand reached across and clenched my mother's tight fist. And I watched as Hyacinth chuckled, her hand tightly gripping my mother's. My mother wanted to laugh, I know she did, but she couldn't. You're not supposed to laugh so soon after your husband's died. Instead she seemed happy to have Hyacinth next to her doing the laughing that she would have been doing had my father been with her. And little tears rolled down my mother's face like silent reminders of my father. I smiled but I didn't laugh and little Ronnie seemed happy enough knowing that Hyacinth was laughing for us. The studio audience seemed to be trying especially hard to make up for my father's absent laughter. They were still in stitches. And that's how it was with Hyacinth. That was how she comforted my mother, how my mother came to trust her; she would arrive when she was most needed. She would laugh for my mother or cry for her or sometimes she would just be still with her and sometimes she would rub her back. And then she would leave, making my mother feel a little bit better than she had before she came. She would leave as quickly as she had come but she would always reach out and touch me too before she left. Always. Some of the darkness would be gone after Hyacinth had left; only a little bit, but a bit all the same. The rest of it would still lurk around the front room and the kitchen and out into the little hallway and when we went to bed, it would follow us up the stairs creeping slowly hoping we wouldn't notice it.

The nearest and dearest gathered in the front room. It was sunny outside but the faces of all the nearest and dearest (my own included) were grey and overcast and on one or two (primarily Mrs Freemantle's) a slight drizzle could be seen. Little could be heard from outside; a car backfiring, a gate swinging shut, the distant drone of a road-digger, an old man coughing up a ball of phlegm and spitting it out on to the street.

We met on a school day and I had been granted the day off. My mother had written to my form teacher, Mr Eustace. Mr Eustace was a tall, striking man who looked like he was famous but wasn't. He looked like he should be a famous rock singer or at least a famous folk singer (who usually weren't as famous as rock singers but were famous nonetheless). Most of us in my class, however, believed Mr Eustace was famous anyway even though we never saw him on television.

'Mr Eustace is famous,' Barry Saddler once said on our way over to the science laboratory.

'I know,' I replied. 'But you never get to see him on television.'

'That's because he's too busy teaching us lot.'

Mr Eustace, as if to add to our created mythology, would often (at the end of a lesson) get out his sparkling acoustic guitar and begin to sing us a song from his limited canon of folk hits. His favourites were Simon and Garfunkel's 'Scarborough Fair' and Ralph McTell's 'Streets of London'. He would sing, eyes closed, head bowed, his long hair hanging limply over his shoulders, the guitar resting on his knee, his Adam's apple jumping up and down in his throat like an excited toddler on a trampoline, his flared jeans flapping in time to the music. Sometimes, if Mr Eustace really got going, he rose to his feet, his guitar hanging by its brightly coloured strap over his broad shoulders and he sang loudly, almost shouting . . .

> . . . *so if you think you're l-o-oonely and say for you that the sun don't shine. Let me take you by the hand and lead you through the streets of London. I'll show you something that'll make you change your mind . . . oh..o.o.ooh . . . make you change your mind . . . mmmmmmh.*

And we would shout and whoop and sing along with joy.

My mother's letter to Mr Eustace, to get me the day off, was short and to the point:

> Dear Mr Eustace,
>   As you know Fitzgerald's father has recently been killed. Tomorrow we are gathering to decide where his ashes (Fitzgerald's father that is) should finally be scattered.
>   Therefore I would like Fitzgerald to have the day off school in order to attend this important yet tragic meeting.
> - Yours, Fitzgerald's mother.
> p.s. if you have any suggestions as to where the ashes should go please let me know.

Although Mr Eustace granted me the day off he declined to offer my mother any suggestions as to where my father's ashes should rest. 'I can think of several places, Fitzgerald,' he told me as he folded the note tightly into a tiny wedge and slipped it into his cardigan pocket, 'but it's not my place to comment, I'm only your teacher.'

As we sat in the front room the mood became markedly

sombre. Once everyone had exhausted the initial formalities, introductions and trivialities, the sad and dark purpose of the meeting fell upon us all. It weighed us down like millstones around our necks.

'We are gathered here . . .' my mother spoke, her choice of words echoing the funeral service or even a wedding, '. . . to decide on the final resting place of my late husband, Fitzgerald's father, your friend . . . and, er . . . loved one.

'The ashes, as you can see' (everyone's heads pre-empted my mother and turned toward the red casket) 'are currently in this red casket . . . here on the mantelpiece. In my opinion, this is not where they should remain. I do not believe my husband, my late husband, would have thought it fitting to spend his final days, in perpetuum, sitting idly on a mantelpiece. I firmly believe he would have got bored . . . very bored.'

My mother stopped talking and gazed wistfully at the red casket as if waiting for my father's voice to boom out of the restricted space and shout:

'You're right, Paulie, I'm bored already and I've only been in here a few weeks!'

Sadly it was not my father's voice that broke the silence. It was left to Uncle Albie to speak for him.

'Paulie's right,' he said, rising from his chair as if to address a vast audience. 'A red casket, albeit a finely crafted one, on a mantelpiece is no place for a man of his size to end his days. It's a lovely casket, beautiful and red, and we must all thank Ernie Devlin for the loving attention he must have put into making it. However, a casket of such paltry proportions is no place for my late brother-in-law to remain. He would scarcely have been able to fit his baccy pouch in there for goodness' sake.'

Uncle Albie sat down heavily, looking quite flushed, his temple throbbing, a bead of sweat on his brow. He looked around as if expecting a round of applause. I'm sure he looked a little disappointed when all he got was a general murmur of approval.

Uncle Albie was my favourite relative of all (not that I had many to choose from). He was a ghost hunter. I remember the first day he came over to our house with his first picture of a ghost, two or three years previously. My mother had made me stay in.

'Your Uncle Albie is coming over with a picture of a ghost,' she said as she polished the oven door with the same stained, off-white cloth that she also used to dry the dishes. 'I want you to stay in.'

My best friend, Michael Sawyer, had asked me to go with him to the building site on Frenarby Grove, but I'd had to tell him, as he stood at our door bouncing a multicoloured jet ball up and down, that I couldn't because my uncle was coming over with a picture of a ghost. 'Oh,' Michael said and the bouncing stopped.

Michael and I liked going up to the building site on Frenarby Grove where they were building a new postal sorting depot that seemed to be taking years to complete. When we got there we would jump from the scaffolding into the deep pile of damp sand fifteen feet below. The sign at the entrance of the site read ominously 'Authorised Persons Only – No Entry Without Hard Hats'. So Michael, who was good at making things out of relatively little, had carefully made tight-fitting hats out of two of his mother's old wicker baskets (the hardest head-shaped things he could find), some carpet tape and two pairs of his older sister's tights to keep the hats secured to our heads.

'They're not that hard,' I said, tapping the hats with a pen when Michael first brought them round.

'Can you think of anything better?' he asked.

'No,' I said.

I kept the basket-hats in my room, under my bed, and whenever we journeyed to Frenarby Grove I would sneak them out and smuggle them carefully up to the building site. Fortunately for us, Frenarby Grove was usually quite deserted, so no one ever saw us jumping from the scaffolding into the damp sand with wicker baskets strapped to our heads.

Uncle Albie had phoned my mother from Toynton-All-Saints near Skegness, to say he needed to see her urgently, as he had seen a ghost the night before and had managed to take a picture of it. Uncle Albie hadn't actually phoned my mother directly as, at the time, we didn't own a phone. He'd phoned Mr Plucker, next door, and asked him to deliver the ghostly news to my mother. Mr Plucker delivered the message without a hint of emotion as my mother stood ironing my father's vests.

'Your brother rang,' he intoned, 'from Toynton-All-Saints. He's seen a ghost and wants you to see a picture of it. He said he'll be here tomorrow morning.'

'Where's Toynton-All-Saints?' my mother asked, turning a vest and ironing over a stain that my father had acquired whilst he'd been emptying the dirty water from a radiator at Brady's Waxworks Well.

'Near Skegness,' Mr Plucker replied, 'I think.'

My mother thanked Mr Plucker and he left, pulling up his ill-fitting trousers before closing the door behind him. Mr Pucker had delivered messages to my mother and father ever since he had generously offered to take phone messages for them until we could afford to buy a phone of our own. We were one of the last families in our street to get a phone and the very last to be able to get ITV on our television set (our dial only picked up BBC 1 and 2).

When we eventually did get a phone it took a lot of getting used to. Whenever the phone rang (which in our house was not very often) my mother and father would look at each other in stony silence as if telepathically discussing who should answer it. Neither of them seemed particularly keen (or perhaps they were a little afraid of it) and I was not allowed to, as I was considered too young for such a responsible task. My father usually (though not always) won the silent-deciding battle, leaving my mother with the awkward and onerous task of picking up the receiver and self-consciously saying, 'Wistful, 4331 – who is it?'

In the beginning, before we got used to the fact that people could phone us direct, my mother would phone Mr Plucker and ask if anyone had phoned him to leave us any messages. 'No,' he'd reply 'Why would they have? You have your own phone now.'

The day Uncle Albie arrived, with his picture of the ghost, was autumnal brown; crispy leaves swirled through the sky, a frosty chill was in the air. Uncle Albie had large fingers, a lumbering gait and poor centre of balance and looked nothing like my mother. He worked as an itinerant plumber. He lived nowhere in particular and would travel the length and breadth of the country finding casual plumbing jobs. He had plumbed in Halifax, he had plumbed in Aberdeen, he had plumbed in St Ives. In fact, he claimed, there wasn't anywhere in mainland Britain that he hadn't at least passed through on his way to a plumbing job. He once told me, during one of his whistle-stop visits to our house, that he reckoned at least one in every thousand people in Britain had sat on a toilet that, at some stage, had been manhandled by his large fingers.

When Uncle Albie wasn't fitting new washers and stopcocks and lifting toilet seats he would be engaged in his real passion . . . ghost-hunting. Uncle Albie really only plumbed across the country so that he would be able to stop at famous ghost sightings along the way, carrying with him, in his toolbox, a weather-beaten Polaroid Instamatic with which he would try to catch pictures of ghosts. He told me that he hunted for ghosts everywhere. He had looked for the friendly spirit of the Little Old Lady at Horton Court in Chipping Sodbury (even though the last recorded sighting was in 1937). He had searched for the ghost of the Girl in the Yellow Dress at Thorington Hall in Suffolk. He had waited silently at midnight on the Bossiney Mound at Tintagel for King Arthur's legendary Round Table to rise to the surface and shimmer in the sparkling moonlight. And he had even joined a party of Ghost Club members at the Assembly Rooms in Bath to wait for the famed Man in the Black Hat to appear. But to this day Uncle Albie had never been able to get a picture of any of the ghosts he may or may not have seen. The day he came with his first picture of a ghost promised to be very special indeed.

He'd arrived in his battered and bruised Opel Kadett. Our street was deserted, except for a few of the swirling leaves, the fat cat from number thirty-four slowly winding its way home, and the two Granite children from number eighteen who passed our house on their way to their weekly piano lessons at Mrs Labwicka's on Municipal Lane. The Granite children, who looked like twins but weren't (there were fourteen months between them), walked in unison toward the bus stop. They wore long, ankle-length black coats and their faces were stern, their eyes fixed straight ahead. Both hummed a tune they had learned, I imagined, at last week's lesson.

Once again we had been gathered in our front room; my father, my mother and me, Mr Plucker, who sat swamped in a beige sweater, sipping milky tea, and Mrs Freemantle who had popped in to see my mother on her way to the butchers on Drummond Street to pick up half a pound of corned beef and some off-cuts for the cats' tea. My mother ushered Uncle Albie into the front room like a visiting dignitary. He planted himself down heavily on the threadbare chair by the standard lamp. Uncle Albie's face was red and worn. I noticed that, as was often the case, he had something written in Biro on the back of his hand. I couldn't quite make it out but I think it said 'Sunderland 0 – Grimsby 2'.

After my mother had served Uncle Albie with some milky tea and a slice of battenburg cake, an expectant hush had fallen on the gathering. We watched Uncle Albie as he slowly and deliberately ate his battenburg cake, leaving pink and yellow crumbs on his lap and on his cracked lips. Mr Plucker shifted uncomfortably in his seat and Mrs Freemantle coughed discreetly as my mother topped up her tea. My father's weighty voice broke the silence, the boom of it causing Mr Plucker to shake a little, spilling milky dregs into his china saucer.

'Well, Albie!' he said. 'Where is it?'

'Where's what?' Uncle Albie replied, dipping the last piece of his battenburg into his tea and sucking the tea from the cake, relishing the attention (and the cake).

'The ghost, Albie. Where's the ghost?'

'Oh, the picture you mean? The picture of the ghost?'

'Yes,' my father replied, the little patience he had wearing thin, 'the picture of the ghost.'

'It's here.' Uncle Albie's eyes glinted as he rummaged through the distressed rucksack at his feet. He pulled out a colour photograph, slightly bent at each corner. He thrust the photo out in front of him, showing its image to each of us in turn. Then he placed it on to the seat of a stool.

'There she is,' he said. 'The Ghost of Friary Manor, Toynton-All-Saints . . . near Skegness.' Mr Plucker shot a glance at my mother and smiled knowingly.

We all moved forward in our chairs and craned our necks to get a clearer view of the photograph. My view was slightly obscured by Mrs Freemantle's tidy hair, but what I could see was not promising at all. I could make out what appeared to be a dressing table in a room that could have been Edwardian. I could make out a mirror on the dressing table littered with tools of various kinds, tools that I assumed Uncle Albie used for his many plumbing jobs. Two extremely dirty mugs could also be seen amongst the chaos. One section of the wall could be seen in the photograph and an oil painting could just be made out hanging on it. It looked like a man in military garb sitting astride a white charger. To the right of the picture, on the floor, was a battered pair of working boots. The photograph appeared to have been taken at night, the only light coming from what must have been some type of lamp just out of the frame. What I assumed was the Ghost of Friary Manor could be seen in reflection in the mirror. It looked nothing more than a faint white blur with grey slashes running parallel to the mirror on the dressing table. To me it simply looked like the photo had not been developed very well. It did not look like a ghost, not that I had ever seen one.

The picture of the Ghost of Friary Manor was only the first. Uncle Albie brought several photographs of ghosts to our house after that and each one looked less like a ghost than the last. With each ghost would come a story. We would always gather to look at the picture and hear the story no matter how poor the quality of the picture or how fanciful the story.

VII

Over the Hill and Far Away

After more malt loaf and another pot of tea, the sombre meeting continued long into the afternoon. As the discussion neared a conclusion, I could hear a symphony of sounds outside the window; orchestrated, harmonious normal life playing out its daily, familiar tune. I could hear children returning from school and part of me wished that I could flee the funereal atmosphere of the house and dart up to the park for a game of football (a game I was not too keen on, all the technical bits that is, but a game I enjoyed because of all the darting around, dodging and weaving chasing a bright orange Trophy ball). Or we would play 'forty-four save all' (a game with virtually no technical bits but one that, technically, involved less running around). Most of us should have outgrown 'forty-four save all' but it was like a Class A drug to us and hard to give up.

I could hear familiar voices passing my door; no one knocked. They all knew that the Sombre Meeting was in progress. Some had even seen the note from my mother to Mr Eustace. It was, as Emerson Darkly had referred to it, 'A Note of Import'. I could hear Clive Barrington shouting up the road to one of our friends (I'm not sure who but it was probably Wayne Haynes who usually shouted back unless his mouth was full of rhubarb-and-custards.

As he didn't shout back his mouth must have been full.) I also heard Barry Saddler go past talking to himself. At least I assumed he was talking to himself as Barry Saddler often talked to himself, even when he was in company. 'You're great, Barry Saddler,' I heard him mumble, and he must have actually stopped outside my house, perhaps in his own sad way he wanted his words to be heard by my own sober gathering.

'You know you're great,' he continued, 'you're just great. And you, Barry Saddler, are going places.'

Then I was sure I heard him crying but I might have been wrong. I'd never actually seen Barry Saddler cry in school before but rumour had it that he cried an awful lot out of school, although only two people could actually claim to have seen him; Claudia Shinkel (who claimed she once saw him crying behind O'Casey's Launderette at the top of Passover Crescent) and most notably Emerson Darkly, who claimed he had seen, or at least heard, Barry Saddler crying on several occasions.

'I saw Barry Saddler crying again last night,' he once told me and Michael Sawyer as we sat in the school library quietly trying to research for our summer Geography project that we had named *The Changing Climates Around the Globe – A Study in Great Climatic Changes Around the World*. It was a long and cumbersome title we realised, with more than a hint of repetition, but I had thought of the first part and Michael Sawyer the second part, so we stuck with it, neither of us wishing to lose our chosen titles.

'And where did you see Barry Saddler crying?' Michael asked as he scribbled down the fuel consumption of India into his notepad.

'I didn't actually *see* Barry Saddler crying. I only *heard* him.'

'Well, where did you *hear* Barry Saddler crying then?' I asked, getting up to pull out a slim volume entitled *Climate Changes Around the World – All You Need to Know Vol. 1* from the shelf above Emerson Darkly's head.

'I was on the wall in Parson's Park, spinning, and Barry Saddler was down below me, in the bushes . . . crying.' The wall at

Parson's Park was wide and we would stand on it, twelve feet up, and take turns to spin until we were dizzy, the risk of falling off making it all the more exciting. It was perhaps another of our youthful equivalents to taking drugs.

'How do you know it was Barry Saddler crying?' I said as I sat down with the book. I flicked it open at a page headed 'Climate Changes in Europe – All You Need to Know' (the authors were obviously not overly imaginative types).

'Because when he stopped crying he kept saying to himself, over and over again, "Don't be a stupid boy, Barry Saddler. You stop that silly crying now. STOP IT NOW! DO YOU HEAR ME?"'

'But you didn't actually see that it was Barry Saddler,' Michael said in a stern, almost protective voice.

'No,' Emerson Darkly confessed, 'I didn't see him, I only heard him. The bushes were too thick.'

Shortly after Barry Saddler had gone I heard Timothy Drinkwater, an older boy from Cranbourne Avenue, the street that ran parallel to ours, pass by. I could hear a slow, creaking sound and knew that he was pushing his little sister, Lily, on her derelict, rusty tricycle. The piercing creaks of the wheels sent a shiver through my body. Timothy Drinkwater thought he was a meteorologist despite the fact that he was only fifteen and had never worked for a day in his life. He had difficulty spelling 'meteorologist' (we all did) but this did not prevent Timothy Drinkwater from claiming weather-forecasting as his chosen vocation.

'I'm a Metre Rologist,' he'd tell us, holding his head aloft and looking at the clouds as he spoke (his hair was blond and fluffy and was often itself mistaken for a low-lying cloud formation), 'and no one knows more about clouds or rain or frost formation than me. I am the King of the Cumulo-Nimbus.'

When it was raining, Timothy Drinkwater would gather a group of us under the roof of the bus garage in Franklin Street. We would sit, perched on old tyres, Lily on her tricycle, and for two and a half pence each, Timothy would claim that he could predict the exact time to the nearest fifteen minutes that the rain would stop. We would dutifully hand over our coins and Timothy would scribble his prediction on a piece of paper which would be then passed on to Lily who would hold it tightly in her tiny fist until the rain stopped. No one dared to peek at the predictions while they were clenched in little Lily's tiny hand. Once we sat for almost two hours until the sun had begun to sparkle and Lily opened her clenched fist to reveal her brother's mystical prediction. Timothy's predictions were rarely, if ever, right but we wanted to believe in his magical powers and so it didn't take a great deal of persuasion for him to get us to part with our copper coins. We needed to have a mystic in our otherwise bland neighbourhood.

Timothy's father, Mr Drinkwater, had brought Lily and Timothy up on his own for most of their childhood. Theirs was one of the first broken homes in our neighbourhood, possibly the first. Mr Drinkwater believed he was a Native American Indian. 'I'm a Red Indian!' he told us if he passed us in the street and then he would spin around dancing and whooping with his hand cupping his mouth as we often saw Red Indians do in the films on television. My mother had once told me that Mr Drinkwater had first believed himself to be a Red Indian following a brief spell in hospital. He'd been hospitalised at St Roderick's due to a particularly bad case of septicaemia. In the worst throes of his illness he suffered a short psychotic episode. During his psychotic hallucinations, Mr Drinkwater was convinced that he had been visited by a stunningly handsome golden eagle that had told him, in a deep American drawl, that he was in fact a Native American Indian called 'Dry River Come Drink Water'. The golden eagle told him, he believed, that he had really been hospitalised by the arrow of an opposing tribe intent on killing him.

Fortunately the psychotic episode was short-lived (a reaction to the medication, his consultant told him) and Mr Drinkwater was soon discharged. Unfortunately, whilst he realised that it was highly unlikely that an eagle had visited him, Mr Drinkwater still held firm to the 'revelation'. Thereafter he began to buy authentic Red Indian costumes, the full regalia, and would sit watching his favourite TV programmes wearing them; *Crossroads* and *Nationwide*, *Songs of Praise* on Sundays, the long eagle feathers standing proudly on his headdress as Sue Lawley spoke morosely into the camera or Hughie McPhee chirped away in his kitchen.

Word soon spread in our neighbourhood that Mr Drinkwater began to go to Red Indian Appreciation Society conferences, usually in London but sometimes as far afield as Inverness or Belfast. It was when he set up a wigwam in the back garden, my mother told me, and asked to take his tea in it that his wife, at the time, Mrs Drinkwater, a portly lady with poor sight and a reluctance to smile, left him and he, Lily and Timothy became a single-parent family. Their home broke. It was shortly after Mrs Drinkwater left the family home on Cranbourne Avenue and Mr Drinkwater began taking his tea in the wigwam that Timothy began to believe he was a meteorologist and little Lily's tricycle began to rust.

The sound of Uncle Albie clearing his throat brought me back to the voices of the Sombre Meeting. The sounds outside dissipated; Clive Barrington's shouts, Barry Saddler's tears, the piercing creaks of little Lily Drinkwater's tricycle.

'So . . .' Uncle Albie spoke, his voice heavy and laboured (it had been a long meeting fuelled by copious amounts of tea and malt loaf swirling around in the bellies of all present), '. . . are those all of your considered and final thoughts?'

Everyone nodded.

'So . . . I shall just recap then?' Uncle Albie then took a sip of his milky tea, slurping the fluid into his mouth.

Everyone nodded.

'OK, I'll recap.' Uncle Albie stood again. He held his hands behind his back, rocked gently on his heels and addressed the gathering like a politician in the House of Commons.

'Nerys –' he looked at Auntie Nerys sitting by his side. He almost placed his hand on her head like a priest about to offer her blessings but didn't. 'You, Nerys, think that Fitzgerald's father's ashes should remain in the red casket and be put to rest in the cupboard under the stairs. The cupboard under the stairs, you feel, is a place that would be warm, comfortable and somewhere where he could rest in quiet with very little disturbance. Is that correct?'

'That is correct, Albie,' Auntie Nerys replied as if under oath. As she looked up at Uncle Albie her cheeks flushed a little. Auntie Nerys was a nervous woman, with permanently flushed cheeks.

'Mr Plucker,' Uncle Albie spoke and Mr Plucker half stood in his seat and then thought better of it and sat down again on the stool, his beige sweater billowing as if a breeze had just passed through the house, the flesh under his chin flapped, 'you think that the ashes should remain in the red casket and should rest in the back garden, on the current site of the shed. You feel that the shed should be dismantled and the pieces of wood donated to an appropriate charity and that Erik Stanislaw, the stonemason on Municipal Lane, should be asked to erect a small but digni-fied monument symbolising Fitzgerald's father's hands. The oars. Is that correct?'

'That is correct.' Mr Plucker chose this opportunity to stand. He also nodded at everyone in turn. 'It would be a fitting gesture. To behold a monument of those great hands every time one was to step into the garden would, I think, be very fitting. The ashes should be near the oars.' He sat down again repeating his final words to himself under his breath as if needing to reassure himself of his final decision.

'Mrs Freemantle,' Uncle Albie continued, 'you believe the ashes should be taken, in the red casket, out on a boat and scattered in the sea. You recognise that my late brother-in-law had no real interest in the sea and would not have described himself as a great swimmer, but you still believe this to be an appropriate choice. Is that correct?'

'That is correct,' Mrs Freemantle replied, adjusting herself on the stool by the door, being careful to avoid looking at the unbroken piece of wood. 'I just feel it would be the right thing to do. A dear old friend of mine was once scattered at sea and

91

it was one of the happiest days of her life. She wasn't a very good swimmer either.'

Uncle Albie raised his eyebrows looking slightly puzzled but continued with his summation.

'Paulie,' he said and my mother looked up, not at Uncle Albie but at the red casket. 'Paulie, you feel that your late husband's ashes should not remain in the red casket, but should be placed, covered, in a scented bowl of dried leaves on a wooden base, on the mantelpiece. You believe it is right and proper for him to remain in the house he so loved and above all to be in a place where he is able to listen to you and to be able to keep an eye on young Fitzgerald . . .'

Everybody looked at me, the women cooed and I looked at my feet.

'. . . Is that correct?'

'That is correct, Albie,' my mother sighed and Hyacinth placed a hand on her shoulder. 'That is correct.'

'Hyacinth –' Uncle Albie turned to Hyacinth, 'am I right in saying that it is your considered opinion that it would not be fitting for you to have any influence over the final decision as to where the ashes should finally rest, as you did not actually know Fitzgerald's father? You believe that the final decision should be left to a close member of the family. Is that correct?'

'That is correct.' Hyacinth leaned forward to offer her bag of boiled sweets to us all. 'A close and *significant* member of the family.'

'Thank you,' Uncle Albie said and chose an orange-flavoured sweet. He slotted it into his mouth and pondered Hyacinth's last words. Everybody sucked their chosen sweets for a few moments, the fruity smells like a fresh fruit salad, and pondered Hyacinth's last words along with Uncle Albie.

'Anyway,' Uncle Albie continued, the pondering complete, the sweet in his mouth causing the word to sound like '*Ebiway*'. 'As for me I think the ashes should remain in my care, in the red casket (for transit purposes only) and for one year only. They can then travel with me on a tour of the British Isles. Fitzgerald's father never had the chance to travel a great deal and I'm sure he would have loved the opportunity to explore this the land that was his home. After the completion of the year-long pilgrimage the ashes should be returned to this dwelling to rest, as Paulie has so tenderly said, with his loved ones, on the mantelpiece, but not in the red casket. He'll need more space than that. That's my final and considered opinion.'

'Thank you, Albie,' we all said in unison (only I added an 'Uncle' which slightly disrupted the harmony of the voices).

The nearest and dearest continued their deliberations. As they spoke, Hyacinth drew back in her chair slightly and looked across at me, her boiled sweet causing her left cheek to swell a little, like a molehill. She didn't say anything but looked at me, intensely, for a moment or two. Her eyes appeared almost too bright and she held my gaze for a few more moments and then returned to the heat of the conversation. I looked at the unbroken piece of wood under the bay of the window. It seemed to glow, just slightly. I looked at the red casket on the mantelpiece. It too seemed to glow, just slightly. I felt compelled to look at my hands. They seemed bigger, just slightly, and they felt unnaturally warm. Another strange shiver ran down my spine. Shivers down my spine were becoming a regular occurrence recently.

'You can get a lot more done with large hands,' I heard my father's voice say to me and I caught a vision in my mind's eye of him chipping away at a piece of wood in the shed at the bottom of the garden with his mallet and chisel.

'You can get a lot more done with large hands,' I heard his voice again only this time it appeared not to be in my head or my mind's eye, but in the room itself, booming. I looked around the room at the nearest and dearest. They continued normally, nodding and talking, talking and nodding, trying to come to some agreement about the ashes. Mrs Freemantle's cup and saucer rattled on her knees.

'And in a lot less time.' The voice again. My father's voice. In the room. I looked at my hands, still bigger. Still glowing. Hyacinth, smiling. The red casket. Still glowing. The unbroken

piece of wood. Still glowing. As I looked at the wood it slipped from its resting place under the bay and fell to the carpeted floor. A dull thud. Dust swirling in the air. Still it glowed, perhaps a little brighter. The conversation stopped. All eyes turned toward the unbroken piece of wood. Silence. It continued to glow. I looked at Mrs Freemantle and thought she would burst into tears. She didn't but her eyelids did flutter as if she was holding the tears back. My mother got up from her seat.

'I'm sorry,' she said, reaching down to pick up the unbroken piece of wood. She appeared not to notice that it was glowing. She leaned it back up against the wall and returned to her seat. No one else appeared to notice that it was glowing either. At least, no one commented. They returned to their conversation. Hyacinth looked at me and smiled.

I heard the clock on the wall ticking. It was getting dark outside; the street lamps were coming on. I heard someone running past our front door, a jogger perhaps? Heavy feet . . . a man's feet, followed by a heavy male cough. I heard a cat meow, a long, strangulated whine, too screeching to be the fat cat from number thirty-four. I heard the sound of someone whistling a tune. A familiar tune. A tune I'd often heard my mother whistling around the house or playing on the record player when she wasn't playing Bix or Cab or some other big-band number. It was 'It's a Most Unusual Day' by Andy Williams. My mother once said to me – 'I'm in love with Andy Williams. If I hadn't married your father, I'd have married Andy Williams.'

'Who's Andy Williams?' I asked. 'And where does he live?'

'He's someone who has never known how much I love him,' my mother said clutching her hands to her breasts, 'and he lives in a perpetual state of unrequited love. Even though he doesn't know it.'

'Is that far away?'

'Where? Is where far away?'

'The State of Unrequited Love.'

'Farther than the east is from the west,' my mother said and skipped on the spot, her hand still clutching at her breast, her heart.

'Does Dad know you're in love with Andy Williams?' I continued.
'No, Fitzgerald, he does not. Let that be our little secret.'

The smell of my father's baccy balls caught me by surprise. I'd
not smelled his baccy since the day that the last drop had been
absorbed into the unbroken piece of wood. It was also the first
thing I had been able to smell all day. My nose appeared to have
unblocked which was surprisingly sudden. The sight of my father
standing by the door leaning against the doorframe surprised me
even more. There he was, at the very least a vision of my father,
his tight brown curls, his light brown skin (the European
beech), his freckles, his baggy, grey clothes, his oars hanging heavily
by his side. I was rooted to the Wonky Stool of New Cross.
I could not move. No one else in the room noticed my father.
Their protracted conversation continued.

'Hello, Fitzgerald,' the vision spoke and he smiled. I noticed a
small piece of baccy wedged between his two front teeth.

'Hello, Dad,' I said, shaking slightly, my palms beginning to
sweat. 'Are you dead, Dad?'

'I suppose I am.' He nodded, his head moving in slow-motion.

'Are you a ghost, Dad?'

'I'm not sure I believe in ghosts, Fitzgerald, but I wouldn't ever tell
Uncle Albie that.'

I looked across at Uncle Albie but he seemed completely
oblivious to my father's presence; he wasn't rushing to get his
camera anyway.

'Are you OK, Dad? Are you in Heaven?'

'Yes son, I'm fine. And I don't think I can tell you where I am.
Some things you have to work out for yourself. All I know is there's
lots of trees, lots of wood, lots of singing and lots of dancing . . . lots of
dancing and it smells nice. Wherever it is, it feels like home.'

'Will you be staying with us long, Dad?'

'No son, only for a very short while.'

'Why have you come back?'

'I wanted to see you, son. To talk to you.'

'To talk to me about what, Dad?'

'*About the ashes, son. About my ashes.*' My father pointed to the red casket on the mantelpiece.

'What about the ashes, Dad?'

'*It's important that they go to the right place son, that they're scattered in the right place.*'

'That's why we're here. To find the final resting place for the . . . I mean your ashes . . . to . . . well you know . . . to rest.'

'*I know you are, son. But none of them . . .*' he nodded in the direction of the nearest and dearest, '*. . . none of the relatives really know where is the right place for my ashes to rest, son. Not even your mother, much as she loves me. None of them could even begin to guess. Could they, son?*'

'Couldn't they, Dad?

'*I don't think so, son.*'

'Not even Mum, Dad?'

'*Maybe, but I'm not so sure. I don't think she would really know. Now, where's me spittin' cup?*'

'It's in the kitchen, Dad, by the breadbin. Where it always is. Shall I get it?' My father nodded. I leapt up from my stool and dashed into the kitchen. I grabbed the spittin' cup, which had not been moved since he had been killed by the lorry, and rushed back into the front room. No one else appeared to be at all aware that my father was in the room; they talked on apparently oblivious to his presence. As I rushed past my father, I felt a warmth emanating from his body and I could see tiny specks of sawdust floating in the air around him. The air was thick with the comforting aroma of his baccy balls. He spat the baccy ball into the spittin' cup and popped another into his mouth. More sawdust leapt from his hair and danced in the air around his head, some of it came toward me and danced around me. I grabbed at the specks with my hand, trying to hold them in my closed palms. They had disappeared when I opened my hand to look at them.

'Mum's not whistling, Dad. Not since you've been gone.'

'*I know that, son. I do feel bad about that.*'

'Don't be, Dad. It's not your fault.'

My father, the vision, didn't reply. Instead he chewed harder on his baccy ball and the smell of the baccy was so much stronger than I could ever recall it being before. I breathed it in.

'Where is the right place for your ashes to rest, Dad?' I continued.

'Has anyone asked you where my ashes should rest, son?'

'Me?'

'Yes, son, you.'

'But I've no idea where they should go, Dad.'

'Yes you do, son. Have you really thought about it?'

'I guess I have a little bit, Dad.'

'Really thought about it, Fitzgerald?'

'Well there have been other things on my mind lately, Dad.'

'Like what, son?'

'Like missing you, Dad. Like wondering why you had to die. Like wishing Mum would whistle again or dance even. Like . . .'

'Stop it, son. I'm sorry, Fitzgerald.' My father seemed to want to hold me, to ruffle my hair, but he held back. Perhaps he was not allowed to or perhaps he was just in my imagination and no amount of imagining on my part could get him to hold me again.

'Do you remember that first time I told you about being proud to be African, Fitzgerald? You were on the stool outside my shed?'

'And my ears were still wet. I could feel the water in them, they were making a popping sound.'

'I wanted you to be so proud to be African. As proud as you were to have passed your swimming test.'

'Did you, Dad?

'Yes, son, I did. And I wanted to be proud to be African too, Fitzgerald. I wanted to know that in both my body and spirit I would one day be able to be truly proud to be African.'

'I did think of Africa, Dad. I did want to tell the nearest and dearest that the ashes should go to Africa but I thought they'd think I was mad. You want your ashes to be laid to rest in Africa. That's it isn't it?'

My father smiled and moved towards me. He reached out his oarlike hand and it seemed as if he was about to place it on my shoulder. He didn't but let it hang in the air between us as if it was part of some invisible family tree. I could smell his arm and it smelled of damp wood.

'*That's right, son,*' he said, '*It would make me very happy. And it would make you very happy too, son.*'

'It would? How would it make me happy, Dad?'

'*You'll see, son. You'll see when you get there.*'

'When *I* get there? Me? How can I go to Africa, Dad? I'm only thirteen and . . . and I don't even know how to get there. How will I get to Africa at my age?'

'*You know where it is, son. Africa is in your heart. It's over that hill and far away,*' my father's blue eyes sparkled, '*and besides someone will help you to get there. You won't be on your own. Someone will take you there. You'll never be on your own, son.*'

'Who will help me to get there? Who will go with me? Is it Hyacinth, Dad? Does Hyacinth know how to get there?'

'*No more questions, son. Look, the meeting's come to an end, they've made a decision. And, Fitzgerald, I hope you'll be able to forgive me. I always loved you, always. More than you can ever imagine.*' My father pointed to the nearest and dearest. I followed his immense finger, still more sawdust falling from the end of it and I looked at the doleful gathering. I could hear their voices again, coming back into my world. It was my mother's voice that I was first aware of.

'So we're all agreed then,' she said, her voice ethereal, distant, other-wordly. I looked back to where the vision of my father had been standing. He was gone, just the faintest of whiffs of baccy in the air and the memory of his presence.

'DAD!' I shouted, my voice raised and urgent, 'DAD, COME BACK!'

'Fitzgerald.' My mother came over to me. She put out her hands and with her moist fingers began to chub my cheeks (a habit she had not stopped despite my advancing years). 'Fitzgerald love, are you all right?'

My mother's words echoed, she seemed to be talking from another place, far away from me. The room was hazy, dark, hot, close, overwhelming. By now everyone in the room had risen from their seats and gathered around me. Their faces appeared too close to me. Ghoulish. Uncle Albie's eyes bulged. Mrs Freemantle's hair seemed too tidy, much too tidy. Mr Plucker seemed thinner than was humanly possible, skeletal. Auntie Nerys seemed so nervous she looked about to scream, like Munch's picture *The Scream*, that I had seen in an art book at school. It was only Hyacinth and my mother's chubbing that seemed normal, bringing me some comfort. The last thing I remember noticing before I fainted was one last overwhelming smell of my father's baccy balls, and then . . . nothing.

VIII

The Hinterland

I awoke from a dream-filled sleep. In my dream planks of wood were dancing in my tiny front room, twirling around and jiving to a stomping beat. Bix was in the room blowing so hard on his horn that it looked as if his cheeks would explode and Cab was next to him, Minnie the mooching. Other pieces of wood leaned against the bay of the window and chose not to dance, preferring to watch instead. One or two sipped drinks; others made a point of refusing to drink. Waxwork images of my father filled my dream, his lifeless body lying still amidst the dancing wood. Some of the pieces of wood leaned over him, begging him to wake up. Hyacinth was in my dream glowing brighter than the midday sun, offering bags of baccy balls to the nearest and dearest, asking them to smell them which they did and, in my dream, I knew they were all thinking about my father. Outside the house Barry Saddler was riding up and down our street squashed on to little Lucy's rusty tricycle holding the fat cat from number thirty-four and crying, 'You're going places, fat cat.' Uncle Albie, dressed as a Red Indian, was taking a picture of a ghost sitting on a huge red casket. Ernie Devlin stood beside the casket singing 'You'll Never Walk Alone'. As the dream began to fade I could see my father waking up and he looked at me and began mouthing the same words over and over. I couldn't hear him but I could lip-read the words and I knew what he was saying.

When I awoke I was in my bed. I was damp; I was sweating. Crisp, early morning sunshine filled the room. Warmth. It was clean and fresh. I breathed in deeply, letting the air fill my lungs. I looked over the side of my bed and noted with relief that the unbroken piece of wood was safely in its place. I lifted my pillow and, unfolding my balled tissue, blew my nose. As I blew, the events of the previous evening slowly began to filter back into my mind. I lay back down and sighed heavily. A crow cawed outside my window and I could hear its wings flap like washing on a line.

After I had fainted, Uncle Albie carefully lifted me off the floor and placed me on the bright orange sofa. I remember the first sounds I heard as I began to come round . . .

'Get him some water!' (My mother.)

'Call an ambulance!' (Mrs Freemantle.)

'Does he do that often?' (Auntie Nerys.)

'Is he dead? He looks dead.' (Mr Plucker.)

'It could be epilepsy. Put a spoon in his mouth.' (Auntie Nerys.)

'Stop it, all of you. He's just fainted. Now give him some space to breathe.' (Uncle Albie.)

'I think he *is* dead you know. He's not moving.' (Mr Plucker, again.)

As I slowly began to come around I became aware of the faces staring at me, no longer ghoulish but concerned faces.

'Are you all right Fitzgerald, love?' my mother spoke; there was a noticeable tremor in her voice and sweat appeared on her brow.

'You just fainted, lad,' Uncle Albie declared.

'Did I, Uncle Albie?' I said and tried to get up. Uncle Albie pushed me back down and told me to take it easy. Mrs Freemantle got up and went to the kitchen to get a glass of water.

'I saw Dad, Mum,' I said and the nearest and dearest went quiet. 'He was here, Mum, in the room. I saw him, right there, over by the door.'

'What did he want?' my mother said, breaking the silence. 'And if it was grim news how come I didn't know it was coming?'

'The lad's had a shock,' Mr Plucker said, his neck quivering. 'He must have imagined it.'

'I didn't imagine it, Mum, and it wasn't grim news. It was about the ashes. He wanted to tell us where they should go. Where they should rest. He wanted me to know. He wanted all of us to know.'

As I was speaking Mrs Freemantle returned from the kitchen with the glass of water. She took a sip herself, as if testing it, and then handed it to me, licking her lips.

'Are you chewing baccy yourself now, Pauline?' she asked.

'Why do you ask?' my mother replied and we looked at Mrs Freemantle as she approached.

'It's only that there's a freshly chewed baccy ball in the spittin' cup.'

Everyone looked at Mrs Freemantle and then they all looked at me. Hyacinth smiled, again.

'Was he a ghost, Fitzgerald? Your father?' Uncle Albie asked hopefully.

'I don't really know, Uncle Albie. I've never seen a ghost. He was clear as day though, not all fuzzy and white like ghosts are supposed to look like.'

'Was he all right?' Mr Plucker asked. 'Was he in good health?' I could hear the sound of loose change as Mr Plucker fiddled with items in his pocket.

'He looked fine,' I replied, 'considering he was dead. He said he was happy where he was. He said there were lots of trees and it smelled nice. He said none of you really knew where his ashes ought to go. He wasn't even sure you would know, Mum. I asked him if Hyacinth would know but he went before I got an answer.'

The nearest and dearest took a collective sharp intake of breath and eyed Hyacinth suspiciously as she stood behind the orange sofa, her gnarled hand resting on the back. She seemed to puff her chest out a little, taking on a slightly regal air. My mother reached out and grasped at my hands, holding them tightly. The moistness of her palms comforted me.

'Your hands, Fitzgerald!' Mr Plucker exclaimed.

'They look bigger,' Mrs Freemantle said.

'They seem to have grown a little,' Uncle Albie said, reaching out to touch them.

'And he's got sawdust in his hair,' Auntie Nerys said and she reached up to my hair. She extracted a small piece of sawdust and held it up to the light bulb to examine it. It was bright sawdust, quite beautiful. It held us spellbound for several moments as we looked at it.

'You can get more done with large hands, Auntie Nerys,' the words seemed to jump out of my mouth, I had no control over them. The boom of my own voice shocked me. Mr Plucker jumped in his seat as he heard it, the flesh around his neck quivering again.

'And your voice, Fitzgerald,' my mother said.

'It sounds different,' Auntie Nerys said.

'Like it's broken,' Uncle Albie said.

'More gravelly,' Mr Plucker said.

'It has, Fitzgerald,' my mother said. 'I think your voice has broken.'

Everyone looked at me with surprise. They asked me to say something else, so they could hear the voice.

'What shall I say?' I asked.

'Anything,' they said.

'The rain in Spain falls mainly on the plain,' I said.

They listened. They smiled. Uncle Albie smiled the most and I knew that he was thinking of Spain as well as my new voice. They gave me a small round of applause.

'It has,' they agreed. 'His voice has broken.'

'Fitzgerald is almost a man now,' Hyacinth spoke and Auntie Nerys looked more nervous than ever. Mrs Freemantle straightened the creases in her floral-print dress and Mr Plucker sat up straight, holding on to the flesh around his neck to stop it quivering. 'He has a job to do,' Hyacinth announced.

'The ashes?' my mother spoke, tightening the grip on my hand. I almost winced.

'That is correct, my dear,' Hyacinth replied and she nodded toward the red casket. We all looked at the red casket. 'Fitzgerald must take them on a journey. When he returns he will be a man. Kind of. Won't you, Fitzgerald?'

I nodded. Something deep inside me agreed completely with what Hyacinth was saying, as if it was my destiny to go on this journey she spoke of. I thought of Saint Roderick of Leicester the Patron Saint of Unsound Minds, and wondered if this was how he had felt when he had received his calling.

'Fitzgerald's father . . .' Hyacinth continued and bowed her head solemnly; we all followed suit; '. . . came from a place that, in life, he sadly never got to see. He wasn't born there mind, but he held that place close to his heart. He very rarely spoke of it, except to Fitzgerald and occasionally to Pauline, but it was dear to him. It was part of him and he was more proud of it than words can truly tell. He kept that place alive in his heart, even though he never saw it. Unless his ashes are returned to that place he won't be able to find complete rest. His spirit will not be as happy as it should be, my dears.'

'What place are you talking about, Hyacinth?' Uncle Albie asked, furrowing his brow.

'The place that he came from, Albie. The place where he really started from,' Hyacinth said.

'She means Africa, Uncle Albie. My father was from Africa. That's where he wants his ashes to go,' I said and I could feel my Adam's apple adjusting in my throat to the boom of my new voice.

'Africa?' Uncle Albie puzzled. 'But your father wasn't African, Fitzgerald, he was from Wistful.'

'I can't say I ever thought of him as African, he wasn't even very brown, not brown so's you'd notice,' said Mr Plucker, adjusting the belt on his trousers. 'I know he was part African, but he was British really, wasn't he? He never spoke of being African to me.'

'He did to me,' I said. 'Well, kind of anyway. He said that even though I was only part African, I had as much right to be as proud of being African as someone who was fully African.'

My mother nodded in recognition. She'd heard my father telling me these things and of course there had been the great *jollof* rice and *moin moin* debacle. And I'd often heard them having other, darker discussions about being African that they kept from me. Whenever my father had spoken to me about being African, my mother had always left the room or gone out of the house. If she went out my father would say, 'I hope she doesn't go to the *Hinterland*.' I remembered another time, several years previously, when my father had spoken to me about being African. It was the first time he had referred to the *Hinterland*.

It was an Easter Sunday morning, my mother was whistling that week and my father had just completed a piano stool for Mrs Labwicka, the piano teacher.

'I've just finished the stool for Mrs Labwicka,' he had said as he came in from the garden removing a splinter from his finger (he usually got up early to work in his shed before breakfast). He sat down heavily on a chair at the kitchen table. It creaked under his weight. My mother was at the cooker frying eggs and mushrooms. My mother never fried eggs and bacon, eggs on their own, yes, bacon on its own, yes, but never eggs and bacon together. She said it was too conventional to cook eggs and bacon together. If, she said, the whole nation is up at the same time cooking eggs and bacon together then she wanted no part of it. So, in rebellion, she would cook eggs and mushrooms, eggs and tomatoes, bacon and black pudding, bacon and mushrooms; any combination to be different, but she never cooked eggs and bacon together on the same plate. She carried on whistling and frying whilst my father extracted the tiny splinter.

'Are you pleased with it?' my mother said, taking a brief respite from her whistling (she'd been whistling Bix Beiderbecke's 'Royal Garden Blues').

'Yes,' my father replied and my mother resumed her whistling. My father looked over at me. I was next to him at the table

105

and I had some paper and felt-tip pens sprawled in front of me.

'What are you drawing, son?' my father had asked, leaning forward to look at my picture.

'I'm drawing a picture of Mrs Braithwaite, my teacher,' I replied and I held my picture up in front of my father. He took it in his hands and held it up to the light. He looked intently at my squiggles of browns and blacks and yellows and reds on the paper.

'It's beautiful, son,' he said. 'It looks just like her.'

'It does?' I said, amazed.

'Yes son, it does. And it looks like so many other beautiful African women who have gone before. *C'est magnifique!*'

'It does?' I said again.

'Yes son, it does.'

'But Mrs Braithwaite said she comes from Jamaica,' I said, looking at my picture as it dangled in the light of the window.

'I know she did, son,' my father said, returning the picture to me and leaning back in his chair. He pulled out his baccy pouch and rolled a small baccy ball. He popped it between his broad lips and continued, 'But like all black people across the world, Mrs Braithwaite originally came from Africa.'

'She did?' I said in awe. 'And is Mrs Braithwaite proud to be African too, Dad?'

'I don't really know the answer to that, Fitzgerald, but I hope she is,' my father said and my mother came over to the table and placed two plates of eggs and mushrooms in front of us.

'Eggs and mushrooms,' she proclaimed. 'They're Easter eggs. I couldn't get any Easter mushrooms, they'd sold out, you'll have to make do with these,' my mother chuckled to herself. 'What were you two talking about?'

'About being African,' my father replied, picking up his knife and fork and removing the baccy ball from his mouth, 'I was telling Fitzgerald about being proud to be African.'

'But he's only part African.'

'But part enough,' my father said and I could hear the first mouthful of mushrooms squidging around in his mouth.

106

'Well, carry on then,' my mother said, retreating to the front room. 'If you need me I'll be in the living room and don't forget to wash up your plates.' She closed the door behind her.

My father looked at me. His face was deadly serious. 'Your mother's gone to the *Hinterland*, son,' he said.

'Where's the *Hinterland*, Dad?' I asked. 'Is it further away than the Netherlands?'

'Yes, son, it is and it's flat like the Netherlands but it's also foggy, grey and very, very cold.' A drop of egg yolk ran down his chin. 'Your mother goes there occasionally, so do a lot of white folks. When they don't want to talk about Africa.' He wiped the yolk off on the back of his hand.

'They do? Will Mum come back?'

'Of course she will, son, she always does. She doesn't usually stay there for long – she loves us too much. But some white folks stay there a long time, son. And some never come back at all. Your mother will stop going there altogether soon. It's just a habit. She'll probably give it up for Lent next year.' My father laughed. I didn't know what Lent was but I laughed too.

'Will I ever have to go to the *Hinterland*, Dad?'

'Not really, son. You're African.' My father's face became serious again. 'Some Africans do go to the *Hinterland* for a little while, if they get confused or take the wrong turn, but they don't usually stay there for long. They soon realise they can't be them-selves in the *Hinterland*. They're not allowed to talk about Africa, they're not allowed to eat *jollof* rice and it's very cold.'

'Have you ever been to the *Hinterland*?'

'Yes son, I'm afraid I have. I spent several years living there, but that was before I realised I was African. So I left. Sometimes I think I may have stayed there too long.'

I noticed a brief look of pain across my father's face. Although it was only brief, it seemed a very deep pain.

'You did?'

'Yes son, I believe I did.'

'Do they dance in the *Hinterland*, Dad?'

'Yes son, they do. But not very much and quite slowly, kind

of like chess pieces being moved around a chessboard. That's partly why your mother doesn't stay there very long.'

I munched on a mouthful of eggs and mushroom, the thick lard sliding over my tongue, and tried to imagine the *Hinterland*.

'But, Fitzgerald,' my father boomed, 'you need never worry about having to go to the *Hinterland*. As long as you always remember to be proud to be African, you'll never have to go to there. That's a fact.'

The following week in school, I had asked Mrs Eugena Braithwaite about the *Hinterland*.

'I was drawing a picture of you last week, Mrs Braithwaite, when we were having breakfast,' I had said when the class had shuffled out for playtime, 'when my father told me about the *Hinterland*. Do you know anything about the *Hinterland*, Mrs Braithwaite?'

'No, Fitzgerald, I don't believe I do,' Mrs Braithwaite had replied, wiping the white chalk off of the blackboard with her duster. She turned to face me, her beautiful black skin oily and shining. The hairs on her top lip standing neatly together like a regiment on parade.

'My father says it's a place where white folks go when they don't want to talk about Africa,' I said and I gazed at the regiment.

'Then yes, Fitzgerald,' Mrs Braithwaite said putting her hands on her hips and nodding. 'Then yes, I believe I do know about the *Hinterland*. In fact I think I may have been there on one or two occasions.'

'You have? Did you get the wrong bus? What was it like?'

'Fitzgerald,' Mrs Braithwaite leaned forward close to my face, her breath warm on my face, her whiskers comfortably close, 'my sweet lickle pickney. The *Hinterland* was rather cold and unfriendly. I did not find it very welcoming. I did not stay long. And do you know, Fitzgerald, I think most of the white folks didn't seem to like it there either. Some of them said they only went there out of habit, said they found it hard to give up even though they didn't like it. Some said they only went there because their parents had taken them there every year when they were children and it was kind of a ritual. Most of them said that if they knew how then they would stop going altogether. I have to say, Fitzgerald, I've since met lots of white people who have stopped going to the *Hinterland* altogether and they won't let their children go there at all, y'know. You have nothing to fear about the *Hinterland*, Fitzgerald.'

My father once told me of another conversation he had had about being African when he had worked as a security guard at Brady's Waxworks Well. We were on our way to the dentist's on Passover Crescent (just down the road from St Roderick's). My mother usually took me to the dentist but, rarely for her, she was in bed with the flu.

'I've got the flu,' she informed my father, snot dripping from her red nose. 'You'll have to take Fitzgerald to his dental appointment.'

'Is it the real flu?' my father asked, stirring two teaspoons of sugar into his tea.

'Real enough,' my mother had replied. 'I'm going to bed.'

I didn't see her again for four days.

As we turned the corner into Passover Crescent my father began to tell me of the need for me to be proud to be African.

'Son,' he began, 'I want you to know that you must always be proud to be African, despite what others may say.' He then went on to tell me about the conversation . . .

My father had been sitting in the staff room with Norman Wreckin, another of the security guards he worked with. Norman Wreckin, my father said, was a tall, carnal man with unnecessary gaps in between his teeth and an elongated nose, like a snout; a weasel's snout. He was a pest, my father said, and was always sniffing around, sticking his long snout into other people's business. They were taking a break, listening to the radio when a news item about Africa came up.

'Have you ever been to Africa, Norman?' my father asked.

'No,' Norman had replied, twitching his long snout, 'and neither would I ever want to go.'

'Why not?'

'Because there's too many fucking Africans over there that's why.'

'Don't you like Africans, Norman?'

'Not really,' Norman said, leaning back in his chair, his snout sniffing at the air around him.

'Why not?'

'Well, one . . .' Norman replied holding one finger up in front of my father's face, '. . . because they're fucking African and two,' (he held up a second finger in the universal sign for peace) 'because they're fucking black. That's fucking why.'

My father said he had shifted awkwardly in his seat.

'But . . .' he said leaning closer to Norman Wreckin's face, his nose almost touching the snout; my father could smell his breath which, he said, smelled like rotten fish, '. . . one, Norman, *I'm* fucking African and two, *I'm* fucking black.' My father held up two fingers in Norman's face (an inverted peace sign).

'No, mate,' Norman said unperturbed, 'don't be fucking stupid. One, you're not fucking African and two, you ain't fucking black. You was fucking born here so you're fucking British and you ain't fucking black you're fucking brown. You ain't a fucking coon, not like them fucking coons in Africa anyway, with their big fucking lips, matty fucking hair and mud-fucking-huts. We don't want that fucking lot fucking coming over here causing any bongo-bongo fucking trouble. No, don't you fucking worry mate you're fucking well one of us.'

'Oh,' my father said, 'I never thought of it like that before.' My father smiled as he told me that he had risen from his seat and towered over Norman Wreckin like a chimney stack. 'Excuse me,' he said, and he told me that he removed the smoking Players No. 6 from between Norman's thin, dry lips with his left hand and placed it carefully in an ashtray (a Spanish ashtray that Norman had brought back the previous year after two weeks of sun and sex on the Costa Blanca). 'You can finish it later,' my father told him and with his monstrous right hand, before Norman had time to reply, my father punched him, with crashing force

110

straight on the bridge of his long nose; the snout. The force sent Norman Wreckin sprawling across the floor. Blood began to trickle from his broken nose before he had even hit the floor. My father told me he was sure he could see stars floating in the air above Norman's head. He'd stood over Norman as he trembled and shook on the staff-room floor.

'Don't worry, mate,' my father said and returned the No. 6 to Norman's mouth. The blood from his nose had trickled over his thin lips and on to the cigarette, 'you was born here, Norman, you're entitled to free healthcare for that nose. Get yourself up to St Roderick's and maybe one of them fucking coon doctors will fix it for you, unless of course they've all gone back to fucking Africa.'

My father smiled broadly when he'd finished recounting his story and apologised for having used the 'f' word. 'It wasn't me you understand, that used it? It was Norman Wreckin. I was just mimicking him.' And I nodded; but he didn't apologise for hitting Norman Wreckin on his long snout. It was shortly after the incident that my father was made redundant. He never told my mother about the incident (or the fact that he'd used the 'f' word). Neither did I. By the time my father got to the end of his story we were sitting in the dentist's waiting room, the grating sound of her drill buzzing in the background.

'Never let anyone say stupid things to you about Africa or Africans, son,' my father said, wrapping his arm around my shoulder. 'Be proud to be African, son.'

'I will, Dad,' I said just as my name was called and I felt a stirring in my stomach. As I walked into the dismal dentist's surgery wishing that I'd cleaned my teeth just one more time to add to the three I'd already managed, I looked back at my father, who smiled encouragingly at me. I looked down at his enormous hands and thought of them crashing into Norman Wreckin's long snout. I felt a little shiver of fear as I tried to imagine how hands that could create such wonders could also be responsible for such a brutal act, justified perhaps, but brutal nonetheless. As the dentist's door closed behind me, I caught one last fleeting glimpse of my father as he lifted his monstrous right hand and waved with tenderness in my direction.

Whilst it is true to say that my father would tell me to be proud to be African, he told me very little about Africa itself. Apart from the uneasy discussion with Mrs Sharratt, the dinner-lady, I had asked no one else about Africa until my middle years in primary school. It was then that I decided to ask Mrs Braithwaite.

We had been playing one of our favourite games in the school-yard. The game involved the flicking of one of your shoes as high up a wall as you could get it. The highest up the wall was the winner. We called the game the 'flicking game'. You had to be wearing slip-on shoes or you had to remove the laces from the designated shoe. Seven of us were playing. Four of us had laces and we had made a little pile at the foot of the steps. They looked like an abandoned clump of liquorice. We were flicking in alphabetical order. It was a new rule devised by Clive Barrington.

'We must flick in alphabetical order,' he'd said as he carefully removed his laces and folded them neatly, placing them at the foot of the steps to begin the liquorice pile.

'Why?' Rabbit Warren asked, shaking and stretching his right leg in readiness for the great contest.

'Because it makes a lot of sense. It will give some order to things,' Clive replied. 'Can you think of a better suggestion? One with the least amount of fuss and one that stops all the squabbles and fights we've had before.'

'No,' Rabbit said, 'I don't think I can.'

'But the littler kids won't be able to join us,' Michael Sawyer said, pushing his leg up against the wall to stretch his calf muscles.

'Why not?' Clive asked.

'Because most of them don't know their alphabets yet. Not properly anyway. My little cousin thinks that "i" comes before "e" and up until last week he wouldn't believe that "q" was in the alphabet. He thought that the only type of "q"s were the ones outside Gray's Fish and Chip Plaice. The ones his mother is always complaining about. He said you wouldn't be able to fit a "q" that long into the alphabet.'

'It does by the way, except after "c",' I said and they had all looked at me and frowned. 'The "i" I mean.'

'I don't think we need worry about the littler kids,' Clive proclaimed. 'Firstly, it is very rare for any littler kids to join us as their legs are too bleedin' teeny to get a good flick. And secondly, if they do we'll just have to put them in alphabetical order ourselves.' We conceded and nodded in agreement.

'How do you spell "h"?' Barry Saddler asked.

'A-I-T-C-H,' Clive Barrington replied.

'Shouldn't there be an "h" in that?' Barry Saddler queried.

'There is,' Clive said, 'at the end.'

'But shouldn't there be one at the beginning?'

'There could be,' Clive said, knowingly, 'but then it would be *haitch* and the "h" would have to be silent and there would be no point in putting it there.'

'Oh,' Barry Saddler mumbled. 'But I always thought it was *haitch*'

'No Barry, it's *aitch* not *haitch*. It doesn't need a silent "h" because it's just *aitch*.'

'Like "oh" you mean,' Barry Saddler mused. '"Oh" has a silent "h" in it. What was the point in putting that there?'

'No it doesn't,' Wayne Haynes interjected, '"O" doesn't have a silent anything in it. It's just "o".'

'No,' Barry Saddler spoke, his voice raising slightly, '"Oh" has a silent "h". You know when you say "Oh dear" or "Oh my". It has a silent "h".'

'Oh,' Wayne sighed and nodded his head, 'I see what you mean. You're right.'

'Which also has a silent "h" in it too,' Michael Sawyer said with excitement. He could see the puzzled looks on our faces, '"Right" has a silent "h" in it too,' he explained.

'And a silent "g",' Rabbit Warren said, picking up the theme.

'So it does,' Clive spoke in professorial tones. 'In fact most of it is silent. Most of it is, in fact, almost extinct. Like the Tyrannosaurus Rex or the Engelbert Humperdink.'

'Right,' we said together and we spent a few moments in silence ruminating on the missing letters and thinking about extinct tyrannosauruses and humperdinks.

When the 'flicking game' commenced we stood in our alphabetical line flicking our shoes up against the school wall. The school wall backed on to a church; the Church of the Holy and Immaculate Resurrection Dawn, a small but well-attended Anglican church with round windows along the sides and huge stained-glass affairs at the front. It looked rather like a reverential boat or a smaller version of Noah's Ark. The vicar at the Church of the Holy and Immaculate Resurrection Dawn was called the Reverend James Alabaster. The Reverend Alabaster was a small, unusually muscular middle-aged man with the widest bow legs I had ever seen. When he stood still, the view between his legs was panoramic. He would come into our school to take rather long and tedious Religious Assemblies.

'You'd want to be bowling against him in a game of cricket,' Michael Sawyer once whispered to me as we sat in the back row of a particularly harrowing assembly.

'Why?' I asked.

'Look at those legs,' Michael said. 'You could bowl the ball clean through that bow and straight out the other side on to the wicket.' We giggled for several minutes as we gazed at the bow and the shaft of sunlight shining between the legs, while the Reverend Alabaster continued his homily on the dangers of hypocrisy.

'I am reading from Saint Matthew, chapter six, verse one,' he said adjusting his dog-collar,

'Beware of practising your righteousness before men to be noticed by them; otherwise you have no reward with your Father who is in heaven. When therefore you give alms, do not sound a trumpet before you as the hypocrites do in the Synagogues and in the streets, that they may be honoured by men.

Truly I say to you, they have their reward in full . . .'

'Who would want to give away their arms anyway?' I whispered in disgust.

'They used to in the olden days,' replied Michael keeping his voice low, not wanting to be heard. 'Jesus told them it was better to give away their arms or legs or even their eyeballs than to be thrown into Hell with all their bits in place.'

'Why?' I asked in disbelief.

'Dunno. It was meant to be a way of making it harder to sin.'

'Oh,' I said, 'and who was Trudy?'

'She was the person Jesus was talking to, a friend of the Virgin Mary, one of the epistles. He was always saying . . . "Trudy I say to you" this and "Trudy I say to you" that. I think he liked Trudy a lot. She had a sister called Verity.'

It was as the 'flicking game' neared its natural conclusion that my flicking shoe flicked too far. It flew from the end of my foot and sailed like a swooping seagull over the school wall and into the overgrown rear garden of the Church of the Holy and Immaculate Resurrection Dawn. In fact, after it had disappeared, a seagull swooped above the church, which was strange as we very rarely saw seagulls in Wistful.

'WOW!' we all said in awe and wonder, looking up at the wall.

'That's the biggest flick I've ever seen,' said Emerson Darkly, vocalising our thoughts.

'A New World Flick Record,' said Rabbit Warren (the wall was at least fifteen feet high).

'A *European* Flick Record, at least,' rectified Clive Barrington. 'You'll have to ask Mrs Braithwaite if she'll take you to go and find it. You can't hop for the rest of the day.'

And so I hopped over to Mrs Eugena Braithwaite, who was on playground patrol.

'Mrs Braithwaite,' I said, balancing precariously on my one remaining shoe.

'Yes, Fitzgerald,' Mrs Braithwaite said staring at my shoeless foot.

'I've lost my shoe,' I said.

'Yes, Fitzgerald, I can see that. And just how did that happen?'

'It's in the Church of the Holy and Immaculate Resurrection Dawn,' said Michael Sawyer, who had now joined me. 'In the garden.'

'And how did it manage to get there, Fitzgerald?' Mrs Braithwaite said. 'Were you playing that flicking game again?'

'Yes Mrs Braithwaite, we were,' I confessed contritely.

'But it was a New European Flick Record,' Michael Sawyer interjected and held my arm aloft like a victorious boxer. When he let go of my arm my standing foot began to wobble. I could feel myself about to topple when Mrs Braithwaite grabbed hold of me and steadied me, preventing my fall.

Wearing one of Michael Sawyer's shoes whilst he remained in class, I went with Mrs Braithwaite to hunt for the missing shoe in the garden of the Church of the Holy and Immaculate Resurrection Dawn.

'We'll be in the garden,' Mrs Braithwaite announced from the front of the class, holding her hands on her wide hips, 'looking for Fitzgerald's shoe. Karen Carpenter will be in charge whilst I'm gone.' Karen Carpenter smiled rather smugly. She often smiled smugly, 'the Smug Smirk' we would call it in later years. 'Stay awake. Keep watch!' Mrs Braithwaite added mysteriously.

The class cheered as we left the room. I turned and waved to them all, Fitzgerald – Flicking-Shoe Champion. European Record Holder.

We slipped into the garden through the side gate. Mrs Braithwaite in front, me behind. Teachers were allowed to slip into the garden of the church at any time they liked, but not children.

'Teachers are allowed to slip into the garden of the Church of the Holy and Immaculate Resurrection Dawn whenever they wish,' the Reverend Alabaster had once informed us on a cold winter's morning. It was so cold, due to the radiators packing up, that we all were wearing two jumpers and thick mittens or gloves. Some of us even wore scarves. 'For contemplation purposes only, but not children, unless of course they are accompanied by a teacher and then only for contemplation purposes. In addition, the group of the children must not exceed twelve and the children must all come from good church-going homes.' The Reverend Alabaster did not seem to have taken into account the fact that we were unlikely to be able to muster up a group of twelve children from church-going homes from any one class at any given time. In our class we only had about five children whose families regularly went to church; most notable of those was Mary Lamb, a Catholic, whose family religiously attended Our Gracious Lady of the Morning Dew every Sunday morning and Zacharias Jones, a Baptist, whose family zealously attended the Strict Baptist Tabernacle of Wistful on Tapestry Street twice every Sunday and once during the week. As for the rest of us we only ever went to church if someone was christened, married or dead or if we thought we might get a Christmas present. 'I'd rather scratch me nuts than go to church,' was how Rabbit Warren put it.

'What's contemplation?' Emerson Darkly asked.

'It's thinking about something that is really horrible. Like treating someone or something with disgust,' Clive Barrington replied from his encyclopaedic head of misinformation.

'Oh I see,' Emerson replied. 'So the teacher and the twelve would go or be sent to the garden to think about something naughty or bad they had done.'

'Exactly. Like a punishment,' Clive said. 'Now shush, he's about to talk about the Ten Commandments again. Last week he spoke about covering your neighbour's house. I want to ask him why you would want to cover your neighbour's house when you are supposed to love your neighbour. And if you do have to cover your neighbour's house, what should you cover it with?'

Mrs Braithwaite and I trod carefully up the contemplation path to the rear of the garden. The area that backed on to our school was wild, overgrown and full of brambles and nettles. It reminded me of what my mother had told me secondary school would be like.

'What are secondary schools like, Mum?' I had asked – we were watching a documentary on teenage children in America.

'Wild, overcrowded and full of brambles and nettles,' she had said. 'Watch out when you're old enough to go there!'

'Will we have to contemplate whilst we're here?' I asked Mrs Braithwaite, fixing the bottom of my trousers into my socks to prevent my legs from being stung by the nettles.

'No, Fitzgerald,' she replied, hitching her skirt and stepping into the brambles. 'We won't have time. We're only here to find your shoe.' We trampled the nettles down together and our search began. A pigeon watched us as we trod, its head bobbed from side to side, its eyes rolling in their little sockets. The sun was warm and I could smell the lovely aroma of roses in the air.

'Do you know anything about Africa, Mrs Braithwaite?' I asked, lifting a bramble bush to peer underneath it, being careful not to prick my fingers.

'Africa?' Mrs Braithwaite replied, wiping sweat from her brow. 'Yes Fitzgerald, I do. Africa is such a huge place, such a vast continent, it's so many miles away from here. It's made up of lots of countries y'know, and each and every one is much bigger than this tiny island. Africa is a place that's rich in colour; reds and golds and greens and bright blue skies. And it is hot and sticky like a treacle sponge. Does your mother make treacle sponge, Fitzgerald?'

I nodded and I thought of my mother's treacle sponges, Dad usually got most of the hot treacle.

'And the sky, Fitzgerald. The sky in Africa is so much bluer than blue ought to be, y'know. And the sun is a bright ball of fire and the sea laps gently around the shores like lickle children coming home from school. And do you know, Fitzgerald, Africa is full of black people, of all shades, every kind of black and brown you can imagine.'

'Like you, Mrs Braithwaite?'

'Yes, Fitzgerald, like me and like *you* y'know, Fitzgerald, and like your father too.'

'But I'm not very black, Mrs Braithwaite,' I said and I showed her my bare arm as if to prove it. 'Neither is my Dad.'

'Oh yes you are, Fitzgerald. You're skin may be a lighter brown than mine but you're as black as any boy that's ever lived in Africa.'

'Are there any white people in Africa, Mrs Braithwaite?'

'Yes Fitzgerald, there are. But some of them haven't always treated black people very nicely. In fact, some of them have treated black people very badly.'

The pigeon cooed and, as I stepped forward, I snagged my sock on a thorn. It pierced my flesh through the sock. 'Ouch,' I winced quietly to myself. 'Will they always treat the black people badly?' I said as a tiny patch of blood oozed through my sock, staining the white cotton.

'No, Fitzgerald,' Mrs Braithwaite said, stopping to catch her breath, 'no one can be nasty for ever, the earth gets fed up with nasty people and they begin to feel kinda self-conscious and ignorant. It's rather like that thorn that's just pricked you. That thorn can be as nasty as it likes to you but you can still trample it down. You can still mash it down under your feet. And one day anyway the Reverend Alabaster will probably get out his Alabaster shears and clear all these thorns and brambles away.'

'Are you from Africa, Mrs Braithwaite?'

'I was actually born in Jamaica, Fitzgerald, but my ancestors all came from Africa.'

'Do all black people come from Africa?'

'I like to believe *all* people come from Africa, Fitzgerald, not just black people.'

'Are you proud to be African, Mrs Braithwaite?'

'Yes, Fitzgerald. In a strange kind of way I believe I am. Are *you* proud to be African, Fitzgerald?'

I thought for a moment as I stood, one foot in the bramble bush, the other pressed firmly on a clump of grass. I looked at Mrs Braithwaite, her chest puffed out, her dark black face, the sweat oozing from her brow. I took a deep breath, the smell of roses filling my nostrils.

'Yes, Mrs Braithwaite,' I said and held my head up high, 'I believe I am too.'

We continued to look for the victorious flicking-shoe for a further half hour or so but to no avail. It was never found. We left the contemplation garden and returned to Karen Carpenter and her temporary charges. She was still smiling smugly. I gave Michael Sawyer his shoe back and he slipped it on. I hopped home from school that day. It took a long time. When I got home my mother asked me why I had hopped home.

'Because I lost my shoe,' I told her, balancing on my one good shoe.

'Where?' she asked.

'In the garden. The contemplation garden at the back of the Church of the Holy and Immaculate Resurrection Dawn.'

'Well you'd better go and look for it then,' my mother said sucking in her cheeks.

'I did, with Mrs Braithwaite. We couldn't find it. It's lost, missing. Like a silent "h".'

My mother let out the air in her cheeks and said no more, not even to ask about the silent 'h' which I wished she had so that I could have explained to her my newly acquired knowledge of the intricacies of the alphabet. My mother and father could not afford to buy me a new pair of shoes for three weeks. In the meantime I had to pull out an old pair from the bottom of my cupboard. They were two sizes too small and squeezed my toes from all angles; they were also wholly inappropriate for the flicking-shoe game, which meant I had to watch from the side-lines for the next three weeks.

Several weeks later as we walked past the contemplation garden we saw the Reverend Alabaster with his mighty Alabaster shears hacking away at the thorns and I thought of what Mrs Braithwaite had told me in the garden. When the Reverend had finished I went over to the railings and, putting my head over the top, asked him if he had found my flicking-shoe.

'No, young lad,' he said in his usual authoritative tone. 'There's no flicking-shoes in here. In fact there are no shoes here at all. If there was I'm sure I would have found it by now just like Jehovah always manages to find the Lost Sheep of Israel.'

IX
Sex

The nearest and dearest had gone home. The decision had been made. My father's ashes would go to Africa. Hyacinth had summed up like a High Court judge.

'And so,' she began, her teeth jiving wildly, flecks of spittle leaping through the air. I felt inclined to duck to avoid the spray or rush to grab my raincoat. 'We are all in agreement. Fitzgerald's father's ashes will be laid to rest in Africa. Where his spirit will find comfort and peace. Is everyone in agreement?'

'Yes, yes, Hyacinth we're all agreed,' Uncle Albie said, seemingly annoyed that Hyacinth had taken over his role as chair of the meeting. 'If that's what Fitzgerald feels his father would want then I guess we ought to respect his wishes.'

'The wishes of a ghost more like,' Mrs Freemantle said. 'You shouldn't meddle with ghosts.'

'It wasn't a ghost,' Mr Plucker said. 'It was his father. It was the boy's father.'

'And there's nothing wrong with meddling with ghosts,' Uncle Albie added.

'The boy's *dead* father,' Mrs Freemantle said and she turned her back on them both.

'There's nothing wrong with ghosts,' Uncle Albie repeated. 'And I should know, I've been chasing them all my life.'

'Seeing a ghost is one thing but talking to one is another thing altogether,' Mrs Freemantle seemed on the edge of tears. 'It's bloody wrong. See, now you've made me swear.'

'But you believe in angels don't you?' Hyacinth looked directly at Mrs Freemantle. Mrs Freemantle coughed, holding her hand over her mouth.

'So what if I do?' Her tidy hair was beginning to fall apart. 'What have angels got to do with ghosts anyway?'

'Well,' Hyacinth said, and her teeth could easily have been mistaken for ghouls themselves, 'ghosts, angels, visions, who really knows how God chooses to communicate with us? It's not for us to know, you've just got to have faith. Isn't that what you've always believed?'

'We're not talking about *my* faith, we're talking about ghosts. Stuff and bloody nonsense, that's what it is, stuff and bloody nonsense,' Mrs Freemantle defended herself. 'Oh Pauline, I am sorry, they've made me swear twice now.'

'Three times actually,' Mr Plucker said.

'That's all right, Agnes, we're all a little bit uptight. It's been a difficult day,' my mother said.

'But the point is,' Uncle Albie said, trying to gain some control over the meeting again, 'the point is that the ashes should be taken to Africa. Are we all agreed?'

The nearest and dearest nodded, even Mrs Freemantle despite her reservations. My mother squeezed my hands again. A tear rolled down her cheek and splashed on to the malt loaf plate that lay on her lap.

'Well, how are we going to get him there?' said Mr Plucker, tucking his sweater into his belt. 'The ashes I mean.'

'In the red casket of course,' said Uncle Albie.

'I realised that, Albie,' said Mr Plucker. 'I mean how will whoever goes get to Africa?'

'On a plane would be my suggestion,' said Hyacinth.

'I realise that too, Hyacinth,' said Mr Plucker, patiently.

'Although I suppose you're going to tell us you've got wings and can fly them there.'

Hyacinth smiled at Mr Plucker and flapped her arms. She didn't take off.

'No, what I meant was,' continued Mr Plucker, 'how will we be able to afford to get the ashes to Africa?'

'We could have a whip-round,' Auntie Nerys said.

'It would have to be a bloody big whip-round,' said Mr Plucker and he looked at my mother. 'Oops,' he said.

'Look,' my mother said. 'Will everyone please stop using the "bloody" word. You all know how much I hate it.'

The nearest and dearest mumbled apologies, except Auntie Nerys who mumbled that she had nothing to apologise for, as she had not used the 'bloody' word.

'But perhaps Albie is right,' Hyacinth said. 'Maybe a whip-round would be the solution.'

'I've got a couple of hundred pounds I've still got saved from Henry's will,' Mrs Freemantle said. 'I'd be more than happy to give you some of that. An old biddy like me will never get round to spending it all and I've got no children, only my cats.'

'And I've got a little nest egg,' said Mr Plucker. 'You could use some of that. I've been saving it for a rainy day but it always seems to rain in my life anyway.'

My mother reached over and rubbed Mr Plucker's hand. 'Thank you,' she whispered.

'And I could sell some of my dusty old ornaments,' Auntie Nerys said. 'They're bound to be worth a bob or two. I've been meaning to have a spring clean anyway.'

'And we could ask some of the neighbours,' said Uncle Albie, thrusting a note he had been scribbling under my mother's nose. 'I've written a note; we'll copy it and stick it up in the street.'

Friends + neighbours. At this sad time we would like to ask for any financial donations (small or large) in

order to help young Fitzgerald take his
father's ashes on a journey. Fitzgerald
would like to take the ashes to Africa
and to sprinkle them in a place where
his father could never go in life. He
was after all African. Pauline &
Fitzgerald would never be able to raise
the finances without your help. Any
donations would be more than grate-
fully received. Signed, the nearest &
dearest of the young Fitzgerald.
P.S. On his return from Africa,
Fitzgerald will repay your kindness
by doing any odd jobs you require.

'And *you* could do some free plumbing jobs too, Uncle Albie,'
I said.

'Free?' Uncle Albie said looking a little worried. 'Well, maybe
one or two.'

'I'm not sure it'll work,' Mrs Freemantle said. 'No one's got
any money round here and you know what it's like, unless you're
in church no one ever gives money away and even then no one
really wants to.'

'What about his wood?' Hyacinth asked and the room went
silent.

'What do you mean?' Auntie Nerys spoke.

'What about selling off some of his wood; some of his
creations?' Hyacinth said.

'But would that be right?' Mrs Freemantle asked. 'To sell off
a dead man's creations?'

'What do you need them for?' Hyacinth asked. 'Do you think
Fitzgerald's father made things just to sit in his shed for ever?'

'There is an awful lot in the shed,' I said. 'Chairs, stools, a

bookcase, loads of stuff and they're all finished, every last one.'
There was a further silence and the nearest and dearest looked
at my mother.

'I think it's what he would have wanted,' Hyacinth said.

'She's right,' my mother said. 'We'll sell it all. What good is
it doing sitting in the shed?'

'Are you sure, Pauline?' Uncle Albie asked, leaning forward
in his chair. 'Are you sure that's really what you want to do?'

'No Albie, I'm not,' my mother said. 'But Hyacinth's right, he
wouldn't have wanted his creations just sitting in the shed
collecting dust. It's better that they're put to good use.'

'And what about you, Hyacinth?' Auntie Nerys said, eyeing
Hyacinth suspiciously. 'What will you be able to give towards
the trip?'

'I've no money I'm afraid,' Hyacinth said and her teeth
appeared to want leap out of her mouth and testify to the fact.
'No money at all really but I would like to volunteer to go with
Fitzgerald.'

'One of *us* should go, surely?' Auntie Nerys said and the
thought of a journey so far with Auntie Nerys terrified me. She
wasn't my favourite relative.

'What makes you think you should go?' Uncle Albie said.

'No other reason than the fact that I've been to Africa many
times, in my younger days of course,' Hyacinth said. 'And I've
grown rather fond of Fitzgerald.'

'Well I certainly couldn't go,' said Mr Plucker, his flesh quivering. 'The journey would kill me.'

'And it would be too hot for me,' Mrs Freemantle said, adjusting
her collar as if just thinking about it made her hot.

'So you know Africa well, Hyacinth?' my mother asked.

'Yes,' Hyacinth spoke and she leaned forward, her sparkling
eyes lighting up the sombre room, 'very well indeed. I've journeyed there many times.'

'For what reason?' Auntie Nerys queried.

'Let's just say for work-related reasons,' Hyacinth said and it
was clear she would say no more.

'How would we know he would be safe travelling with you?'
my mother asked.

'Sometimes in life, Pauline, we just have to take a leap of faith,'
Hyacinth replied. 'He will be safe with me. You're in no fit state
to go yourself are you, Pauline? And we'd never raise enough
money for more than two of us to go. My contribution would
be my knowledge of the place and a promise to care for Fitzgerald.
I shall take great care of him, my dear. It would be a privilege
for an old lady like me to go with him. Fitzgerald, is there anything
you would like to say, my dear?'

I stood up and smoothed the creases out of my trousers. I
coughed and addressed the gathering.

'My father was here,' I said. 'Or, at least, a vision of him was
here. He came to me for just a few minutes; he was here. He
made it clear to me where he wants his ashes to go; where he
wants them to rest. The way I see it is that, as his only child, I
should be the one to take his ashes, the casket, to Africa. It would
be like taking him home. I'd be proud to take my dad home.
Hyacinth, I'm sure, will look after me and help me to get around.
I just feel I've known her for a lot longer than I really have. I
know that sounds strange but I do. I won't be alone, not with
her by my side. She'll be my guardian angel.'

I was surprised by the confidence in my own voice. I sat down
heavily. The room was quiet. I could hear Hyacinth's rasping as
she breathed and Mr Plucker cracking his knuckles. Hyacinth
rummaged in her pocket and withdrew her crumpled bag of boiled
sweets. She offered them around. Some had stuck together. We
each took one, some of us having to prise two sweets apart to
choose our favoured flavour. We popped the sweets into our
mouths and sucked. The room remained quiet except for the
sounds of sucking. I sucked hard on mine (a strawberry one) and
let the sweetness ooze across my tongue and in between the gaps
in my teeth. I thought about how confident I now felt and looked
again at my hands. I turned them over and over, looking at them
from every angle, holding them up to the light.

'They look like oars,' Uncle Albie said, noticing me. 'Like

your father's, great big wooden oars, shaped out of the finest wood. Take care of them, Fitzgerald. Don't let them splinter.'

'I will,' I said and my oars felt heavy.

'Do you have any malt loaf left, Pauline?' Mr Plucker asked. 'It's all gone,' my mother replied. 'But there's some carrot cake in the tin. I'll make another pot of tea and bring out the carrot cake. Everyone for carrot cake?' There was a general murmuring of approval.

I looked at my mother. 'Thanks, Mum, but not for me. I don't like carrots.' My mother looked at me and the colour flushed from her cheeks. 'No, of course you don't, Fitzgerald.'

'Mum,' I said, 'are you happy for Hyacinth to be the one who goes with me?'

My mother didn't reply. Instead she gazed into my eyes and my reflection in her eyes smiled back at me, like it always did even when I wasn't smiling, and then she turned on her heels and slipped into the kitchen.

After further milky tea and my mother's carrot cake, the nearest and dearest began to leave. Uncle Albie had to drive off in his Opel Kadett. ' I've got to dash,' he said, 'I've got to be in Plymouth by tomorrow morning, for a plumbing job. I'll drive through the night.' And as an aside to my mother, he whispered, 'I'm sure Fitzgerald is right. Hyacinth is the best person to be going with him, Paulie. What choice do we have?' My mother nodded and they held each other's hands for a moment. As he opened the front door the Granite children passed by, on their way to Mrs Labwicka's for their piano lesson. They were whistling Scott Joplin's 'The Entertainer' and marching like newly drafted soldiers.

Mr Plucker returned to his home, next door. 'I'd better be off,' he said as he stood swamped in his sweater, leaning slightly to one side, 'if I leave it too late I'll miss the last bus.' We laughed despite the fact that he said the same joke nearly every time he left our house. 'Thank you, Pauline. It's been an interesting day.'

Mrs Freemantle hurried off down our road eager to return to Albion Hill. 'The cats will be waiting for their tea,' she said as she departed, 'and Noah's been a little under the weather lately,

I want to make sure he gets an early night. I hope we've made the right decision.'

Auntie Nerys got a lift to the station with Uncle Albie. She'd be just in time to catch her train, she said. 'Goodbye, Pauline,' she said and the door closed behind her, bringing to an end the sombre meeting.

Auntie Nerys lived near Chessington, in Surrey, which housed one of the largest zoos in the country. She had only moved to Chessington because of her love of monkeys and she wanted to be as near to some as possible. She loved all primates – except humans. Humans made her nervous, she once told me, she could only tolerate humans in small doses.

I didn't go to Auntie Nerys's house very much and I was pleased that it was not more often. I hated going to Auntie Nerys's house. On several occasions, when my mother and father had gone away for a short holiday together or if my father was having a particularly bad 'dark' period, I had had to stay with Auntie Nerys. Her house was a small, white-washed cottage with dirty net curtains and a boot scraper by the front door (the only thing I liked about her house). Whenever I went out, I would deliberately get mud on my boots so I would be able to scrape them off on the boot scraper. The door of the house opened almost immediately on to a busy through road. It was always very noisy inside, the sound of cars and lorries rumbling past the front door. 'Is it always this noisy?' I once asked Auntie Nerys over a plate of fishpaste sandwiches and a mug of lukewarm tea.

'Usually, Fitzgerald, it is,' she replied dryly, 'unless the cars are wearing their slippers.'

Auntie Nerys was always nervous having me in the house and I was nervous being there. She would talk to me about nothing but monkeys. Her voice would drone on for hours, boring me rigid with the intricate details of various members of the primate family. Did I know, she would ask, that ring-tailed lemurs live together in small groups but occasionally could be found in groups numbering as many as thirty? Did I know, she would ask, why the lemur smears branches with scent from glands on its body? What was the difference between the Western Tarsier and the Spectral Tarsier? Did I know that the scientific name for the Allen's swamp monkey was the *Allenopithecus Nigrovindis*? Why, she would ask, did the male Barbary ape 'lip-smack' when it held its own offspring? I knew not, nor cared what the answers were or even could be to these grotesque questions. The fiery passion with which Auntie Nerys dispensed the questions frightened me. As a very young child, during my earliest visits, I would sit and stare at Auntie Nerys blankly, my hands trembling, as she pummelled me with her primatial interrogation. On one horrific occasion she stood in front of me, her arms flailing by her side, and demonstrated the pouting face and grooming technique of the pig-tailed macaque. When she began to mimic its mating call, her contorted face just a few inches from my face, her breath hot and putrid, smelling of fishpaste, I felt a slight squirt of wee seep into my pants, such was my terror. I reached my hand quickly down to my trousers and squeezed the end of my penis, to stop the wee from flooding out. Auntie Nerys had seen my hand and noted the squeeze. She stopped her mating call and told me to stop doing dirty things with my 'thing'. I was far too young for all that nonsense, she said and sent me to my room without any tea.

As I climbed up the wooden stairs to the spare bedroom, a sparse, bleak affair, with only one small window and wooden floors, I felt more trickles of warm wee seep into my pants and run down the inside of my leg. Despite my discomfort, I felt neither embarrassed nor upset at my spillage but, in truth, I was rather relieved that Mother Nature had seen fit to release me from the horrors of Auntie Nerys's animal farm.

When I finally reached the toilet and could release my wee in its entirety, on to the back of the enamel toilet pan, I sighed out loud and watched the jet of urine splashing into the pan with fascination. Auntie Nerys must have heard my sigh and had shouted up the stairs – 'And don't you be doing anything dirty with your thing up there either, you hear me, Fitzgerald!'

129

'I'm not!' I shouted back, my jet now turning to a terrified trickle. 'I'm peeing in the pan!'

'Make sure that's all you do!'

At the time I was too young to know what the 'dirty' things that I could do with my 'thing' were, so I made sure that I scrubbed my penis thoroughly with soap and water every night in case Auntie Nerys chose to come up the wooden stairs and inspect it. As I lay in bed that night, sleep eluding me, I frantically tried to imagine all the 'dirty' things it might be possible to do with my penis. Could I perhaps hold it out of the water every time I took a bath and never let it get clean? Could I get handfuls of dirt from the garden and rub them into my penis on a regular basis? Had Auntie Nerys thought that I had been rubbing dirt into my penis under my trousers? I eventually fell asleep, my head filled with 'dirty' imaginings and my hand clutching my penis. I was still clutching it when I awoke the next morning. Thereafter, clutching my penis to help me get to sleep became a habit of mine, particularly if I was worried or nervous.

On the few dark and sinister nights that I was forced to stay in Auntie Nerys's circus of horrors I would lay in my bed holding on to my penis tightly. Whenever I heard a creak on the wooden stairs I'd be afraid that she was on her way to my room. That the door would creak open and she would suddenly appear, demanding to inspect my penis and check its cleanliness. Worse still, I feared she might cut it off and carry it downstairs for a closer inspection under the fiendish glow of her reading lamp.

In time, of course, I became aware of what Auntie Nerys had really meant. My clutching of my penis under the bedcovers for comfort began to loosen and I began instead to rub it gently, which made me feel even nicer. I don't remember exactly how old I was, but the first time I rubbed it so much that a pleasant sticky fluid shot out of the end, my body tingled for what seemed like hours afterwards and I held the fluid in my hand and gazed at it with fascination. I rubbed my penis again, hard, through my pants, until more sticky fluid came out and then I left the fluid in my pants, enjoying the sticky feeling, and fell asleep. When I woke up the next morning the fluid had vanished. It was a miracle. Masturbating like that, surreptitiously under the covers, became my night-comforter when I couldn't sleep. Sometimes, because of that day at Auntie Nerys's when the wee had squirted into my pants and the consequent association with 'dirtiness', I enjoyed masturbating with a full bladder. The fear that my wee might spill out instead of the warm sticky fluid was a thrill. In my early years of sexual awakening, wee and masturbation became entwined.

As I grew older, my visits to Auntie Nerys became less frequent. Sometimes when I was at home watching wildlife documentaries with my mother and father I would expect Auntie Nerys to appear suddenly from the steaming depths of the jungle and terrify the camera crew with the blood-curdling mating call of the pig-tailed macaque. On another occasion a real group of pig-tailed macaques appeared on the tiny screen in our tiny front room, screeching wildly. I instinctively clutched at my penis and squeezed it hard. My mother and father both looked at me and then they looked down at my hand. Neither of them said anything. There was certainly no mention of going to my room. My mother leaned over to my father, who was stretching his giant toes out in front of him and spoke quietly into his ear. His toes wiggled as she spoke. I could just about make out the last few words she had said – 'He's at that age. Talk to him tonight, won't you? Before it's too late.' My father nodded and his toes wiggled again.

Later that night as I lay in bed, clutching my penis, the door eased open. The shaft of light from the landing caught my face and the mound that was my clutching hand under the covers.

'You can let go of it for a while, son,' my father said as he slipped into my room. He flicked on my bedside lamp and sat at the foot of my bed. I let go of my penis. My father folded his arms, which that night seemed cumbersome and heavy. He leaned back slightly. He looked a little like the Leaning Tower of Pisa, which I had read about in school. The glow of the lamp shone on one side of his face, leaving the other in shadow.

'Son,' he said sternly, 'your mother has said I need to talk to you about your willy and other things, like vaginas and sexual

131

intercourse. Do you know anything about sexual intercourse, son?' I shook my head. 'Well it won't take long,' my father reassured me.

'Was it the pig-tailed monkeys, Dad?' I asked nervously, awaiting some form of punishment. 'I just didn't want any wee to go down my legs.' (I had never told my parents of the terrors of Auntie Nerys's.)

'It wouldn't have been wee, son,' my father said. 'It would have been sperm. Spunk. And it shouldn't happen when you watch pig-tailed macaques on TV. Or when you watch pig-tailed macaques any place for that matter. It would upset your mother.'

Quite what my father meant eluded me but I was pleased that he did not appear to be telling me off. He then unfolded his arms and leaned forward and grabbed my hands. They disappeared into the depths of his own huge hands.

'I've always told you never to let your hands be idle, son,' he spoke, turning my hands over in his and gazing at them. 'But never let them be over-active either. Avoid extremes. Especially when it comes to pig-tailed macaques or any other member of the animal kingdom, for that matter. It's not right, is it, son?'

I didn't know what he meant but I shook my head anyway.

'Would it not be better to think of someone on the television, one of Charlie's Angels perhaps, the blonde one maybe or a pop-singer? What about Suzi Quattro or one of The Three Degrees?'

My father then went on to give me *The Sex Talk*. Everything I would ever need to know about sex in ten bedside minutes. He talked about my 'willy', about what to do with it when it got hard and why it was good to let it stay soft at least some of the time. He warned me that when I became a teenager, apart from getting spots and feet that would begin to smell, it would also become almost impossible for me to stop my willy from getting hard. He said it would go hard on buses, when I was having my tea or watching *Nationwide* and even in the classroom. I was terrified and worried that I might bang it on my classroom desk and that it might snap. My father told me about vaginas. He said they were wonderful and mysterious and nice and that when your willy was hard and you were old enough and you knew and loved a woman well, that a vagina was a good place to put your willy – 'Unless you're bent of course,' he had said. 'Then you wouldn't want to put your willy anywhere near a vagina.'

'What's bent, Dad?' I had asked.

'Someone that isn't straight, son, but you're too young to have to worry about things like that,' he had replied mysteriously. 'Ask your mother when you're older. She's good at explaining why some people are bent and some people are straight. It's beyond me.'

'Like roads, Dad?' I said. 'The road outside our school is bent, just by the telephone box.'

'Exactly,' my father said, seemingly relieved that the road outside my school was enough of an analogy to satisfy my curiosity.

My father then went on to say that every month women had something called a period. 'The Period', he said, 'is strange and more mysterious than The Vagina. Many men have tried to fathom the darkest depths of The Period but they have returned more baffled than when they set off. The Period is the eighth great wonder of the world. But a dark wonder. Your mother never whistles during The Period and she most certainly never dances.'

My father concluded his lamplight instruction with a brief résumé of all the male body parts followed by a rather longer summation of the female body parts. He paid particular attention to what he termed as 'The Universally Acknowledged Erogenous Zones' (which to me sounded like the parking area at Maybank University). When he got to the description of a woman's nipples, he took rather longer than he had on the other body parts. He seemed quite excited, especially when he began to describe how they became hard like bullets if you touched or sucked them. He stood to make one final comment – 'By the way, son. Sperm is what comes out of your willy when you're happy and if you've rubbed it a lot or put it inside a woman's vagina. Sometimes if your sperm meets her eggs, she'll have a baby. If you don't want a baby always use a johnny bag, you can buy some at Butler's chemist on Drummond Street when you're old enough. Always keep a tissue by your bedside and don't rub your willy too often and never when you're watching pig-tailed macaques on TV. Try to think about nipples instead. Human ones.'

My father left the room as quietly as he had slipped in. I was confused and a little afraid. I tried to erase all thoughts of vaginas and nipples from my mind. I made a mental note that I would have to ask my mother the next morning to tell me what my father had actually meant. What was The Period? Why would nipples turn into bullets if you rubbed them and if they did wouldn't they be dangerous? And why had my father kept referring to the pig-tailed macaques? Had Auntie Nerys spoken to him about the squeeze? I put my hand back under my cover and felt for my penis. I held it firmly in my hand. There was a gentle tap at the door. It eased open. My father appeared again. He stood in the doorway, his vastness silhouetted by the landing light. I couldn't see his face – 'I almost forgot,' he said. '*Sexual Intercourse; the act of sexual procreation in which a male's erect penis is inserted into the female vagina; copulation; coitus.* That's a much tidier way of describing the whole affair.' With that he was gone. They were the last words my father ever spoke to me on the matter of sex.

As a consequence of *The Sex Talk* and my father's barely concealed excitement over nipples, I began to develop my own interest in women's nipples, as did most of the boys in my class. I remember one cold winter morning in our final year at junior school. We were being taught by Miss Shawn, a student teacher who had been assigned to our class for a term. Miss Shawn was a young blonde woman, with red cheeks and small ears (so small in fact that they were almost not ears but simply holes in the side of her head). Despite her minuscule ears, she appeared to be bopping constantly to some mystical rhythm that only she seemed to be able to hear. Miss Shawn wore the obligatory faded, flared jeans that all teachers seemed to wear at that time and, despite the season, a tight T-shirt. Miss Shawn also never wore a bra and, as a consequence, the outline of her nipples (which were rather large) could be clearly made out under the fabric of her T-shirt. It was a pair of outlines that fascinated us. Miss Shawn appeared oblivious to our fascination with her protruding projectiles; they, however, became, for a term, the most important things in our lives.

'It's because she's cold,' Barry Saddler informed us as we gazed at her twin peaks. 'You can only really notice a woman's nipples when she is cold.'

'Or if she's excited,' Emerson Darkly added.

'Do you think she's excited? Teaching us?' I asked. 'Do you think it's possible to get that excited teaching us about Roman History?'

'No,' Clive Barrington announced sagely. 'It's because she's cold. Roman History would never make anyone *that* excited.'

We looked at Miss Shawn's nipples. Clive Barrington was right. Her nipples were too large and so obviously protruding it had to be because she was cold and had nothing to do with Hadrian's wall or underground drainage systems.

'Perhaps she's pregnant,' Michael Sawyer speculated. 'I read a book once and it said that a woman's nipples grow bigger when she's pregnant. You know, ready to feed the baby?'

'Oh! Yuk!' Clive Barrington replied. 'She's not pregnant. If she was pregnant she'd be being sick every morning and she'd be having labour pains. Have any of you seen her being sick? Has anyone heard her complain of having labour pains?'

We shook our heads but kept our eyes firmly fixed on the protuberant nipples. They appeared to live a life separate from the rest of Miss Shawn's body.

'My dad told me that when you get older it's nice to rub nipples or suck them,' I broke the silence. 'He says sucking them makes them grow bigger.'

'Your Dad sucks nipples? Your mother's nipples?' Clive Barrington was clearly unnerved. 'To make them grow bigger? Ugh!'

'That's what he said. But he said you should only do it to someone you know well.'

'That's disgusting,' Emerson Darkly said. 'I'm quite interested in Miss Shawn's nipples but I don't think I would want to suck them.'

'You couldn't anyway,' Barry Saddler said knowledgeably. 'It's against the law to suck a teacher's nipples. They'd send you to prison. And besides think of all that milk you would have to swallow.'

'But I'd like to see them though,' Emerson Darkly said, expressing all of our thoughts. 'Just once.'

A hush fell upon us all, the light from the sun bathed us in a golden glow. Miss Shawn continued her oral history from the front of the class. She spoke through her nose and her sentences went up to a higher note at the end. As she spoke her breasts appeared to be wrestling with the tightness of her T-shirt, as if they were trying to free themselves. We stared in a pre-lustful way at them, willing them to break out, like two bald prisoners digging themselves out of a tunnel. None of us would have known what to do with them if they had been suddenly exposed and we would certainly not have wanted to suck them but we were in total agreement with Emerson Darkly: it would have been nice to be able to see them, just once.

Rabbit Warren spread a rumour around our class. Rabbit Warren often spread rumours around our class. The rumour that school would finish one lunch break, that the Head had decreed that we were all free to go home at lunchtime, had been spread by Rabbit Warren. It had not been true. The Head had been none too pleased when he and his staff had had to round up hordes of eager children as they headed, *en masse*, for the school gates after eating their cornflake tarts. The rumour that the school was about to be demolished to make way for a motorway, meaning that we would all be off school for several months while they tried to find us another school, was not true. Rabbit Warren had spread the rumour. The rumour that Mr and Mrs Warren (Rabbit's parents) had won half a million pounds on the football pools and were moving to a mansion in California was not true. Rabbit Warren had spread the rumour. Mr and Mrs Warren didn't even do the pools. The rumour that the Queen was about to abdicate her throne because she'd fallen in love with the lead singer of Mud when she'd met him at a Royal Variety Performance, and wanted to live on the road with him, was not true. Even though we'd all watched the evening news that night because Rabbit had said it was going to be announced. Of course it was Rabbit Warren who had spread the rumour that, in our next Art and Craft lesson, Miss Shawn was going to pose naked, for a life drawing. Despite the fact that we all knew of Rabbit's appalling record for spreading falsehood, we chose to believe him. We needed to believe him. The belief that our wish to see those wonderfully pronounced nipples, in the flesh, might be about to come true overrode any grain of corporate common sense we may have had between us.

'Miss Shawn is going to pose naked,' he said, running around the classroom like a junior town cryer.

'How do you know?' Michael Sawyer asked.

'Because I heard her talking to Mrs Braithwaite, in the corridor, that's how,' Rabbit replied, stopping to catch his breath. '"I'm going to pose naked," she said to Mrs Braithwaite. "It will be good for the children to be able to draw a real naked person, don't you agree?" "Yes I do agree," Mrs Braithwaite said to her. "You can do it today, in the next lesson." "But Miss Shawn," she said, "you must take off all your clothes and let them pay particular attention to your nipples. Nipples can be particularly hard to draw, wouldn't you say, Miss Shawn? The children must have sufficient time to be able to look at them and get them right."'

We salivated together, little droplets of saliva dripping on to our desktops, forming lustful puddles. Barry Saddler said 'Wow!' but the rest of us were speechless.

Had anyone decided to drop a pin when Miss Shawn entered the classroom it would have been heard. She closed the door. We sat open-mouthed, the girls giggled. Our hearts beat frantically. Miss Shawn's T-shirt, white, emblazoned with a yellow smiley face, was suitably tight. The nipples stood to attention like two Apollo rockets about to be launched at Cape Canaveral. Miss Shawn put her bag of clutter on to her table and, placing her hands on her hips, smiled at the class. It was the smile of an artist's model, of someone not ashamed to go topless on a beach. We smiled back, eager for the great unveiling.

'Today, children . . .' she began and we willed the T-shirt to be removed, to be abandoned hastily and artistically on to the wooden floor, ' . . . we will be doing papier mâché. To begin with we will need to tear up lots of pieces of newspaper. It will be a long and arduous task but by the end of the lesson your little fingers will have made some wonderful and fascinating creations. Hills, mountains, lots of wonderful things like that. I just love papier mâché.' She then proceeded to hand out boxes of newspaper from a collection of boxes stacked in the corner. There was to be no unveiling of the pert nipples. No gazing at their fascinating form, pencil in one hand, eraser in the other. We looked across at Rabbit Warren who smiled feebly. Soon, with our hands covered in glue and sticky newspaper, our thoughts did indeed turn to the altogether infinitely less erotic undulations of our papier mâché hills and mountains. Thoughts of Miss Shawn's nipples began to filter from our minds. The nipples would remain a mystery.

It was many weeks later that Miss Shawn left our school. Not surprisingly she took her nipples with her. We never got to see them. She did leave behind, however, a classroom full of papier mâché creations. Wonders of all shapes and sizes adorned every available space, undulations here and undulations there. Silent reminders of Miss Shawn's own perfectly peaked mounds. Mrs Braithwaite told us that Miss Shawn had passed her teacher training successfully and had been offered her first real teaching post in a little school on the Isle of Man.

'It's a lickle school,' Mrs Braithwaite said, as we readied ourselves for PE in the schoolyard, tucking our white vests into our shorts and pulling on our black plimsolls. 'A lickle bit smaller than our school and a lot colder. Miss Shawn will be very happy there. The children on the Isle of Man are called Manx children, like Manx cats but without the claws.'

'Or tails,' Barry Saddler said.

'Manx cats don't have tails anyway,' Mrs Braithwaite said. 'They're tailless.'

We were sure too that Miss Shawn would be happy there and so too would the little Manx children, especially the boys. If what Mrs Braithwaite said was true and it was colder on the Isle of Man, then Miss Shawn's wonderful nipples would be even bigger.

The jealousy consumed us; we hated the Manx boys. It became too painful to think of them, sitting happily in their cold classrooms, oblivious to the bitter chill, staring at Miss Shawn's delicious peaks. One or two of us considered moving to the Isle of Man, but the twin complications of, firstly, not knowing where it was and, secondly, knowing it would be impossible to persuade our parents to move to colder climes, put paid to our relocation plans. Soon, after a suitable period of mourning, the subject of nipples, anyone's nipples (but especially Miss Shawn's), was dropped from our conversations. It was easier for us all that way.

It was many months after Miss Shawn's departure that I did in fact see my first pair of exposed breasts and indeed of nipples. It was my first sexual encounter, of a kind. I was ten years old and it was at the end of the spring term. Miss Shawn was now long gone and only remnants of our grief remained (and only remnants too of the papier mâché). I had been in the playground by the prefab classroom, playing conkers with Michael Sawyer (Michael stored conkers to use all year round), when I was approached by Carrie Abraham-Wender and her friend Susan Strong. Carrie and Susan were in another class in our year group. Carrie was the only person we knew with a double-barrelled surname. Most of us were quite jealous of the double-barrel and thought she must be more important than all of us because she had two surnames. Carrie did nothing to shatter the myth and acted as if she *was* more important than all of us. She flouted her surnames, exaggerated them when she spoke, emphasising the doubleness. When asked by a new teacher to the school or by the nit-nurse who she was, Carrie would not simply reply 'Carrie, miss' (or sir) like most of us would have done; no, she would reply, 'My name is Carrie. Carrie *Abraham-Wender*. The Abraham and the Wender are double-barrelled. I have *two* surnames. Abraham and Wender!'

Carrie could make an epic novel out of explaining her surname. Sometimes she would reply – 'My name is Carrie. Carrie Abraham-Wender. It's a double-barrelled name as you will have noticed. Double-barrelled names are quite a rarity. The Abraham is from my mother, she comes from a Jewish family. They were Jewish, although my mother is not practising. She is a circular Jew. The Wender is from my father. Although the Wender sounds Jewish, so I am told, my father is not Jewish, not directly. He says that maybe one half of his family were Jewish way back down his ancestral line but they are not now; not so's you'd know anyway. So that's my name, Carrie Abraham-Wender.'

It came as a blessed relief to us all (although not to Carrie) when her parents divorced. Her father, Mr Wender (the possibly ancestral Jew) left Mrs Abraham (the circular Jew) for a bohemian art teacher from Maybank University, whom we never saw but who could often be heard playing Bob Dylan's *Bringing It All Back Home* album at full volume in her tiny flat above Macy's Watch & Clock Mender's on Tapestry Street. She was ten years younger than Mrs Abraham, my mother told me, and had hair down to the base of her spine and a bottom that older men craved. Carrie stayed in the family home with her mother and her two older brothers, Marvin and Benjamin, two large, leaden characters who smiled only when they ate chocolate (which was quite difficult and often resulted in chocolate dribbling down their chins). When the divorce was completed Mrs Abraham, who won custody of the children, had all their names changed to the single-barrelled, Abraham. It was something that caused Carrie infinite heartache. She grieved the loss of her second surname more than the loss of her father.

It was with Carrie that I was to have my first sexual encounter. She was still the double-barrelled Abraham-Wender then. As I steadied myself to aim my conker at Michael Sawyer's, Carrie spoke: 'Do you want to make love to me?' She flicked her auburn hair casually in an effort to appear seductive, like Jaclyn Smith on the opening credits of *Charlie's Angels*. It fell back across her face obscuring her eyes and she had to flick it away with her hand. I missed my shot and my conker smashed into Michael Sawyer's nose. He yelped. Carrie and Susan giggled.

'Yes . . . please,' I said to Carrie nervously, I couldn't look her in the eyes, which were still partially obscured by her hair anyway.

'Come on then,' Carrie said and holding my hand she pulled

me behind the prefab classroom. We stood opposite each other amongst a pile of discarded empty crisp packets. I could hear Michael Sawyer still yelping and Susan Strong giggling at him. My heart was beating faster than usual.

'How do we start?' I asked, nervously fingering my frayed shirtsleeve.

'Have you done it before?' Carrie asked, the sound of crisp packets rustling under her feet. I could smell the cheesy aroma of the crisps.

'No, never. Have you?'

'No, but I know all about it from a book I read in the library.'

'Oh.'

'I let you touch my sex parts and look at them and then you let me hold your thing.'

'Your vagina and your breasts?' I clarified.

'Yes. And then I hold your thing.'

'My penis?'

'Yes, your penis.'

'Will we have sexual intercourse?'

'If your thing becomes hard we will, if not we'll just have to make love. Besides, we haven't got long, we can't be late for Mr Humber, you know how moody he gets.' Carrie looked at her watch. 'We've got five minutes.' It seemed more than enough time to me.

Carrie then lifted her maroon sweater and her white polo shirt. Her bare chest was exposed. 'Quick,' she said, her face partly obscured by her clothing, 'you can touch them if you want to.'

I looked at her exposed chest, my rising excitement now sapping away. It was a disappointment. The only thing it had in common with Miss Shawn's wondrous chest was that it was braless. There were no supple swellings, no mountainous erect peaks. In fact her chest looked little different from my own, except for the skin colour. There were no real breasts to speak of – only the slightest of bumps – and her nipples were nothing more than pink imitations of my own rather dull and flat nipples. Nothing stood to attention. Nothing was hard like a bullet. Nothing was like my fevered imaginings had imagined Miss Shawn's perfect points to have been. As I gazed at the naked flesh I felt a stab of sorrow and a brief reminder of my loss, our loss, at the departure of Miss Shawn. I no longer wanted to continue making love to Carrie. I wanted to return to Michael Sawyer and our conkers. I wanted to flee Carrie and her disappointing breasts.

'Do you want to touch them?' Carrie said, still holding her clothes up.

'No,' I replied a little too hastily. 'There's not enough time.'

'Will you touch my vagina then?' Carrie asked and she grabbed my hand and thrust it down the front of her skirt. She tried to push it into her underpants but I resisted, instead I simply let my hand rest in the general vicinity of her vagina, which felt like a little bump.

'Do you like it?' Carrie queried, closing her eyes.

I nodded and realising she couldn't see me I said, rather too loudly, 'Yes, Carrie, it's nice!'

'Good,' she said and then quickly removed my hand and looked at her watch. 'Two minutes. Now let me hold your willy.'

I backed away slightly. Carrie grabbed clumsily at my shorts, I didn't resist, a slight swell of excitement returning as her hand yanked at my shorts. I helped her with the belt buckle and the fly, loosening it to allow her deft fingers to slip inside my shorts. She rummaged around until she found the entrance to my purple Y-fronts and then her cold hand slipped in. I felt a combination of fear and exhilaration as her icy fingers clasped my penis. It was the fear that prevented it from becoming hard. Carrie fondled it like she was kneading a lump of dough.

'It's not very big,' she announced.

'I'm only ten years old,' I replied. 'It'll get bigger as I grow won't it?'

''S'pose so. It's not very hard either.'

'No,' I replied ruefully and looked away, avoiding eye contact. 'My dad said it'll get a lot harder more often when I'm a teenager. When I go to secondary school. He said then it'll be hard most of the time.'

'But we've only got a minute left, I can't wait that long. Can I squeeze it?'

'If you want to.'

And so she did. She squeezed with a firm, almost painful grip. And as Carrie's icy fingers squeezed my penis the school bell went off to signify the end of break. The shock of the bell brought a vivid picture to my mind of Auntie Nerys, her face contorted, her neck muscles straining as she shrieked, at full volume, the mating call of the pig-tailed macaque. The mental picture, the shrill of the bell and the squeeze were too much and the tiniest of drops of wee squirted from the end of my penis on to Carrie's hand. She let go of my penis instantly and withdrew her hand.

'You've weed on my hand,' she said and she stared at the squirt on the palm of her hand.

'I'm sorry,' I said frantically zipping up my fly. 'It was the squeeze.'

'It's warm,' Carrie, said, continuing her examination of the droplets in her palm. I expected her to shout at me, to scold me, to run off to report me to the teacher, but she didn't.

'I couldn't help it. It was the squeeze and the bell.' I felt like crying.

'Never mind,' she said, and with one deft swipe she wiped the droplets of wee on to one of the legs of my school shorts. 'Thank you for making love to me. You were my first.'

'That's all right,' I replied, relieved (in more ways than one). 'You were my first too.'

We returned to our classroom, two minutes late. Mr Humber, who looked more dour than usual, frowned as we entered. He didn't speak, just frowned and tutted. Mr Humber rarely spoke unless it was absolutely necessary and then only if it was in relation to science and nature, his subject. I remembered one chillingly miserable lesson, on a dark winter's day, when he managed to take the whole lesson without uttering a single word, just a series of expressions, grunts and glances each one more dour than the last. Rabbit Warren had once spread a rumour that Mr Humber was dead, that he had been killed slipping on a fallen science book in the science section of the public library. Rabbit Warren said that Mr Humber had been planning to bring the book to our next lesson. The book, according to Rabbit Warren, was apparently the dullest book to be found in the entire library, so dull in fact that several people had died reading it. We sat and waited in the classroom for his replacement to turn up for our Science and Nature lesson. There had been a huge sigh of disappointment from all of us when it was, in fact, Mr Humber who walked in, still very much alive.

Several of our classmates giggled as we entered the room (it was the only lesson when our class doubled up with Carrie's class for a joint lesson). I looked at Michael Sawyer, whose nose was red and swollen from the conker. He had a thick plaster stuck across the bridge. He winked at me and grinned, the plaster moving up and down as he winked. I knew that he'd told everyone in the class that Carrie and I had gone to make love behind the prefab classroom. I realised that my belt buckle was still loose and I hastily tightened it and took my seat next to Michael. The whole class cheered and a few boys ruffled my hair. Carrie blushed and held her head in her hands. Mr Humber looked sourly at each and every one of us until order was restored.

'Today, children,' he began, loosening the tie around his loose and blotchy neck, 'we are going to be looking at the reproductive system of mammals. In other words we will be looking at how animals mate. How they make babies.' Another cheer went up, my hair was ruffled and Carrie blushed again. I put my hand up to get Mr Humber's sullen attention.

'Yes Fitzgerald, what is it?' he asked reluctantly.

'Can I be excused sir? I need to use the toilet.'

'Yes boy, if you must. Please hurry back, we're going to dissect a mouse.'

As I left the room for the toilet another cheer went up. I caught Carrie's eye as I departed. She grinned awkwardly and I knew she was thinking of the squirt of wee.

X
Wood

We sat together in our tiny front room – the remaining three;
Hyacinth, my mother and me – and we quietly began to make
our plans for the return of the ashes. It was getting late in the
day, the light was beginning to fade, night was closing in. The
rumble of evening traffic could be heard outside the front door.
The street's workforce returning home, car doors slamming,
gates opening and shutting. The familiar smells of evening
meals seeped through the cracks under our doors and windows.
Fish fingers from one house; cheese on toast from another;
liver and bacon from still another. The distant wail of an
ambulance could be heard and, for a fleeting moment, I had
a picture in my mind of someone else sitting in their front
room hearing the distant wail of an ambulance on the day my
father had been killed by the lorry. I had another mental
picture of the driver of the lorry, overweight, face flushed from
the shock, standing, trancelike over my father's lifeless body,
his eyes riveted to the sickening angle of my father's broken
neck. Next to my father I could picture the unbroken piece of
wood.

'Make sure it goes with us.' Hyacinth's voice broke my spell.
I looked over at her as she nodded in the direction of the unbroken

piece of wood, still standing against the bay of the window. 'You might need it when we get there.'

'I will?' I queried, eyeing the wood, noticing its smooth, unsplintered edges.

'Yes,' Hyacinth replied, 'I think you'll find you might. It should just about fit in a suitcase. I'll put it in mine.'

'Will they allow it through Customs?' my mother asked.

'If it's in my suitcase I think they will,' Hyacinth said. 'And besides there won't be a great deal in my suitcase, I always travel light.' Her eyes twinkled as she spoke. My mother and I stared at her, momentarily bewitched.

I got up from my chair and went over to the unbroken piece of wood. I put my cheeks close to its surface and rubbed it tenderly. I slid my hands across the smooth surface. The wood was warm, its odour calming. I felt compelled to kiss it but didn't. 'I'll keep it safe,' I said and Hyacinth and my mother nodded in agreement.

That night, instead of putting the unbroken piece of wood on the floor beside my bed, I put it on my bed, next to me, so that I could keep a close eye on it. There it lay, three foot of fine teak. The smoothest wooden surface I had ever seen. Its smell . . . glorious! It smelt like all the wood in an entire forest. I leaned across the bed and put my nose close to the wood. I sniffed, letting its fragrance fill my nostrils. I swooned a little, like a leading actor falling in love with the leading lady. Had I been standing and not lying on my bed I may have fainted again, but I wasn't, so I didn't. The woody fragrance conjured a sense again of my father. His hugeness filling my mind, like a train through a tunnel. I remembered the first time I asked him what wood was. I was very little, perhaps four at the time.

'WOOD!' I shouted, as loudly as my little lungs would allow. I had been holding my father's hand as he and my mother and I wandered aimlessly through a leafy glade in Fragrance Wood near Maybank. 'Wood! Wood! Wood! What's wood, Dad?'

My father looked down at me, his frame temporarily blocking out the light. '*The hard fibrous substance consisting of xylem tissue* that occurs beneath the bark in trees, shrubs and similar plants,' he answered as if his dictionary was open in front of him. 'A collection of trees, shrubs, grasses etc. usually dominated by one or a few species of tree; usually smaller than a forest.'

'Don't fill his head with too much wordy nonsense,' my mother said. 'He's only little so how will he understand that? Make it simpler for him. Close that dictionary in your head. Use your own words.'

My father stopped and looked at the trees around us, a shaft of sunlight bathing him in a resplendent glow. He jumped from one foot to the other, skipping like a Shakespearean minstrel. Twigs cracked under the weight of his giant frame, echoing through the trees, like gunshots.

'In the beginning . . . !' he chanted, his voice filling the glade, '. . . was the Wood. And the Wood was with God. And the Wood was Good. Wood was in the beginning in heaven. That's what wood is. Wood is from God and it's Good. If you love wood and treat it well son, then wood will be good to you and God will be good to you too. Wood is for the making of all things.' My father then leaned forward and slipped his arms under my armpits and lifted me from the ground, my feet dangling in the air like divers swimming to the surface of the ocean. Then my father began to spin me. Round and round I went, the trees flashing by, the light dancing across my face, the harmonious perfumes of the glade tickling my nostrils. I giggled with undisguised delight. As he spun me, my father chanted with clear rhythm – 'The wood is Good!' over and over again, 'The wood is Good!', and my mother skipped in time to the chant from one foot to the other, twigs cracking under her feet too, only not as loudly. When he put me down I struggled to keep my balance. The trees in the glade swayed from side to side and bowed down, as if they too were dancing with my mother to my father's chant. The fragrances from the trees and plants encircled me. I liked the dizzy feeling. I liked the woody fragrances. I liked the fact that wood was good and it made my father chant, my mother skip and caused the trees themselves to dance and bow.

My father lifted me again but this time he planted me firmly on his solid shoulders and we turned to leave the glade, our trip now over. As we left, the sound of cracking twigs under my parents' feet, my mother began to whistle. I recognised the song from her collection of records. It was one of the songs she often put on if she wanted me to dance with her. It was 'The People Tree' by Sammy Davis Jr. I tried to whistle along with her but at the time I wasn't very good at whistling. A bird sitting high in a tree appeared to hear my pitiful attempt to whistle and began to chirp, as if to show me how it should be done.

The preparations for the journey were brief but necessary. Mrs Freemantle volunteered to act as treasurer and collate all the money. 'You don't need to worry about that, dear,' she told my mother. 'You've got enough on your plate to have to worry about.' Uncle Albie was true to his word and had stuck copies of his note up in our neighbourhood and donations were coming in in dribs and drabs. My father's creations, as expected, sold well. People came from all over Wistful to rummage, under mine and my mother's guidance, through the shed to choose what to buy. After a while my mother began to find it all too distressing and Uncle Albie took over.

'Get her inside,' Uncle Albie told Mrs Freemantle. 'Get her away from the wood, away from the shed. You can still smell him in there for goodness' sake.' Mrs Freemantle obediently ushered my mother inside away from the smell and away from the disappearing memories of my father as they were sold off one by one.

Once most of my father's things had been sold, Mrs Freemantle assured us that, together with the contributions from the nearest and dearest and our neighbours, there would be more than enough for the journey.

'We'll need to get you vaccinated I suppose,' my mother said as she and I ambled along Drummond Street in the direction of the florist's (my mother had decided to buy some gladioli – 'They'll brighten up the kitchen,' she said). When we entered the florist's a little bell rang to signify our entrance. Mrs Aderley the florist appeared.

'Good, morning,' she said. Mrs Aderley was a short, thin woman with stiff, spiky hair. Had her hair been green she may well have resembled one of her own potted plants on sale in the window; a spineless Yucca perhaps or a Majesty palm. As it was, her hair was mousy brown so she just looked like a short, thin florist with spiky hair.

'Gladioli,' my mother said, seeming to forget the usual formalities. It was the grief that took away the formalities. 'To brighten the kitchen.'

Mrs Aderley nodded. 'I suppose it will help after the dea. . . I mean . . .'

'Yes,' my mother said. 'After the death.'

'I'm sorry.' Mrs Aderley seemed to be having difficulty swallowing.

'That's all right,' my mother said. 'I understand. One bunch will be fine.'

Mrs Aderley began to busy herself preparing the bunch. Behind her, in the back room, I could see her sixteen-year-old daughter, Sharon, sitting on a stool flicking through a copy of a *Jackie* magazine. She was chewing at her nails and spitting bits on to the floor.

'He's off to Africa,' my mother said, her voice monotone, without emotion. 'With the ashes.'

'I know,' Mrs Aderley said. 'I've seen the note. It was on a lamp-post up by St Roderick's.' I was going to ask her if she had made a contribution but I didn't think it the right time. And besides, if she had I might have had to volunteer to help out for a day or two in the florist's when I got back and I wasn't sure I fancied sitting in the back room with Sharon spitting her nails at me.

'He'll need vaccinations won't he?' my mother queried.

'I'm sure he will, Pauline. There's all kinds of diseases over there.' Mrs Aderley put some Sellotape up to her mouth and bit a piece off.

'YELLOW FEVER, CHOLERA, MALARIA!' Sharon shouted from the back room. 'THAT'S WHAT HE'LL NEED. I SAW IT ON THE TELLY ONCE; *NATIONWIDE* OR *WORLD IN ACTION* OR SUMMINK!'

'Oh thank you, Sharon,' my mother said and I could see Sharon spit out another nail. It landed on a freshly cut bunch of roses.

'AND WHERE IN AFRICA IS HE GOING?' Sharon shouted.

'Nigeria,' I said. 'That's where my father was from. Originally. Nigeria.'

'WHERE DID YOU SAY?' Sharon shouted.

'Nigeria!' I shouted it this time, for Sharon's benefit. I shouted perhaps a little too loud and Mrs Aderley looked slightly nervous as she arranged the gladioli.

'THEN YOU'LL NEED A VISA. YOU GETS IT FROM THE HIGH COMMISSION! IN LONDON! TAKES A WHILE TO PROCESS MIND! I SAW THAT ON THE TELLY TOO!'

'Thank you, Sharon,' my mother said. 'You've been most helpful.'

'Oh she can be you know,' Mrs Aderley said, tightening the tape around the wrapped gladioli and leaning forward to whisper. 'She can be a blimmin' lazy sod, barely lifts a finger in the shop but she gets a lot of useful information from the telly, you know. She watches a lot of telly. I wouldn't know half the things I know if Sharon didn't watch so much telly. I learnt that Prince Philip was Greek from Sharon watching the telly, you know, and I learnt that Cliff Richard was born in India from her watching the telly.'

'AND 'E MUST 'AVE A PASSPORT MIND!' Sharon shouted. 'DOES 'E 'AVE A PASSPORT?'

'I do,' I said.

'Though the furthest he's been abroad is the Isle of Wight,' my mother said. 'Isn't it, Fitzgerald?'

'Yes, Mum,' I nodded. 'Blackgang Chine.'

'THAT'S ALL RIGHT THEN!' Sharon shouted. 'IF 'E'S GOT A PASSPORT YOU'RE 'ALFWAY THERE ALREADY!'

'There you are.' Mrs Aderley thrust the flowers at my mother. 'Gladioli. I hope they work.'

'I'm sorry?' my mother queried.

'I think she means she hopes they brighten up the kitchen,' I said and Mrs Aderley nodded and attempted a smile.

'Thank you,' my mother said and, as she took the gladioli, I noticed her hand shake a little, 'I'm sure they will.'

As we left the florist's the little bell rang again, like a sleigh bell at Christmas. I looked back and saw one last glimpse of Sharon gnawing at her nails in the back room. She was a ruddy girl and the more she chewed the redder her face became. Mrs Aderley caught my eye and attempted to smile again. It looked more like a grimace or as if she was trying to suppress breaking wind. Or perhaps, I thought, some of that Sellotape had got caught in her mouth and was preventing her lips from parting.

Outside we bumped into Hyacinth, returning, she said, from posting a parcel at the post office. She joined us as we continued up Drummond Street. Hyacinth was a comfort to my mother and she offered to put the gladioli in a vase when we got home. We continued to walk and talk until we got to the timberyard. When we got there we stopped and turned to face it. It was the first time we had seen it since the day we received the grim news; the day we passed it on the way home from St Roderick's after my father had been killed by the lorry. We stood in a row looking at it, the gladioli having been temporarily forgotten. I could hear the sound of Hyacinth's teeth clicking in her mouth, she appeared to be moving them around with her tongue. It seemed as if she was using her tongue to prevent the teeth from escaping, so few had she left. The sound of a chainsaw sawing through wood, coming from the timberyard, drowned out Hyacinth's clicking teeth. The saw was loud, very loud; its grating made the nerve endings in my teeth feel raw. I winced. The sound of male voices, loud voices, followed the grate of the saw. The voices were swearing. Expletives. Loud expletives!

'Oh fuck it!'; 'Bollocks!'; 'Sod it!'; 'Fucking Bastard!'. My mother winced. The voices did not appear to be having conversations. There were no sentences, no pauses, no question marks, just expletives. The men were sawing and swearing. Swearing and sawing.

The smell of the sawn wood was powerful. I breathed in and it filled my lungs. I held my breath and held the wood in my lungs. I wanted the wood to become part of me, part of my being. I wanted not only to have hands that looked like oars but a whole body that looked like it had been made out of wood; a wooden body. Flakes of sawdust for hair; a smooth pine chest that I could varnish and polish, and legs that were made of heavy oak, which would need to be treated to protect them from the rain. The woody aroma from the timberyard was all-consuming and to a degree I could feel what my father must have felt on that fateful day when he had been wooed by the wood.

My mother held her arms across her chest, her hands covering her breasts, her heart. She clutched her chest as if she had been stabbed by an invisible knife. Tears began to roll down her cheeks like a waterfall. Cascading. Flowing. She whined like a wounded dog. Hyacinth edged closer to her and put a comforting arm around her heaving shoulders.

'It's all right, Pauline,' she said. 'It's all right.'

I moved aside and stood behind Hyacinth and my mother. Something told me it was the right thing to do; to let my mother have her own private moment of grief without having to worry about me. I watched Hyacinth as she supported her. My mother continued to cry, the tears dropping like rain at her feet. Hyacinth held my mother, whispering quietly to her. Then, from the depths of sorrow, my mother tilted her head back and screamed at the timberyard, at the wood, mustering all her strength. Her voice, a plaintive rage, filling the sky around us. Starlings flew out of their trees in shock desperately trying to maintain their formation. And then my mother fell to the ground, a crumpled heap of quivering flesh. Hyacinth knelt down beside her and continued her ministrations, like a priest giving the last rites. She spoke gently and kindly and rubbed my mother's quivering back. As she rubbed, she cooed.

From the bowels of the timberyard three men who had heard the banshee wail appeared. They stood together by the wooden door. Each held a piece of wood in his firm hands and each had sawdust in his hair. Their clothes were grey and baggy, as were their faces. Each was indistinguishable from the other, except one who was short, very short (under five feet tall). Their swearing had now ceased. They looked at my mother and at Hyacinth and at me. Recognition dawned on their faces. They knew who my mother was. They knew she was my father's wife. Widow of the Wood-Addict. They knew he had been killed by the lorry, in part, I knew they had been told, because of his addiction. They knew that the crumpled heap in front of them was the Whistling Woman. They bowed their heads appropriately. I suspect that if they had been wearing hats they would have removed them in respect. The sawing inside ground to a halt and, as if part of some national Synchronised Timberyard display team, all the men began to file out of the timberyard. On seeing my crumpled mother they too bowed their heads and joined the original three, standing quietly. Not a sound could be heard except the pitiful sobs from my mother's broken body and Hyacinth's tender cooing.

Specks of sawdust danced through the air coming from within the timberyard. Some specks appeared to leap and somersault through the air heading, seemingly deliberately, towards my mother and settling in her sandy hair and on her heaving back. I watched the sawdust. So did Hyacinth. Then, as I stood surveying the dazzling scene before me, I felt drops of rain on my head. Gentle drops at first, like a close friend tapping me on the shoulder. And as my mother sobbed and Hyacinth ministered and the wooden men stood, heads bowed, the rain began to fall.

We stood for a long time in the rain as it poured like tears from an invisible God. My mother remained crumpled on the paving, Hyacinth at her side. The men, aware of their need to return to their sawing and swearing, gradually began to drift back inside, their respect to the Whistling Woman (now the Sobbing Woman) having been paid. Through the driving rain the sounds of working began to start again, the loud sawing of wood, the general clunking of men at work and the swearing. Now however, as if in respect for the dead and my mother's grief, the expletives they used were slightly milder. 'Oh fuck it!' was exchanged for 'Shit!'; 'Bollocks!' for the more digestible 'Damn!'; 'Sod it!' was substituted for the arguably milder 'Flaming hell!' and 'Fucking bastard!' was exchanged for the far more gentle and nostalgic 'Cobblers!'

Due to the moisture in the air, caused by the sheets of rain, the sawdust disappeared and the woody fragrance changed to a mustier, dirtier, less alluring smell. Hyacinth lifted my mother to her feet and, wiping rain from her brow, began to walk her slowly, painfully, and with caution away from the timberyard. My mother's shoulders continued to shake, like a refrigerator in the middle of the night. As they walked past me Hyacinth, her pastoral care now in full flow and sensing my own sadness, rummaged into the well of her pocket and withdrew her bag of boiled sweets (slightly damp from the rain). She offered the bag to me and I slipped my sodden hand quietly into the bag. I withdrew one, a lime one, and popped it into my mouth and sucked.

Hyacinth and my mother continued to walk, slowly, carefully, like refugees from a war zone, past Kenny the Keycutter's. As we shuffled past, our clothes completely drenched, our faces wet with rain, Kenny the Keycutter appeared at his door. His orange hair dangled over the collar of a loud yellow and purple shirt. He smiled at me. In his hand he clutched a black top hat. With his other hand he pulled a rabbit from the hat, a large, fluffy white rabbit, docile but very much alive. I looked back as we edged slowly back up Drummond Street. As I did, Kenny the Keycutter smiled again and pulled out another white rabbit and yet another, followed by a white dove. I smiled too and Kenny the Keycutter smiled again, his smile so broad his lips nearly touched the borders of his cornflake hair. He let the dove go and it flew into the rain-filled sky, circled above my head twice and then fluttered back down to land on Kenny the Keycutter's hairy head. In its tiny beak I was sure I could see a small leaf, but I may have been wrong.

We continued the short walk home. When we got there Hyacinth gave me the gladioli and took my mother upstairs to lay her down on her bed, I went into the kitchen. The kitchen looked particularly sad on this grey and wet afternoon. I put the gladioli into a vase. The flowers were bruised and battered from the rain.

Several nights later I had a dream. I'd fallen asleep with one hand on the unbroken piece of wood (which lay next to me) and the other clutching my penis. The unbroken piece of wood and my penis were both hard but the wood was harder. In the dream I was walking slowly down Drummond Street in the pouring rain. I was holding a length of rope that was attached to little Lily Drinkwater's rusty tricycle which trailed behind me. As it moved and the rain fell in torrents, the tricycle was becoming rustier by the second. Little Lily Drinkwater was not sitting on her tricycle but Hyacinth was. Hyacinth held in her hand a red casket full of boiled sweets, sweets that were gold and silver in colour. Children of all sizes and colours were taking the boiled sweets from the casket and popping them into their mouths. Birds (starlings and doves mainly) were plucking some of the sweets from the outstretched hands of the littlest children, not out of spite but just for fun. Some of the children however (including Barry Saddler who was amongst them), began to cry. Tall wooden women, some wearing baggy, grey clothes, comforted them. None of the women was swearing, instead they were saying pleasant things like 'Isn't this rain lovely' and 'What beautifully coloured boiled sweets'. Wooden men stood next to the wooden women and seemed to be learning from them, taking notes with wooden pencils on wooden pads. Running along behind Hyacinth (in my dream) was Timothy Drinkwater, surrounded by the boys from my class. He was looking up at the sky, rain splashing on to his face. He appeared to be telling the rain that it should stop but the rain was ignoring him.

At the end of Drummond Street outside the timberyard sat my mother, staring off into the distance and crying. My mother was shouting but no words could be heard. I could just see her mouthing my father's name. She appeared to be able to see him on the horizon. With one of her hands she was passing keys to Kenny the Keycutter who stood behind her, dressed in a garish white suit with yellow collars. Kenny the Keycutter was putting the keys on top of his crispy hair and was making them disappear. Just as I was feeling a little bit scared of my dream and wanted to wake myself up, a huge black horse began to appear through the driving rain, coming up Drummond Street from the opposite direction, from the direction of the library. It pulled up outside the grocery store and neighed, shaking the rain from its silvery mane. On its back sat a young man dressed in purple garments. Behind him sat my father, smiling (only he was made of wood). I realised that the man dressed in purple was none other than Saint Roderick of Leicester the Patron Saint of Unsound Minds. Saint Roderick dismounted his charger. He stood before my mother and pulled a large, gleaming sword from a scabbard around his waist.

'Arise Sister Pauline, sister of Albie, sister of Nerys,' he said and softly placed the sword on each of her shoulders. 'Wipe away those tears.'

My mother obeyed him and stood up. Kenny the Keycutter took his keys and disappeared into the shadows of his shop.

'Look,' Saint Roderick continued, pointing to my wooden father, who smiled again, 'here is your husband, safe and well in another place. You cannot see him, but know this, Sister Pauline, he is SAFE!'

Then Saint Roderick of Leicester pointed the sword in my direction. As he did so Mrs Eugena Braithwaite appeared from the shadows of the grocery store and stood beside him.

'Look at your son, Fitzgerald,' he said to my mother. 'Look at him, Sister Pauline. Know that his destiny is in his hands.'

As my mother looked at me the rain increased. Everything in my dream began to blur and then it ended. I awoke, my head felt muggy and confused; I had the lingering feeling that my dream had been more than a dream. I felt as if Saint Roderick may actually have visited my mother, so clear had been the images in my head. I could hear the last drops of rain splattering against my bedroom window as the sky outside began to clear and the morning sun began to break through. I glanced across at my bedside clock, a Westclox – *Big Ben*. It was seven o'clock. As I scratched the back of my head, trying to wake myself up, I remembered that this was the day. Hyacinth and I were travelling to Africa. My journey was about to begin.

XI

Mr Plucker's Blues

When the day finally came for me to leave for Africa, the sun, a hazy, burning ball, was high in the sky. One or two clouds remained, no bigger than large cotton buds or giant sheep waiting to be sheared.

As I dressed in my bedroom, I packed the last essential items for my journey. My mother had packed the bulk of my clothes the night before. She'd not whistled whilst she had packed them into an undersized suitcase, in fact my mother had hardly whistled at all since my father had been killed (which was not surprising).

'I'll not pack too much,' she said, squeezing clothes into the last inch of space. 'If I pack too much you'll be tempted to stay longer.'

'We're only going for a week, Mum,' I said, helping her to hold the case shut as the clothes tried to free themselves, 'ten days at the most.'

'I know, Fitzgerald. But you never know.'

'Temptation can be a terrible thing,' I added before she could say it herself.

Hyacinth and my mother had gone to London a few days previously to book the airline tickets.

'We'll be flying with Nigeria Airways,' Hyacinth had announced before they had left.

'Are they any good?' I had asked.

'Good enough,' Hyacinth had replied. 'They take their time doing things, but at least because they're so slow it puts off hijackers. I've never heard of a Nigeria Airways plane being hijacked.' Hyacinth chuckled at her own observation. My mother did not (hijacking, I'm sure, was not something she wanted to think about). They had left me with Mr Plucker, walking off up our street toward the bus stop around the corner, Hyacinth still chuckling and my mother grimacing. I was to stay with Mr Plucker for the day whilst Hyacinth and my mother were in London. I liked Mr Plucker, despite his melancholic nature.

Mr Plucker had not always lived next door and he'd not always been a melancholic but he had always been very thin and he had always leaned to one side. His thinness was a result of his dislike of most food except my mother's malt loaf and carrot cake and raw vegetables (which he ate in copious amounts). Apart from that, Mr Plucker ate little else. He leaned to one side as a result of being infected with polio as a small child. 'Its full name is *poliomyelitis*,' he once told me, leaning to one side. 'But after what it's done to me it doesn't deserve such a grand title. If it was down to me I'd just call it *po*.'

Mr Plucker also had a keen, possibly obsessive interest in cigarette cards. Cigarette cards, he said, were the only things that could really keep the blues away.

'Fitzgerald,' he once said, as I sat perched on the Wonky Stool of New Cross, him leaning one way, me leaning the other, 'I suffer from the blues, depression, melancholia.'

'It sounds beautiful,' I told him. 'Melancholia. Like a melody.'

'But it isn't, Fitzgerald,' he replied, his sallow eyes darting suspiciously from side to side as if he was afraid someone was listening, 'Melancholia is by no means a beautiful thing, but it is like a melody.'

'How come, Mr Plucker?' I asked, curious to know more.

'Fitzgerald, melancholia is like a melody because it's there but

159

you can't see it. When it comes it takes you over Like a song, you have no control over how it makes you feel. Unlike a melody, however, that can make you feel many things – elated, joyful, curious, nostalgic, excited, sad – melancholia can only make you feel one thing . . . bloody miserable!'

Sometimes, when my father was still alive, Mr Plucker would watch over me if my father was out delivering his finished creations and my mother had to shop in Drummond Street or attend an after-school meeting.

'Can you watch over Fitzgerald?' she would say to Mr Plucker as she stood at his door, Mr Plucker sagging in his cavernous trousers, his sweater billowing as if a wind was gusting down our street.

'Will you be long?' he would ask.

'No, just a little shopping in Drummond Street then I'll be back in time for tea.' Then my mother would usher me into Mr Plucker's overcast hallway. I always felt it was going to rain in Mr Plucker's hallway, it was so grey; I felt that I should have an umbrella with me or, at the very least, a hooded top. Then my mother would head off down the street, trailing her tartan shopping trolley behind her, whistling Cab Calloway's 'Zaz, Zuh, Zaz' or Bix Beiderbecke's 'Singing the Blues'.

Mr Plucker's house mirrored our house. Whereas everything in our house was to the left of the front door as you looked at it, everything in Mr Plucker's was to the right. I always said his house was the wrong way round.

'Did you know', he told me, 'that we really see everything the wrong way round and as the light hits our eyes everything gets turned around? It's all to do with the optics. So it's really your house that's the wrong way round and not mine.'

Mr Plucker's tiny front room (which seemed even tinier than ours due to the clutter) was melancholic too. Everything in it, including the discoloured paintings on the walls, seemed to be suffering from depression. The room seemed to groan in mental anguish. Everything was a mismatch of colours (none of which was at all bright). Colours that may once have been described as *Orange Glow* or *Sunrise Red* were now stained with a deathly brown. The wallpaper was ancient and peeling in places and seemed to be in pain. The chairs (a brown sofa and two wicker chairs) appeared to be waiting for the release of a funeral pyre. In the middle of the front room was a stained coffee table that my father had made for Mr Plucker many years ago. 'But I don't drink coffee,' Mr Plucker had said when my father had delivered it to him as a surprise on his birthday.

'Then don't put coffee on it,' my father had replied, 'put other drinks on it.'

The rest of the room was cluttered with faded magazines (mainly copies of the *Radio Times*) and various discarded items of clothing. A small TV stood in one corner, Mr Plucker's telephone in the other, perched on top of two suitcases. The room smelt musty and despite the fact that Mr Plucker didn't smoke it smelt of smoke, but that may have been because of the cigarette cards. That was the other thing that caused the clutter in his front room, the stacks of leather-bound binders that adorned one wall. In the binders were his sacred cigarette cards. Cards he had been collecting for over twenty years.

'I'm a cartophilist,' he once told me as he reached up for one of his leather-bound binders.

'What's a cartophilist?' I asked, helping him to place the binder on the coffee table.

'Someone who is interested in cartophily,' he explained, opening the pages to reveal the cigarette cards cocooned, like sleeping babies in a maternity ward, under their transparent sheets, – Mr Plucker's children. 'The collecting of cigarette cards. I'm a melancholic cartophilist, although when I'm looking at my cards I don't feel melancholic any more.'

I enjoyed listening to Mr Plucker, I enjoyed all the new words he taught me. Mr Plucker told me that cigarette cards were first issued in Britain in 1888. He told me that his favourite collections were cards from the 1930s (which, he said, was the heyday of the cigarette card). His most prized collection was a set entitled *Modern Dance Steps*, a series of fifty cards.

Mr Plucker had the complete set, except for one – No. 34, *The Blues: The Natural Turn, 1st Step.* 'Keep your eye out for *The Blues*, Fitzgerald,' he said to me. 'If you ever see it come and find me. I'm always looking for *The Blues*. Isn't that ironic? Someone like me actually looking for the blues.' I didn't know what ironing had to do with his card collecting, so I just looked at him blankly.

Mr Plucker would wade through his collections, showing me a world of cigarette-card wonders. He had all sorts; *Famous Films*, a series of fifty issued by Peter Jackson cigarettes; *Screen Stars*, a series of forty issued by Abdulla & Co. (my favourite was No. 36, *Vivien Leigh*, whom I thought was beautiful); *Ships Flags & Cap Badges*, a series that was issued by the Imperial Tobacco Company (I thought it was incredibly dull but Mr Plucker seemed to enjoy it immensely). My own particular favourites of all his collections were a series of fifty entitled *Railway Engines* by Wills' Cigarettes and a smaller but no less exciting series of forty-eight cards issued by Gallaher Ltd entitled *Trains of the World*. When Mr Plucker opened the pages of these particular collections I would stare in fascination at the shiny steam engines with their endless carriages trailing behind them, dreaming of journeys to far-off places.

There were some cards from the film and screen-stars collections that Mr Plucker liked very much but he wouldn't let me look at for too long. He said I would appreciate them more when I was older. He was particularly keen on, from his *Beauties of Today* series, a card featuring the actress Jessie Matthews, standing in the half-light wearing a near-transparent dress. He was also very keen on another print of Jane Woodward from his *Glamour Girls* collection revealing her long, shapely legs. In my opinion neither Jessie Matthews nor Jane Woodward looked as beautiful as the sultry Vivien Leigh.

'I've not always been a melancholic,' Mr Plucker once told me as he showed me another of his leather-bound binders. 'I was married once. I wasn't melancholic then.'

'What was her name, Mr Plucker?' I asked. 'Your wife?'

'Edith,' he replied slowly, fingering the plastic sheets, 'Edith Topaz. Topaz was her maiden name. A topaz is a beautiful gemstone, usually pink or yellow in colour. Edith too was usually a lovely pink or yellow in colour. Sometimes she glowed. She was not very happy about having to change her name to Plucker when we finally got married. Can you imagine it? Having to change your name from Topaz to Plucker? Would you be happy?'

I shook my head, then quickly nodded it, not wanting to offend Mr Plucker. Mr Plucker continued, pulling out another *Glamour Girl* and holding her up to the light. 'Edith was hardly beautiful, however. She was solid and hard like a gemstone but not beautiful like one at all. I fell in love with her solidity, not her beauty. When you're as thin as I am it's nice to have someone solid around. A bit like a wind-break.

'She was like a day of the week, my Edith; like a Monday or a Tuesday. Always there, you know exactly when it's going to be there and what it's going to be doing. Sometimes, I have to admit, you'd wish it wasn't, but you know you'd be awfully upset if it wasn't. Could you imagine if a Monday failed to turn up one week or Tuesday decided to have a lie-in? Sometimes I wished Edith would be a bit more like a Friday or a Saturday, you know, a bit more fun, but she wasn't. I loved her all the same.'

'What happened to her?'

Mr Plucker looked down at his narrow feet. 'Well, Fitzgerald, that was the strangest thing. She left me. She fell in love with a Hungarian trapeze artist. They met at an evening class – *Origami, Folding Can Be Fun.* Within only two months of their meeting she had left with the Hungarian and they both moved to Budapest.'

'What was his name? The trapeze artist?'

'Karina the Flighty,' Mr Plucker replied, the pain etched on to his fleshless face. 'And *he* was a *she* and a beautiful she indeed. I don't think Karina the Flighty was her real name; I never knew her real name. And to cap it all Edith left me on a Friday. Can you imagine that, Fitzgerald? All our years together of solidity, of Mondayness, of predictability and she leaves me on a Friday to run away to Budapest to live with a female, Hungarian trapeze artist that she'd met at a paper-folding class'

'A lesbian,' I said, rather too proudly for the moment (it was shortly after my father's *Sex Talk* and my mother had further enlightened me on the various natures of sexuality).

'Yes Fitzgerald, you're right,' Mr Plucker said, startled a little by my knowledge, 'a lesbian, female, Hungarian trapeze artist. Edith was so much in love with her. I could see it in her eyes. When Edith moved out, Fitzgerald, melancholia moved in. I became married to melancholia and we've stayed together ever since. I've lost count of the times I've asked her to move out, pleaded, begged with her to leave me alone, but she won't go. She's committed to a life of marriage to me, of making my life a misery. There'll be no lesbian trapeze artists for her. Not my melancholia.'

I looked at Mr Plucker, the flesh hanging loosely under his scraggy chin, vibrating as he spoke. His Adam's apple was so prominent it looked as though he had swallowed a small box or an egg cup and it had wedged in his throat. His brow (what little brow he had) furrowed and he held his knobbly hand to his stomach as if he was in pain and for a few moments he seemed to be in another place; the place of sorrow. The place I imagined he would have been when his beloved gemstone, Edith, had fled the familiarity of the matrimonial home for the airborne, altogether more exciting and unconventional Hungarian world of Karina the Flighty. I could picture him standing alone in the house he imagined he would have been sharing with his sturdy wife for the rest of his life. I could see him alone in his voluminous sweater, the tears welling up in his eyes, as he tried to will Edith to return home.

'I never heard from Edith again,' he mumbled, choking up phlegm in his throat as he spoke. He swallowed it and looked up into my face. 'Never. Not a birthday card, not a Christmas card, nothing. It was as if she had never existed. As if I had imagined her pink and yellow skin. As if I had never been married. After she left me I lost so much weight, and God knows I was skinny enough anyway, that my wedding band just fell off. I had been standing in the rain waiting for a bus when it just slipped from my finger and fell into a drain. It was gone.

Disappeared just like Edith. It was the final sign that our marriage was over.'

Mr Plucker held up his wedding finger and thrust it toward my face. 'Look!' he cried. 'No sign it has ever been there.' The bony finger shook in front of my eyes and I examined it carefully, not sure of exactly what I was supposed to be looking for. Not sure of what signs would indicate that a ring had once been present.

'All I'm left with now, Fitzgerald,' he continued, his voice quivering, his finger still shaking, 'is melan-bloody-cholia! I loved my Edith . . .'

I hung my head, unsure of how to respond to Mr Plucker's pained outburst.

'I loved my Edith. I needed her. I never dreamed I would end up living alone being taunted by the misery of melancholia whilst my beloved Edith flies through the skies with a lesbian lover in a distant land. Never!'

Mr Plucker slammed his fist down on to the coffee table, cigarette cards fell to the floor, dust shot up into the air around us. I jumped in my seat in shock.

'Blast you melancholia!' he shouted and then, looking at me, his eyes softening a little as he remembered my tender age, he said quietly, 'Never let melancholia move in with you, Fitzgerald. Fight her with every bone in your body.'

'I will,' I promised and my heart went out to him.

Mr Plucker rarely spoke of melancholia again, at least not with so much passion and fury, but he often spoke of Edith, his precious gemstone. His love for her never died. He once told me that he often had a recurring dream. In his dream he would be dressed in fine clothes and he would be holding Edith, who was wearing a transparent dress, close to his chest. He would be rubbing her pink and yellow skin until it shined and sparkled like the morning sun. Holding Edith close to his heart, he would climb on to a trapeze several miles above the earth and, with one hand supporting his beloved and the other holding on to the trapeze, he would swing back and forth through the clear sky. In his dream, Mr Plucker would swing for ever, never tiring, never stopping and Edith would look into his eyes and whisper words of love to him. Gentle words; words full of light and promise. She would keep on whispering to him, an endless stream of fragrant words and some of the words would run together to make one long word like – *'summerbeautiful'* or *'preciousheartbeat'*. Mr Plucker told me that, as they swung higher on the trapeze, way below him in the darkest depths he could see melancholia covered in slime, struggling to free herself from the mire of the earth. In his dream, melancholia held no fear for him, he knew that he was free from the mire, free to swing in endless harmony with his beloved gemstone, his beloved Edith.

When he awoke from his dream (which he inevitably had to do), Mr Plucker said that the darkness of reality surrounded him, choked him, terrified him all the more. Sometimes, he said, he wished he would never wake up.

On the day that Hyacinth and my mother went to London there was no talk of lesbian trapeze artists or melancholia. We just sat and looked at Mr Plucker's cigarette cards. When Hyacinth and my mother returned home I thanked Mr Plucker and got up to leave.

'Have you seen *The Blues* yet, Fitzgerald?' he asked, his sad eyes momentarily eager with anticipation.

'No,' I had replied, 'but if I find it I'll let you know.'

I never did find *The Blues* although I looked, often.

XII

Swing Low, Sweet Chariot

When I had squeezed the last of my possessions into my suitcase I reached over for the unbroken piece of wood, still laying
on my bed. With one hand clutching the wood and the other
holding on to my suitcase, I managed to shuffle backwards out
of my room and slide, awkwardly, down the stairs. I landed safely
in the hallway by the front door and then shuffled, like an Arctic
explorer fighting the northern winds, into the tiny front room.
I placed the bulging suitcase next to the orange sofa and leaned
the unbroken piece of wood under the bay of the window. The
sun shone through the net curtains, resplendent, noble. It warmed
my face like a pleasant memory. My mother sat in the kitchen
in a purple frock and a yellow cardigan, completing a crossword.
She sipped from a blue and white mug of milky tea. Her face
looked drawn and tired.

'There's warm tea in the pot!' she called out. 'And some bacon
I've kept warm for you under the grill. You'll need to eat well.'

'Thanks, Mum,' I said and joined her in the kitchen. I picked
the bacon off of the grill pan and placed it on to a plate. I
buttered some white bread and poured a mug of tea and then
sat down at the table with her. My mother continued her crossword. We sat in silence for several minutes. I was reminded of

Mrs Freemantle and her silent meals with her beloved Henry. The only real sound that could be heard was my chewing on the bacon, which was amplified by the silence. When my mother finished her crossword, she placed her pen down and picked up my hands.

'Your hands are bigger now, Fitzgerald,' she spoke softly, her sharp eyes looking deeply into mine. 'And so are you. You're growing up, you only have to listen to your own voice to know that. You'd better use your hands wisely, Fitzgerald. Don't waste them. Your father never did. You've got more hand space than two or three children of your own age put together. When you take your father's ashes to Africa, hold the casket firmly. When you've released the ashes you must start to use your hands wisely. It's what your father would have wanted. He would say it would be such a waste to have such large hands and not do anything with them. But whatever you do, Fitzgerald, beware of temptation. It's a terrible thing. It can kill you. Do you understand?'

'Yes Mother, I do,' I said. 'But what shall I do with my hands?'

'You'll find out when you get there, I'm sure,' my mother said and she let go of my hands. Because I'd not been expecting her to let them go, they fell heavily on to the Formica table top. A loud thud, like two blocks of wood being dropped from a great height. As the thud echoed through the house, the doorbell rang. Hyacinth had arrived.

Hyacinth strode down the short hallway and into the front room whilst I held the front door open. Mr Plucker crept in behind her like a shadow, holding her large suitcase in one hand and using the other to steady himself by holding on to the walls. Due to the size of the case he leaned even more to one side than usual. Hyacinth stopped at the threadbare chair. She looked as if she should have been riding a horse so that she could dismount. She removed her bedraggled, brown coat and sat down, sighing, into the chair. My mother appeared in the doorway of the kitchen.

'Hello, Pauline,' Hyacinth said, a bead of sweat trickling down her creased forehead. 'It's hot out there. Just the right sort of day to be flying to Africa.'

Mr Plucker sat down gingerly on the orange sofa, most of his body disappearing into the orange cushions. All that really remained on view were his two bony knees, his sloping shoulders and his undernourished head. 'Too hot for me,' he said, 'I'll be staying in with my cards today.'

Hyacinth and I were due to fly from Heathrow later that afternoon. It would be a nine-hour flight to Murtala Muhammed airport in Lagos, she told us, with a short stopover in Kano in northern Nigeria. Uncle Albie had offered to take us to the airport in his weather-beaten Opel Kadett. My mother had decided not to go with us. 'I'm not that keen on airport noise,' is all she said, adding, 'I'd rather stay at home and imagine you flying.'

Hyacinth leaned over and opened her monstrous suitcase. There was very little inside; two or three carrier bags stuffed full of what appeared to be her clothing, an alarm clock and several bags of boiled sweets.

'There's room enough in here', she said, 'for the unbroken piece of wood and the red casket. We'll need to tape up the casket of course and wrap them both in towels. For safety.'

My mother carefully took the red casket off the mantelpiece and passed it to Hyacinth. 'I'll get some tape,' my mother said and disappeared into the kitchen. She returned with a thick roll of brown carpet tape and, with Hyacinth's help, began carefully to tape around the lid of the casket, sealing the ashes safely in.

'That'll stop them from falling out mid-flight,' Hyacinth said when the taping was complete. She then passed the casket to me. It felt warm in my hands, the red seemingly redder than usual. 'Put it in my suitcase,' Hyacinth said and I placed it neatly between a large bag of boiled sweets and a bag of Hyacinth's clothing.

My mother went upstairs to get some towels from the airing cupboard. She returned with a collection of multicoloured ones. I noted that my favourite towel, a blue and white starfish patterned beach towel was among them (a towel I'd had since I was small, that I used to take to the beach at Marvel's Point near my grandma's every summer). My mother handed me the towels and I carefully wrapped the red casket in two of them, one of them being the beach towel. Hyacinth watched over me like an owl.

'Mr Plucker,' Hyacinth instructed, 'will you pass Fitzgerald the unbroken piece of wood. That'll need to be wrapped too.' Mr Plucker nodded obediently and, with care, extracted himself from the orange sofa, the effort causing him to wheeze a little. He ambled slowly across to the bay of the window and picked up the wood in his scraggy hands.

'It's heavy,' he said as he passed the wood to me. 'I've not felt it before.'

'But it also has a certain lightness to it,' I said. Then I wrapped the wood in two large towels, being careful to make sure that every last bit was covered, and placed it diagonally in Hyacinth's suitcase, from the top right-hand corner to the bottom left. It only just fitted, wedged really, there was no room for movement.

'Perfect,' Hyacinth said, smiling. 'It fits perfectly. Is your bag all packed Fitzgerald?'

I nodded.

'Then I think we're just about ready to leave,' Hyacinth continued. 'It's ten o'clock, we'd better be on our way.'

'But Uncle Albie's not here,' I protested looking at my mother. My mother looked at Hyacinth and Hyacinth looked at Mr Plucker (who was now safely back in the orange sofa). Mr Plucker looked back across at my mother.

'I'll think you'll find he is,' my mother said and they all three smiled. 'He'll be right outside, Fitzgerald. Go see. I think you'll find he has a few other people with him too.'

'He does?' I said, slightly bemused.

'He does, Fitzgerald,' Hyacinth confirmed. 'It's ten o'clock, they should all be here by now. Go and look.'

I sprang from my seat and hurried down the hallway to the front door. I eased the heavy door open, my palms moist with anticipation. Sunlight streamed through the open door, cascading warmth across my face. I blinked, the sun-rays temporarily blinding me. I rubbed my eyes and they watered a little. When my eyes cleared I realised that, standing there before me, were two rows of people running parallel down opposite sides of our street. Familiar, friendly faces. Auntie Nerys (looking friendlier than usual but still a little nervous and still a little terrifying); Kenny the Keycutter (pulling cards out from behind his ears); the Granite children (humming a tune) and their Granite parents from number eighteen; Miss Gossett and her Book of Psalms from number nine, and several other neighbours from our street whose faces I recognised but whose names I couldn't place; three of the wooden men from the timberyard (including the short one); Mr Eustace, my form tutor (with his acoustic guitar); Barry Saddler (wiping away a tear and admonishing himself for doing so); Wayne Haynes, Rabbit Warren, Emerson Darkly, Clive Barrington and of course Michael Sawyer; Ernie Devlin (wearing a red and white Liverpool scarf); Timothy Drinkwater, his father Mr Drinkwater (in full Red Indian regalia) and little Lily Drinkwatwer sitting astride her rusting tricycle; Mrs Freemantle (wearing a new floral-print dress); and, quite surprisingly, as I had not seen him since I had left junior school two summers previously, the Reverend James Alabaster (smiling ecclesiastically).

At the very end of one of the lines (also quite surprisingly as I had not seen her either since leaving junior school) stood the noble Mrs Eugena Braithwaite, the hairs on her top lip more noticeable in the bright sunlight. Parked in the middle of the street, between the two rows was Uncle Albie's distressed Opel Kadett. Uncle Albie stood beside it, wearing an old cap and holding the rear passenger door open, looking for all the world like an underpaid chauffeur.

'Your carriage awaits!' he shouted, his voice rolling down the gap between the two rows of faces and then altogether, as if they had previously rehearsed the moment, everyone cheered. Uncle Albie then bowed, tipping his cap. The cheering subsided, the smiling did not. I looked back at the front door; there stood my mother. She looked at me almost proudly. She waved her hand in the direction of the Opel Kadett. 'Go on,' she said. 'You've a task to complete, young man. I'll be imagining you flying and I'll be waiting for you when you get back.'

Beside my mother stood Hyacinth, a boiled sweet pressed against her wrinkled cheek. She had on her long brown coat and beads of perspiration swam down the grooves of her face. It was strange to see such an old and thin white woman who sweated so much; she sweated like a large African woman. She didn't wipe the beads of sweat off. They looked like little tributaries from a river as they snaked over the crumpled terrain that was her face. Hyacinth looked at my mother lovingly. She had become like a second mother to her since they had met in the grey corridors of St Roderick's. As I gazed at the rows of faces waiting to see me off, Hyacinth and my mother hugged, warmly, softly, holding their cheeks close to each other's for a few seconds. My mother didn't cry, she held on to her tears. But I knew they would come, later when we had gone; in floods, in torrents, into her milky tea.

'Look after him, won't you,' my mother said, dabbing at the sweat on her brow with a balled handkerchief, 'and the ashes.'

'Of course I will, my dear,' Hyacinth promised. 'We'll be back before you know it. Have a pot of tea waiting for us, won't you?'

'I will,' my mother said and looked to the clear blue sky for inspiration, for solace.

Mr Plucker appeared in the doorway, the hem of his sweater almost covering his knees. He held Hyacinth's vast suitcase in one hand and my over-laden smaller case in the other. Due to the uneven weight distribution he leaned dangerously to one side, so much more than usual that the angle was obscene and appeared to defy the laws of natural physics. He looked like a decaying tree that had been uprooted in a storm. My mother rushed to his side to relieve him of his monstrous burden but he shooed her away with sharp hisses. He then proceeded to shuffle slowly, painfully toward Uncle Albie and his battered car some twenty yards away.

Several of those gathered stepped forward to assist him but he shooed them away too. He chose instead to lumber on alone as if commissioned by some higher authority to ensure the safe delivery of the suitcases to the Opel Kadett without prevention (or assistance) from human or element. 'The body may be weak,' he muttered (seemingly to himself), 'but the spirit is willing.'

Once the bags were safely in the boot, Mr Plucker remained standing by the car, panting and still leaning at a surreal angle. Uncle Albie went over to him and helped him to straighten up to his usual leaning angle.

'Thank you,' breathed Mr Plucker and the sweat poured from him, causing his flaxen hair to stick to the scalp of his head, exposing patches of reddened skin.

I stood and surveyed the scene, a lump swelling in my throat. I looked at the two rows of faces, there to see me off. As I looked, Miss Gossett (from number nine) stepped forward as if pushed by an invisible hand. She coughed and began to speak, using formal tones.

'We are all here, Fitzgerald,' she said, 'to see you off on your sad but important journey. All of us here knew your father, some more than others. We did not all think of him as African but we all knew him all the same. Your father made many things for all of us in this neighbourhood. He had large hands and used them well. He made things to sit on, things to put things on and some things just to look at. We were all very grateful to him and very proud of him. It goes without saying that, when that lorry killed him we were all, and still are, very sad. It seemed so sudden.' Miss Gosset paused, the mood of her own words causing her to choke a little.

'One or two of us', she continued, 'have something we'd like to say before you go . . . as a sort of memorial to your father, your late father. I would like to begin by reciting a short psalm for you to remember on your journey with the ashes.' Miss Gossett opened her red leather-bound Book of Psalms and began to read . . .

'Psalm 139, I'm reading from verse thirteen . . .

For thou didst form my inward parts;
Thou didst weave me in my mother's womb.
I will give thanks to Thee, for I am fearfully and wonderfully
*   made;*
Wonderful are Thy works,
And my soul knows it very well.
My frame was not hidden from Thee,
When I was made in secret,
And skilfully wrought in the
depths of the earth.

Thine eyes have seen my unformed substance;
And in Thy book they were all written,
The days that were ordained for me,
When as yet there was not one of them.'

As Miss Gossett's words filled the air, I thought of my father, unformed in God's secret places, being knitted together, woven, his hands being made larger than normal and being shaped to look like oars. I looked at those gathered, who all stood solemnly listening to Miss Gossett's poetic words. The Reverend Alabaster rocked on his feet, mouthing the psalmist's words with a quiet but fiery passion. I could see right to the end of the street through his bow legs.

'I also have a letter here that your mother received.' Miss Gossett slipped a neatly folded letter from her pocket. 'It's from the driver of the lorry that killed your father. As you know, there was nothing he could have done. Your mother has asked Mrs Freemantle to read it out.' Miss Gossett looked over toward my mother, for confirmation. My mother nodded. The neatly folded letter was passed to Mrs Freemantle. Mrs Freemantle slipped on an ivory-framed pair of reading glasses and began to read. Her voice low and suitably sober. The street was silent as she read:

To whom it may concern (wife, son, daughter?), Sadly, I was the driver of the lorry that killed your husband/father. I was delivering rice and milk (mainly) to the grocery store. As you have probably been told there was nothing I could have done, he (your husband/father) stepped out into the road without looking. I wasn't driving very fast. He was holding a piece of wood and he seemed to be floating. His eyes were closed. I am so terribly sorry.

I am told he was a good man with large hands (I too have fairly large hands, but my feet are quite small). I am also told he created things from wood. I don't really make anything myself, I deliver things (groceries mainly), but I do love wood (particularly pine).

I will never forgive myself for driving the lorry that killed him but I hope and pray that you will find it in yourself to be able to forgive me (in time).

With remorse, Larry - the Driver of the Lorry.

Mrs Freemantle folded the letter and returned it to Miss Gossett who carefully slipped it into her Book of Psalms. 'That's it,' Mrs Freemantle said. We stood, our heads bowed, the words of Larry, the Driver of the Lorry, still in the air. There were a few muffled coughs and one or two shuffled their feet but the rest remained quiet and still. Little Lily Drinkwater moved slowly backwards and forwards on her rusting tricycle, the creek of the wheels grating and echoing down the street. One of the wooden men lit a cigarette, the smoke swirling around his head and drifting quietly up until it dissipated in the sky. Three large geese flew over our heads on their way to Fragrance Wood, the sound of their flapping wings causing us all to look up.

'Finally, Fitzgerald,' Miss Gossett announced, breaking the spell, 'it was felt to be appropriate that a song should be sung on this sad yet important day, to mark your departure, to further remember your father by. Mr Eustace, who has brought his guitar, would like to sing a song for us all. It's a tribute.'

Mr Eustace stepped forward, his hair waving mysteriously without the assistance of any breeze, his flared jeans flapping as if in a permanent state of rhythmic arousal. His guitar hung proudly over his firm shoulders, the strap a dazzle of interwoven colours. He looked more famous than he usually did, his finely chiselled features bathed in dazzling sunlight.

'This song . . .' he plucked at the guitar strings with a red plectrum as he spoke addressing us all, '. . . is a song that I'm sure you will all be familiar with. It seemed like the right song to sing. Feel free to join in, won't you.'

Then he started to sing, his mellow voice drifting slowly towards the heavens.

> *'Swing low, sweet chariot,*
> *Comin' for to carry me home!*
>
> *Swing low, sweet chariot,*
> *Comin' for to carry me home!*

I looked over Jordan and what did I see
Comin' for to carry me home!
A band of angels comin' after me,
Comin' for to carry me home!

Swing low, sweet chariot,
Comin' for to carry me home!

Swing low, sweet chariot,
Comin' for to carry me home!'

As Mr Eustace sung some of those gathered began to hum and some provided backing harmonies; the wooden men in their deep baritones; Mrs Freemantle with a pitch-perfect alto; my friends from school a heady mixture of sopranos and tenors. They began to sway too, in time to the music, Mrs Braithwaite clapping on the off-beat. Other neighbours opened their doors, one or two coming out to join the massed choir. One neighbour, Mr Parker from number forty-four, brought with him a shining trumpet and, improvising, he began to blow, filling the street with sultry jazz riffs, causing feet to tap and more hands to clap (most notably my mother's). As the massed choir continued its tribute, Hyacinth pointed toward the Opel Kadett.

'We must be on our way, Fitzgerald,' she said, 'it's getting late, we'll miss our flight.'

We walked slowly toward the open doors, smiling at those around us as they continued to sway. As we approached the end of the two lines Mrs Braithwaite stepped forward, stopping her singing and swaying. She clasped my hands in hers and held them firmly. She could barely fit the largeness of them inside her own hands but she held them all the same. She looked into my eyes, intensely.

'Travel safely, Fitzgerald,' she said. 'Bring back a little more of Africa than you take, won't you, my lickle pickney.'

I nodded.

'Maybe I won't be able to call you pickney again when you get back.'

I nodded again. Mrs Braithwaite stepped back into the line and continued to sing and sway, her voice and movement bringing a much needed rhythm to the whole affair.

As I walked towards the car, Michael Sawyer shouted out.

'Fitzgerald!' he shouted and I turned and faced him. 'See you when you get back!'

'Yep!' I said. 'Yes, I won't be long.' I turned, waved and walked to the car. Uncle Albie held the back door open.

'Step inside, young man,' he said. 'You have a long journey ahead. Mind that tin of sardines, they're for my tea.'

I scrambled into the back seat, moving the sardines to one side and sitting down. Rolls of film littered the other side of the seat and a tool of some kind lay on the floor. Hyacinth climbed into the passenger seat and sat down heavily. The smell of oil and petrol was overwhelming, causing Hyacinth and me to sneeze simultaneously.

'Bless you,' Uncle Albie said and then slipped into the driver's seat. He turned the key and the engine attempted to roar into life, causing the car to tremble and shake. It stalled and shuddered to a halt. Uncle Albie turned the key again and again the engine roared into life. This time there was no stalling and no shuddering just a gentle (albeit slightly clanking) purr of the engine.

'Right,' Uncle Albie said, removing his cap, his hair jutting out from his head like strange antennae, 'we're off.'

The car began to pull away, creeping up our street between the rows of the massed choir. Their singing and swaying continued, the trumpet dipping and diving, the guitar flowing, the voices melting through the air. As we edged past my front door I looked across at my mother who now stood alone (the only person not singing) and she wasn't whistling either. I could see the beginnings of a tear in the corner of her eyes waiting to roll. She looked at me and mouthed, 'I love you', then she turned and slipped quietly into the house, closing the door behind her.

The Opel Kadett crept quietly out of the street, turning left into North Cross Hill, leaving behind the last strains of the massed choir as it continued to sing . . .

> *'I'm sometimes up and sometimes down,*
> *Comin' for to carry me home,*
> *But still my soul feels heavenly bound,*
> *Comin' for to carry me home!'*
>
> *Swing low, sweet chariot,*
> *Comin' for to carry me home!'*

XIII

Roderick

The ebony-skinned man pushed the little wooden rowing boat out into the water, waves gently lapping against the sides. He hopped in, his crusty toes skimming the surface. Tiny droplets fell from his feet back into the water, causing the surface to shimmer. His deftness was magical. He edged past me like a will-o'-the-wisp and sat down delicately at the helm of the little wooden rowing boat. The boat rocked slightly from side to side, the gentle *phut-phut* of the lapping waves against its side soothing my ears. The *phut-phut* of lapping waves was one of my favourite sounds. I remembered once in junior school when Mrs Braithwaite asked the class to name one of their favourite sounds.

'The sound of a toilet flushing,' Emerson Darkly said and Mrs Braithwaite kissed her teeth at him.

'The sound of a stomach when it stops rumbling,' Barry Saddler said, rubbing his hands in circular motions around his ample belly.

'But that's not a sound,' Mrs Braithwaite said. 'When it *stops* rumbling it's no longer a sound.'

'I know but it sure *feels* nice 'cos it means you're going to eat something.'

'The sound of my mother brushing my hair,' said Lucy

Hermington who had the second most beautiful hair I had ever seen (Jasmine Khan's, who by then had already moved to Manchester, had been the best).

'The sound of a well-played piano concerto,' said Mary Lamb (whose parents were not only Catholics but also classically trained musicians).

'The sound of a lid popping off of a new jar of strawberry jam,' said Rabbit Warren (who ate strawberry jam every day in his packed lunch), 'and it's got to be *strawberry* jam.'

'The sound it makes when my feet land in damp sand when I jump from a great height,' Michael Sawyer said (and I knew he was thinking of Frenarby Grove).

'The sound of a kite flying on top of a hill,' said Clive Barrington (and we had all looked up at the ceiling trying to picture his kite flying over the grassy slopes of the Great Green Hills).

'The sound of a seagull in the sky over Marvel's Point,' Karen Carpenter said (she had a grandmother who lived there too).

'The sound of the *phut-phut* of lapping waves,' I said and I felt so moved by the thought that I stood up and made a wave-like motion with my outstretched hands.

Mrs Braithwaite smiled and she too had made a wave-like motion with her hands. 'Yes, Fitzgerald that's a truly beautiful sound,' she said, continuing to make waves with her hands.

'I love the sea,' the ebony man said to me. 'It is my purpose in life to be on or in the sea; to move across its silvery surface. Even though I am not a fish nor a sea mammal I believe I was made to be a part of the sea, to move through its beguiling waves.' His name was Thomas. Thomas was tall and wiry, his muscles taught but not bulging. He wore blue and white striped shorts (held up by a frayed piece of white string), no top and no socks or shoes. His crusty toes were wedged together and looked almost webbed, like paddles. His eyes, the deepest of browns, were set far back into his face as if some invisible hand had squashed them as far back as was possible. His nose spread broadly across his face and his full lips surrounded his teeth like a well-maintained privet hedge. His skin was black, very black, and looked silky to the touch. He was truly magnificent. He was darker even than Mrs Braithwaite. Next to me in the swaying boat sat Hyacinth, mouth full of boiled sweet, perspiring wildly, hands clutching on to the red casket.

'Hurry, Thomas, please!' she commanded, gesticulating toward the horizon. 'We have a job to do!'

'Jus' relax a little, Hyacinth,' Thomas said, picking up two heavy oars gracefully. 'I will get you there in no time. Besides, Hyacinth, you have all the time in the world, you're in Africa now. There is no need to rush. You should know that.'

Hyacinth nodded humbly as the little wooden boat eased out of the bay. Letting go of the red casket and letting it rest in her lap, she reached into her pocket and withdrew a bag of boiled sweets. She offered the crumpled bag to Thomas, he took a lemon one. The sound of the wooden oars sliding between the gentle waves was like the sun slipping from the sky at night, graceful and comforting. A huge white bird swooped by, its bill inches from the surface of the sea, its head turning from side to side searching for prey. I fixed my eyes on the wooden oars as they dunked in and out beneath the swelling sea, obeying the command of Thomas's deft arms. Tiny droplets of clear water fell from each oar every time they came out of the water, glistening in the sun. I looked at the hands at the end of his arms. His hands were large too, larger than mine but (as far as I could remember) smaller than my father's.

As I sat and watched him, sweat sprang from my brow and my hands felt moist, very moist. The African sun was hot, a clammy heat, the coolness of the sea doing nothing to dampen its power. I breathed in the smells of Africa and thought of all those times my father had told me to be proud of this wondrous place. The aromas were warm, colourful; the reds, the yellows, the greens, the hazy blues gelling together like an ancient woven fabric, new to my senses yet strangely familiar. The sky above our heads was bluer than I could imagine blue could ever be, infinitely bluer than on the day, only a few days ago, when I had left our street to the lilting strains of 'Swing Low, Sweet Chariot'. Mr Parker's trumpet still rang in my ears, echoing around the insides of my skull. I held my breath and let the wonder around me fill me to the core of my being.

Between Hyacinth and me, slightly damp from the splashes of water spilling over the edge of the boat, lay the unbroken piece of wood. It was glowing ever so slightly. We were taking the unbroken piece of wood and the ashes to a small island just off the shores of Lagos. The island was a place (the locals had told us) where many 'displaced' Africans came to scatter the ashes of their loved ones. A mystical place, they said. They came, they told us, from many distant lands; from Europe, from the Americas, from Australasia, from Asia.

'Scatter your loved one's ashes on the island,' a sturdy local with pale skin and a broad smile assured us, 'and their spirits will never be lonely again.'

A few days previously when we had finally arrived at our hotel – The Monumental Hotel of Lagos, a tall, narrow, whitewashed building in the heart of a busy street in the Yaba district, nine miles to the north of Lagos – the first thing we did, on entering our twin bedroom, was to unpack the unbroken piece of wood and the red casket. Hyacinth placed the unbroken piece of wood under the sill of the window, 'To let the African sun warm it,' she said. She placed the red casket carefully on the small teak bedside table, patting it like a small dog. The second thing Hyacinth did was to erect a screen between our two beds. She had been able to get the screen from the porter who, at her persistent requests – 'We need a screen in our room to dress behind. I'm an old lady and he's a young boy. It's not right, that we should have to unrobe together' – had managed to find one in the basement of the hotel.

'We can change in private now,' Hyacinth announced as she stood the tall screen between the two beds. I couldn't actually see her and the screen muffled her voice, making it sound like she was locked in a cupboard. 'Make sure you always keep your mosquito net on,' she added.

'I will,' I said and went over to the window. I peered out at the scene below. The street was vibrant, busy, thriving and beyond the street row upon row of corrugated tin roofs spread out like a rather stiff patchwork quilt. I looked out at a sea of black faces; bare arms, shoulders and legs. It was the most black faces in one place I had ever seen, a rich texture of browns and blacks, shining, glowing. The insistent beat of music from a small van with speakers on the roof pounded across the street, pulsating through the air; invisible musical fingers touching several of the massed heads causing their hands to clap and their hips to sway. I noticed one enormous man, with sleepy eyes and hands that looked like baseball catcher's mits, leaning back in a doorway. His giant head was thrown back and he was whistling; the sun glistened on the dome of his bald head. With one of his catcher's mits he flicked clumsily at the persistent flies as he whistled.

A woman, small and round, dressed in a traditional wrap and a white T-shirt with the words *'Viva España!'* stretching across her sumptuous breasts, swayed in time to the music. Her hips gyrated slowly, her arms moving in circular motions toward the ground, vast rings of damp sweat spread under her armpits. Other women carried large flasks on their heads and still others walked with their babies strapped firmly on to their backs. Further up the street, two boys (probably about my own age) took it in turns to breakdance on a faded yellow mat that they had laid out in front of them on the roadside. They were not very good break-dancers but they had lots of enthusiasm. They both wore loose, baggy, grey shorts (coated in red dirt) and nothing else. The red dirt had also mingled with the sheen of sweat on their backs.

Behind the boys stood a man; a man so old it appeared as if his spirit must have already left his body for another place and had not informed its owner that it had gone. The man's eyes were milky, clearly lacking any vision. His head was totally bald and, like the man with the catcher's-mit hands, sparkled in the sun. He chewed persistently at something in his mouth, I couldn't see what it was but I later learned that he was chewing sugarcane. Unlike Hyacinth's suicidal bats, the old man's teeth (at least the ones I could make out) appeared still to be in his mouth. The old man wore a loose-fitting, well-ironed, purple shirt with gold braids running down the sleeves and khaki shorts so vast that they almost covered the length of his decaying legs and were, in fact, like trousers. His feet seemed to have fused with the red dirt of the sidewalk. I wondered if he ever moved from that spot. In his bony and gnarled hands (one of which was adorned with a gold signet ring on the wedding finger) he held a thin, almost inconsequential, walking stick. White tape had been wrapped around the top and middle of the stick, probably to signify his blindness. The tape was now peeling.

As he stood behind the breakdancing boys, I noticed that he leaned slightly to one side, his hip sticking out at an acrobatic angle. I thought of Mr Plucker and imagined the two of them standing next to each other leaning at crazy angles like some bizarre geometric configuration.

The old man was tapping his gnarled fingers in time to the music, pounding out from the two nearby speakers. I recognised the music: it was a song that had been playing on our little radio in the days and weeks leading up to and immediately following my father's death. It was 'Celebration!' by Kool and the Gang.

My mother had had the radio on in the kitchen a few days after my father was killed. 'It keeps the sad thoughts out of my head,' she told me. We were standing together in the kitchen doing nothing in particular. We'd done that often since my father's death; just standing together in various parts of the house doing nothing in particular. Sometimes Hyacinth would be with us but usually it was just the two of us. Most of the songs that the frantic deejay had chosen to play had gelled together, passing us by like a series of bland autumn days, unremarkable and quickly forgotten. Neither my mother nor I could recall any of them, such was the depth of the grief we swam in. When 'Celebration!' had come on, however, its opening 'Yahoos!' had taken us both by surprise, my mother especially. Her body flinched as if shocked by a charge of electricity, her hands began to shake and her left eye began to flicker and jerk involuntarily like Father Ferdinand's from Our Gracious Lady of the Morning Dew. The guitar intro jangled like a gaoler's keys, leaping out hideously and inappropriately from our little radio perched on top of the work surface.

'Are you all right, Mum?' I asked, holding a shaking arm.

'No Fitzgerald, I'm not,' she said, the shake increasing steadily. 'Turn it off please, it's not right, not now!' I reached for the protruding knob of the radio and quickly switched it to the off position. Kool, and his celebratory Gang, left the kitchen quickly, noisily and a little clumsily. Somehow it seemed as if they knew that grief was in the air and that they shouldn't have been singing in our kitchen (not that song anyway). I somehow felt they were pleased to leave, pleased to take their celebration to a more suitable and grief-free kitchen.

My mother then sat down on the chair by the kitchen table. She placed her shaking hands down flat on the Formica top.

'Stop them from shaking will you, Fitzgerald?' she said, looking at me with haunted, faraway eyes. 'Hold them will you? Hold them still.'

I had gone over to her and held her tremulous hands firmly down on the table top. My larger hands swamped hers. We stayed together for several minutes, perhaps even ten, until the shaking subsided and my mother felt strong enough to stand again. Then she gently chubbed my cheeks and we carried on standing in the kitchen, doing nothing in particular, just 'being' together. The radio remained turned off. Every so often, if my mother's hands began to shake again, we would go over to the kitchen table and, sitting down, my mother would place her shaking hands on the Formica top and the ritual would begin once more, me holding my mother's hands down firmly until the shaking subsided.

I eased open the hotel window and let the warm, sticky air and African fragrances drift into the room. Heat and dust, sweat, cooking spices and the distinct smell of urine. It had been the strong smell of urine that had taken me by surprise when we had stepped out of Murtala Muhammed airport on to the bustling, overcrowded streets of Lagos on our arrival. The clammy heat, thick like invisible soup, had also been a shock.

'The Monumental Hotel of Lagos,' Hyacinth said to the back of the taxi driver's domelike head. 'Yaba district.'

'I can smell pee,' I said settling into the back seat of the yellow and green taxi, my sweat-stained shirt sticking to the car seat. 'Urine.'

'Welcome to Nigeria,' the back of the taxi driver's head said (he didn't turn around so I never got to see his face). 'Feel free to relieve yourself whenever and wherever you like. To pee is to be free!' He chuckled to himself.

From outside the open window the boom of the bass from the standing speakers below caused the window frame to shake a little. The jangle of the guitars rising above the myriad African voices drifted up from the street. Kool and his Gang seemed at home now, welcome; their celebrations now appropriate, away from the immediacy of grief. I stood at the window and my eyes surveyed the wondrous scene below, busier and more alive than any place I had ever seen. A multitude of black faces, more than I ever knew existed. It was indeed something to celebrate and I felt my feet begin to jig in time to the music (if my mother had been with me I felt that she too would have been temporarily released from her grief and her feet would have danced too, although deep down I wasn't so sure). I took in the harmony of other sounds aside from the music, the deep voices, the cries and shrieks of scampering children, the hoots of several car horns, the blare of an occasional goat. As if to justify the taxi driver's comment on the freedom to pee, I watched in amazement as a woman of wondrous proportions carefully squatted behind a white van and, in full view of several male passers-by, hitched her skirts and began to relieve herself on the roadside. When she got up and left, there remained, clearly visible, a large wet puddle in the red dirt. The steam from her pee rose in circles heavenwards. The puddle soon began to evaporate as the heat from the sun sucked it in. I thought momentarily of my visits to Auntie Nerys and then quickly banished the thought from my mind.

'Come, my dear,' Hyacinth's voice broke in, 'we must be going.'

'But we've only just arrived,' I said, turning to face her as she stood by the screen holding out a fresh bag of boiled sweets.

'There's someone we have to meet,' Hyacinth said.

'We do?' I dropped my hand into the bag of sweets. Because my hand was now so much bigger I could only really fit in two fingers and my thumb. I took an orange one.

'Yes,' Hyacinth said, turning on her heels and heading for the door, 'we do.'

I followed her as she descended the stairs with the speed of a small child. She handed the keys in at the front desk, nodding at the receptionist, a wide woman like a chest of drawers with a huge mole on her chin, who nodded back without actually lifting her head to make eye contact with us (all I could really see of her face was the mole).

Hyacinth then stepped out into the Lagos streets. 'Keep close,' she said. 'Don't lose sight of me.' I had no intention of losing sight of Hyacinth and I skipped to keep up with her. She strode down the street in the direction of the breakdancing boys and the gnarled blind man in the purple shirt. She dodged and weaved down the street like a featherweight boxer. I dodged and weaved behind her. I was overwhelmed by it all. My head span, buzzing with a combination of joy and trepidation. I looked at the faces around me, I could see Mrs Braithwaite in one or two, and several, although much darker in shade, looked distinctly like my father. No one in Wistful had ever looked vaguely like my father. I also realised that many of the men even walked in the same way as my father had walked, the way he walked when he went to 'wander and ponder' (the way he would have been walking, most probably, when he was killed by the lorry). They walked slowly with one shoulder slung forward, hips at an angle, arm swaying from side to side and their feet almost rolling, rather than stepping, over the red dirt.

Numerous pairs of eyes watched us with curiosity as we dodged and weaved, enjoying the spectacle of the rather strange and ancient-looking white lady pushing through the crowds, being followed by an eager teenager with afrormosia-coloured skin. Other heads, rather mysteriously, nodded at Hyacinth with familiarity. Rather strangely (or so I thought), one voice, coming from a sweating middle-aged man rushing by in a damp grey suit, clutching a crocodile-skin briefcase, spoke to Hyacinth.

'Hello, Hyacinth,' he said, not stopping to break his stride, 'so good to see you again.' Hyacinth smiled at him, revealing her dreadful stumps, as he flew by. As he passed me his jacket brushed my arm, his speed of movement causing me momentarily to lose my balance.

Hyacinth continued for a few more yards, then came to an abrupt halt in front of the two breakdancing boys. The boom of the speakers continued, shaking the very ground we stood on, Kool and the Gang having now been replaced by a heavier, slower American funk band (I could not recall their name). The beat of the song was clearly inappropriate for the two boys to breakdance to and they had given up trying to spin on their heads to it. Instead they sat next to each other on the faded yellow mat and with their fingers made little circles in the red dirt.

'Wait here,' Hyacinth said and she went over to the gnarled blind man in the purple shirt. They stood next to each other, whispering, smiling and touching each other's bony hands. I felt sure that I saw the old man's milky eyes light up and shine but I couldn't have, he was blind. Whilst I stood and waited, I watched the two boys as they drew circles in the dirt. They both looked up at me and smiled. I smiled back.

'My name is Fitzgerald,' I said, 'I'm from England.'

'And my name is Peter,' the bigger of the two boys said. He smiled and I noticed his mouth tilted to one side as if it had forgotten that it was supposed to be straight.

'And my name is Wole,' the smaller of the two boys said. He picked his nose as he spoke to me. 'I'm from Nigeria.'

'And so am I,' I said puffing out my chest a little. 'At least part of me is.'

'Why are you here then?' Peter asked.

'To bring my father home.'

'Your father is here with you?' Peter said, his slanting smile returning after each question.

'No,' I said. 'He's dead.'

'Your father is dead and yet you are bringing him home?' Wole said.

'Yes,' I said. 'He's in a red casket. His ashes I mean.'

Wole and Peter were silent for a while. They seemed a little lost for words; so did I.

'Is your mother alive?' Wole asked, breaking the silence.

'Yes,' I said. 'She's at home; my home, in Wistful.'

'Wistful,' Wole said and I could see him rolling a bogey in his fingers as he spoke. 'I've not heard of Wistful before.'

'Have you heard of *The Wistful Arcs*?' I said and I held my arms aloft and demonstrated the shape of the arcs. They shook their heads, Peter's smile seeming momentarily to straighten itself whilst his head was shaking. As they were shaking their heads I realised that the sounds of a Jam song were beginning to pump out of the speakers behind us. It was a song called 'Going Underground'. I thought it best to start dancing. I wanted to show them that I could dance too. I began to bounce up and down as The Jam shouted in the background. As I jumped I kicked the red dirt into the air each time I landed. Wole and Peter looked a little puzzled.

'This is not a song that is easy to dance to,' Peter said.

'Not a song that we can breakdance to,' Wole said, standing back.

'It's The Jam,' I said, sweat breaking out on my brow. 'They're from England. You can pogo to it. Come on join in.'

Wole and Peter looked unsure.

'What is a pogo?' Wole said and he flicked the bogey on to the ground.

'It's what I'm doing,' I said. 'You just bounce up and down.'

'Do you pogo to all music in England?' Peter asked.

'No, not all!' I shouted. 'Just music like this!'

I continued bouncing up and down as The Jam rattled their pounding tune across the Lagos street. Wole was first; he tentatively began to join me, jumping from foot to foot, slowly at first, unsure of exactly how to pogo. 'Both feet together,' I said. 'And faster.' Wole increased his speed and began to bounce manically. Peter joined in too, catching up with Wole. 'Feel the rhythm!' I shouted. 'It's inside of you!' And as I bounced with Peter and Wole to the urgent beat of The Jam I was aware of how heavy my hands had become and I had a sudden urge to smell some wood. 'THE WOOD IS GOOD!' I wailed and Peter and Wole looked even more puzzled as they pogoed.

'Your hands are big!' Peter shouted over the din of The Jam.

'I KNOW!' I shouted as I bounced.

'They look like oars!' Wole shouted.

'I KNOW!' I shouted and The Jam continued their own shouting. A group had gathered around us and were watching as we pogoed. Some were dancing in a very African way, swaying from the hips, but one or two were trying, not very successfully, to mimic my pogo. The woman with the *Viva España!* T-shirt was one of them. Her large breasts flapping dangerously each time she bounced. The Jam ran out of puff and came out from the Underground to end their song. They were worn out. A different song began to pound out of the speakers, something about a woman feeling like she was in love. This seemed to suit Peter and Wole and the *Viva España!* woman better and they stopped their pogoing and began to move more comfortably to the fluid sound of this new rhythm.

I stood and watched them dancing and became aware, out of the corner of my eye, that I could see Hyacinth gesticulating toward me. She was waving her arm motioning for me to come and join her and the gnarled blind man.

'Fitzgerald,' she said when I reached them, 'may I introduce you to an old friend of mine. His name is Roderick. He's blind.'

'Hello,' I said, stretching my arm in Roderick's direction, allowing him to take hold of my hand. The boniness of Roderick's hands startled me; they felt like the knobbly roots of a tree. The rockiness of his huge signet ring added to my shock. Roderick's milky eyes penetrated me.

'Hello, Fitzgerald,' he said. His Nigerian accent was strong, his voice a deep throb. 'I'm so glad to meet you. Hyacinth has told me so much about you. I've been waiting for you.'

'I'm pleased to meet you,' I said. 'There's a saint who shares your name you know; Saint Roderick of Leicester the Patron Saint of Unsound Minds. Have you heard of him?'

'Yes, I have,' he said. 'My own mother and father were both Catholics. They named me after him. They had both visited England in their youth. They liked it very much, except for the cold of course. I believe Saint Roderick died at a very young age. Such a tragedy when one dies so young. By all accounts I have heard that Saint Roderick was a lovely man.'

'Yes, I believe he was,' I said 'There is a hospital named after him. St Roderick's on Passover Crescent; in Wistful. Have you heard of Wistful?'

'Yes, I have, I've heard of the splendid arcs; to the north and to the south of the town. And yes I've heard of the hospital too,' Roderick said. 'It would be my deepest desire that perhaps one day I too will have a hospital named after me.'

'I'm African, sir,' the words blurted out of my mouth. 'At least I'm part African. My father was part African too. I'm *very* proud to be African.'

'I know you are, Fitzgerald,' Roderick said, finally releasing my hands from his knobbly grip, 'I can tell by the way you speak and by your beautiful light brown skin.'

'But you're blind. How can you see?'

'You don't always need eyes to be able to *see* things, Fitzgerald.'

'Have you known Hyacinth long?'

'Oh yes,' he said smiling, his teeth whiter than I had expected. I had anticipated them to be like Hyacinth's. 'Hyacinth and I go back a long way. Hyacinth has been here many times, she's almost an African herself now.' Hyacinth appeared to kiss her few remaining teeth and they both chuckled. They looked like two ancient trees growing next to each other, bark peeling, branches dying, leaves falling off but full of centuries of knowledge and wisdom. I was sure that if you could peel back their skin you would be able to count the rings and work out their ages. I thought I heard one of them break wind but wasn't sure. As I stood in front of them I was aware, perhaps for the first time, just how old Hyacinth actually was. The deftness and quick mind that I had grown to love and admire since our first meeting concealed a timeworn body. Roderick too looked antique. I struggled to put an age on him but he was very old. I knew that and yet somehow they both looked almost ageless. It was as if their old age superseded any recognised chronological sequence.

'When Hyacinth was made aware of your father's death,' Roderick spoke again, 'she got in touch with me. When she found out where your father was from she knew I would be able to help.'

I had the distinct feeling that Hyacinth was somehow 'made aware' of my father's death long before she'd actually met us in St Roderick's Hospital and perhaps she knew of his death long before he was actually killed. Where this feeling came from I don't know but it was there all the same.

XIV

Light and Dark

As I lay in my hotel bed, sleep eluding me, I looked up at the ceiling. The light of the full moon outside lit up the room, the dark colours of the night softened by the lunar glow. I felt as if I was lying in the middle of a painting. *Boy Unable to Sleep in Lunar Glow* perhaps, by a long dead Spanish or French artist. I imagined our class standing on a school trip to a London art gallery, huddled in a little group around the famed painting, talking in self-assured art-appreciation tones with Miss Clifton our art teacher.

'Why do you feel the boy in the picture ith unable to thleep?' Miss Clifton asks. (She was an unnecessarily narrow woman with thick eyebrows who spoke with a lisp which would be all the more prominent in the quiet of the art gallery.)

'Because he's not tired,' Emerson Darkly replies.

'Or perhaps it's because the moonlight is keeping him awake,' Barry Saddler says.

'No, children,' Miss Clifton lisps. 'Exthplore your inner feel-ingth, the boyth inner feelingth. Don't just thtate the obviouth reathonth why the boy may not be thleeping. *Feel* the reathonth why he may not be able to thleep. Come into the boyth mind, the artisth mind ath to why the boy ith unable to thleep. *Feel the reathonth. Feel them, children!'*

'Maybe he doesn't *feel* tired then,' Emerson Darkly says and I imagine Miss Clifton raising her thick eyebrows.

'Or maybe he *feels* annoyed that the moonlight is keeping him awake when really he wants to go to sleep,' comes Barry Saddler's reply and Miss Clifton breathes heavily, becoming exasperated.

And then I imagine Clive Barrington silencing us all with a scholarly summation.

'No, no, no,' he begins, pushing his way to the front of the huddle and turning to face his inferiors. 'The boy is unable to sleep because if he had been asleep the artist would not have painted him. No respectable artist would sneak into a young boy's room and paint him whilst he's asleep in case the noise of his easel being set up woke the boy.

'No, the artist must have asked the boy not to sleep until he had finished painting him. The moonlight being in the picture is a bonus for us, the viewer, to help us to see that the boy is unable to sleep and is actually awake. If there had been no moonlight I doubt the picture would ever have been painted in the first place as it would have been too dark for the artist to see the boy. And besides, if it had been dark the boy would have been asleep.'

Miss Clifton, by now, would have her narrow head held in her narrow hands and would then quickly move us on to the next set of paintings, hoping I'm sure for something more straightforward like a landscape or a picture of a house (with no one in it).

I looked across at the silhouette of the dividing screen. From behind I could hear the rasping of breath being expelled from Hyacinth's decaying mouth. She was sleeping soundly.

We had stayed in the company of the blind Roderick for some time that afternoon. Hyacinth told me he was a close friend of hers; she said she'd known him many years.

'How many years?' I asked.

'Too many to remember,' she said. 'Sometimes a year is just

a blink of an eye. Sometimes many years pass in the blink of an eye. Let's just say I've known Roderick for the blink of an eye.'

Hyacinth took me round to Roderick's little flat, a short stroll from our hotel. 'It's called an apartment,' Hyacinth said as we entered, 'not a flat. They call them apartments here.'

'Like on *Columbo*,' I said. 'They call them apartments on *Columbo*.'

'Yes,' Hyacinth said, tapping at the door, 'and *Ironside*.'

'Come in!' Roderick called out. Hyacinth nudged the door open and we entered. The front room had a familiar smell to it, not dissimilar to Mr Plucker's front room, musty and old. Everything in the room was old, stained or faded. It was dark. Roderick had not opened the shutters but then, being blind, I suppose he didn't have to. What little light there was in the room flickered nervously as if unsure it really belonged there.

'Hello again, Fitzgerald,' Roderick said, his milky eyes swimming around the room. He was still wearing the same purple shirt and he had circles of sweat in his armpits. A plug of sugarcane was wedged in the corner of his mouth. Roderick's peeling white walking stick leaned against the chair he was sitting on. 'Sit down, please. Hyacinth, come sit down.'

Hyacinth pulled up two wicker chairs and we sat down. I was pleased to have the cooling fan in the room, whispering behind me on my back. The sound of the whirring blades was like a huddle of little children tapping on a window, trying to get my attention.

Roderick leaned forward and pushed a dirty white saucer across the glass coffee table in my direction. 'Welcome,' he said. 'To Africa.' On the saucer there was a handful of small pink nuts.

'Take one, eat,' Roderick said, appearing to sense my hesitation.

'Kola nuts,' Hyacinth explained. 'They're offered as a way to make you feel welcome.'

I hesitated and picked up a kola nut. I held the nut in one hand and the saucer in the other. The nuts looked like strange little sweets; penny chews perhaps. My hand swamped the saucer. Roderick smiled. I put the nut my mouth and began to chew.

My jaws began to ache as I chewed on the nut; it was like chewing a very chewy chewing gum only not as nice. Not as nice as the Wrigley's spearmint gum that me and Michael Sawyer bought from the newsagent on the corner of Drummond Street. I choked and almost spat the nut out. Hyacinth and Roderick laughed, the sugarcane falling out of Roderick's mouth.

'It's bitter isn't it?' Hyacinth said.

I nodded. My eyes watered a little but I persevered, not wanting to appear rude.

'It's nice,' I lied. I had never tasted anything quite so bitter. I chewed harder, this time determined to find something enjoyable about the nut. I was beginning to feel a little light-headed and I could feel my heart racing just a little faster. 'My father never told me about kola nuts when he told me about Africa.'

'I think your father had probably never heard of kola nuts,' Hyacinth said. 'I hate them myself, they get stuck in my teeth. With teeth like mine, it's not nuts you want to be eating.' Hyacinth opened her mouth to laugh and I was reminded again of just how despairing her teeth were.

'No, it's nice,' I still felt the need to lie. It felt like horses were racing in my chest as my heartbeat quickened. The 3.30 at Aintree.

'I'm not a great fan of the taste myself,' Roderick said. 'But please don't tell anyone. I prefer Hyacinth's sweets. You have such lovely sweets in England.'

The bitter taste began to change and a surprising sweetness oozed into my mouth. I felt giddy, a sense of well being spreading throughout my body.

'It tastes sweet now,' I said.

'Keep chewing,' Roderick said. 'Take another.'

I slipped another kola nut into my mouth and chewed it hurriedly.

'That's Africa,' Roderick said. 'You have to overcome the bitterness to find the sweet.'

'In my experience,' Hyacinth said, 'that's the way of the world, Roderick, not just Africa.'

The sweet taste was now exhilarating and my body felt warm

and comfortable like I was inside a hot-water bottle. 'I don't think I would have enjoyed the sweetness so much if it hadn't come after the bitter,' I said and Roderick and Hyacinth nodded in agreement. 'It's like Uncle Albie always tells me, you can't enjoy today without yesterday.'

'And you can't enjoy tomorrow without today,' Roderick said. 'Everything in life has its own order. Death follows life and life follows death and so it goes on.'

'Roderick is a wonderful cook,' Hyacinth said, changing the subject. 'Aren't you, Roderick?'

'Even if I have to say so myself,' Roderick said. 'For a man I am pretty damn good. What kind of foods do you eat at home, Fitzgerald?'

'We have a roast on Sunday and bubble and squeak on Mondays,' I said and I felt a sudden yearning for some bubble or some squeak. 'On Tuesdays we have shepherd's pie or lamb casserole; on Wednesdays and Thursdays we used to have something from the freezer like a pie or something but ever since Mr Josiah and little Bobby took away the freezer we have *moin moin* or *jollof* rice. On Fridays we have fresh fish from the fishmongers and on Saturdays we have something from the chip shop and Dad always has pickled onions or a pickled gherkin.' I stopped to take breath and thought of my father's pickled gherkins. I could almost see one in my mind lying on his dinner plate with the first bite having been taken out. I could see his face too with the pickle juice running down his chin. A lump formed in my throat and I looked across at Hyacinth.

'Isn't that a strange word?' Hyacinth said.

'What?' Roderick asked, his eyebrows raising above his empty eyes.

'Monger,' Hyacinth said. 'You know "fishmonger". Isn't the monger bit an odd word? I've never really thought of it before but it is.'

'Monger,' I said. '*It can be used in combination except in archaic use; a trader or dealer: ironmonger or in combination as a promoter of something: warmonger.*'

'I wonder if you can just be a monger?' Hyacinth asked, her stumps clicking in her mouth as she spoke. 'Then little children could say they want to be a monger when they grow up.'

'I don't think you can,' I said. 'You have to have something to monger. But you can be a mongerer, like a warmongerer.'

'Can you be a shoemonger or a clothesmonger?' Hyacinth asked. 'Or a what about a sweetmonger?'

'No,' I said and I could feel the spirit of Clive Barrington hovering nearby. 'Only fish, iron or war. I don't think you can monger anything else, not that I've heard of anyway.'

'Did I hear you say that your own mother cooks *moin moin* and *jollof* rice?' Roderick asked.

'Yes,' I said. 'She learned to cook them from Mrs Cuthbert.'

'But your mother, she isn't Nigerian, is she?' Roderick said.

'No,' I said. 'She's not, she always says she's one hundred per cent Anglo-Saxon.'

'Then Mrs Cuthbert is Nigerian?'

'No,' I said. 'She's from Dominica.'

'And who is Mr Josiah?' Roderick asked, rolling the sugarcane around his mouth as he spoke.

'The rag-and-bone man,' I said.

'And what is that?' Roderick asked. 'What is a rag-and-bone man?'

'A man who buys and sells things that no one wants any more,' I said.

'A rag-and-bonemonger,' Hyacinth said and we laughed.

Roderick eased himself from his chair, his knees creaking as much as the wicker. 'Come,' he said, picking up his white stick and moving towards a back room. Despite his lack of sight he was able to negotiate the obstacles in his way without problem. 'Let me teach you how to cook another Nigerian dish, then you will be able to teach your mother one day and then she will have three dishes. That would be good would it not?'

I stood up and looked at Hyacinth. She waved her arm in the direction of the back room suggesting I follow. 'I think I'll stay here, dear,' she said. 'I could do with resting my old legs.'

'Make yourself at home, Hyacinth,' Roderick called, as he disappeared into the back room.

'I always do,' Hyacinth replied and she popped one of her boiled sweets into her mouth.

I followed Roderick into the back room, which I discovered was a kitchen of sorts. Smaller even than our kitchen in Wistful. Dirty pans were stacked in unruly heaps and the work surface was corroded and in need of a clean. It smelled of heat and of sweat and of something I felt I ought to be more familiar with but wasn't. Roderick negotiated the mess like a man with sight, seeming to know where everything was amidst the chaos. A little brown transistor radio was perched on a window ledge; two flies were buzzing around it, hungry for food. Roderick flicked the switch on. The sound of the radio was tinny and I could hear Diana Ross's voice asking us to remember her as a big balloon.

'Have you ever eaten *egusi* soup before, Fitzgerald?' Roderick said.

'No,' I said. 'What is it? Is it an animal?'

'No, no, no,' Roderick chuckled. '*Egusi* are seeds. From a vegetable; like a pumpkin. When they are ground down you can make a soup with them. Listen, my friend, I'll pass you the ingredients and tell you what to do with them, I'll show you how to make your first *egusi* soup. It will be easy. What do you think?'

'I would like that very much,' I said. 'I never really get the chance to cook at home.'

Roderick's blindness was of no consequence in his kitchen; he appeared to know where everything was by touch and smell. The shutters were open and I was grateful for the light.

'Bitterleaf,' he said, handing me a bunch of green leaves that looked like spinach and a sharp but dirty knife. 'Chop it finely and put it to one side. You must chop it finely. Make sure of it.' I took the leaves nervously and fingered the sharp edge of the dirty knife. Then I carefully began to chop the leaves on the corroded work surface. Roderick switched on a kettle with a frayed lead and the water hissed gently as it began to boil.

'When the water has boiled,' he said, 'put the bitterleaf in a

200

bowl and cover it with hot water.' I followed his instructions. 'As soon as it's covered in water quickly pour all the water away. Let the bitterleaf cool down then sieve it to drain the excess water.' I did everything as Roderick said.

'Tell me about your home town, Fitzgerald.' Roderick had perched on a stool and was sitting still with his bony hands clamped together on his lap. The sugarcane was back in his mouth; it didn't impair his speech.

'Wistful?' I said and I watched the bitterleaf as it began to cool, waiting for the steam to evaporate.

'Yes, tell me about Wistful,' Roderick said. 'What is it like?'

'Cold usually,' I said, 'and grey, it always seems to be grey, even in the summer it can be cold and grey. Except the hills, they're very green.'

'The Great Green Hills?'

'Yes.'

'And the arcs?' Roderick said, sucking on the sugarcane. 'Tell me about the arcs.'

'They're very big, and my father helped to make them,' I said. 'When we were little, me and Michael Sawyer used to stand under them. We used to think they went right up to heaven. We thought they went up to space, "This is Flight Commander Sawyer on Apollo 9," Michael would say. "We have orbited the earth, we are just coming over Wistful Ground Control, we can see them, we can see the Arcs. We have seen the Great Wall of China and now we can see the Arcs."'

Roderick chuckled. 'Who knows,' he said, 'maybe you can. Who is Michael Sawyer?'

'My friend, my best friend.'

'Now, while you are waiting for this bitterleaf to cool, grind the *egusi* seeds down in that little bowl with some water,' he said and I reached over for the bowl by my side marvelling at how Roderick knew it was there. The bowl was sticky to the touch and I wiped off some dried tomato paste with my thumb. I began to grind the seeds into the water. I mixed them for what seemed hours with Roderick periodically asking me to pass him the bowl so he could put his hands in to feel the texture. 'It must feel like a paste,' he said several times, handing me back the bowl.

'Do you have many friends in Wistful?'

'Yes, I believe I do,' I said. 'There's Wayne Haynes and Barry Saddler and Clive Barrington. And Emerson Darkly and Rabbit Warren of course, they all go to my school. And then there's Mrs Freemantle and Mr Plucker.'

'Who are they?' Roderick asked.

'Neighbours,' I said. 'I've known them all my life. Mr Plucker lives next door, he suffers from polio and melancholia. Mrs Freemantle lives on Albion Hill and she's got six cats. She's a Catholic.'

'Not a nice combination, I mean the polio and melancholia, not the cats and being a Catholic,' Roderick said. 'Now chop up some onions, some tomatoes and the cloves of garlic and the ginger. You'll find them in the cupboard under the sink.'

I reached down and removed the vegetables and spices from a collapsing blue plastic rack under the sink. I wasn't sure what garlic was so I had to ask Roderick. He leaned across and felt the different spices in the rack and picked out the garlic. He separated two cloves and gave them to me. 'Chop these finely,' he said. I found another small knife amidst the chaos and followed his advice and hacked away at the cloves, surprised by the strong smell they left on my fingers.

'It seems a lovely place,' Roderick said. 'Wistful I mean.'

'It's the only place I know,' I said.

'Do you believe in God, Fitzgerald?' Roderick asked, the timbre of his voice changing a little.

'I don't know really. I think so. As a maker of things I do. You know like butterflies, people and trees. Who else could make things as weird and wonderful as that? Especially if you knew what some of the people in our street looked like. I think I believe in God but I believe in heaven more.'

'Why is that?' Roderick asked.

'My mother always taught me to pray to Jesus just in case he was God,' I explained. 'Just to be on the safe side. But I think that was a superstitious thing really. But my father, he always told me that wood was heavenly. Maybe he's in heaven with his wood.'

'Light the gas with those matches and put some oil on. You'll need to fry all those chopped vegetables and spices very gently. Give them about ten or fifteen minutes. Have you cooked before, Fitzgerald?' Roderick's head swayed from side to side a little as he spoke.

'Like I said, not really,' I said but I was surprised at how comfortable I felt cooking. 'Beans-on-toast and cheese-on-toast, that sort of thing. My mother does all the cooking. My father never cooked, except scrambled egg.'

'Do you believe in angels, Fitzgerald?'

The chopped onions were making my eyes water. I wiped my face with the corner of my shirt.

'I don't know. I used to believe in Wood Fairies when I was little but not any more.'

'*I* believe in angels,' Roderick said and I was aware for the first time of how long his eyelashes were.

'Now, when you have cooked the onions and everything in the pan, add the *egusi* with some water and salt and cook it for another ten minutes or so, then put in the bitterleaf. Don't let the oil get too hot and don't cover the pan. We should add some chillies but maybe only a few. They're in the bowl on your left, just add one or two, chopped up, you need to be introduced gently to Nigerian chillies. I'll add some meat later. There you have it, your third recipe, *egusi* soup. At least a kind of *egusi* soup. It takes a lot of practice and you'll need to make it many times before you get it just right.'

I looked into the pan as the stew bubbled. I breathed in the sweet, nutty aroma.

'It should be ready in about twenty or thirty minutes,' Roderick said. It seemed as if he was looking straight into me. 'I think of God as a creator, someone who likes to make things. I like to think if there is a God he would take great pleasure in creating all things.'

'Like wood?'

'Yes, like wood.' Roderick smiled and reached out to feel for his walking stick, which was leaning up against a cupboard; he caressed it. 'Or at least the trees to get the wood from.'

'And my father too? Would God have taken pleasure in making him?'

'Yes, I like to believe that God would have loved creating your father,' Roderick said and he switched the walking stick from hand to hand. I couldn't help but notice how tatty it was and how the edges could do with being smoothed down. 'And do you know what, Fitzgerald . . . ?'

Roderick stopped mid-sentence.

'What?' I said, still looking at the walking stick and sniffing at the smell of garlic on my fingers.

'I believe', Roderick said, 'that any God that could have made so many interesting things must have really big hands, don't you think?'

I looked across at Roderick, with his strange, milky yet all-seeing eyes and his long, curling lashes as his head swayed from side to side seeking the light, the sugarcane still wedged into the corner of his mouth. I watched as the two flies buzzed around the open window. The tinny radio was still rattling away in the background, by now an advertisement was telling me to buy a drink called Milo for a healthy heart and a sound mind. I could hear a snoring sound coming from the front room followed by the unmistakable sound of Hyacinth's rattling teeth. I knew she had fallen asleep.

I think it was the thought of a God with large hands making things that made me start to believe in God. I could picture Him carefully carving the bones that He would hang my father on, paying particular attention to the hands. 'I'll give him hands like my own,' God would say. 'Large hands that he can make things with.' I wanted to believe in angels too. I wondered if Mr Plucker and his graciousness in the light of his depression might be an angel of sorts, albeit a melancholic one. My mother always said he was.

'You're such an angel, Mr Plucker,' she would say after he had minded me whilst she went shopping on Drummond Street. Or, 'Mr Plucker, you are a little angel,' after he had told us Uncle Albie had phoned in the days before we had a phone. But would angels really lean that far to one side? Would an angel really collect cigarette cards and treat them as if he was caring for his own children?

If it were possible for female angels to have hair on their top lip, then Mrs Braithwaite would be a high-ranking angel. She certainly smelled like she could be. And I wondered if it were possible that Miss Gossett and her Book of Psalms were in fact on a visit from the heavenly realms (who else but an angel would be able to recite words from the Bible with such ease and clarity?). I bumped into her once in the street on my way back from the bus garage on Franklin Street.

'Fitzgerald,' she said and she stood blocking my path. ' "Do not neglect to show hospitality to strangers, for by this some have entertained angels without knowing it." ' I don't know why she stopped me to say that but she did.

What about Mrs Freemantle? She had delivered the unbroken piece of wood. And she had been there when the policeman with the curling fingers had delivered his grim news. But would an angel have so many cats and would an angel need to have such tidy hair? And what about Uncle Albie? But I wasn't sure that an angel would need to be so good at mending toilets; and could I actually be related to one?

As I sat and watched Roderick and Hyacinth speaking together later on, I chewed on another kola nut. After the initial bitterness I felt warm inside again and, more importantly, I had the feeling that my father was safe. It was like that with Hyacinth and now with Roderick; they had a way of making me feel safe. Their voices, when they spoke together, hummed and rattled like the comforting sound our fridge made at home. If, as Roderick had said, God's hands were even bigger than my father's hands then there was no way He was going to let my father go – dead or otherwise. I didn't know for sure what my father's visitation had meant but I was sure then that he was not a *stranger* in Paradise but was very much amongst friends (and heavenly wood). Had I known how to, I believe I would have got on my knees and prayed out loud there and then, but, despite all his other religious instructions, the Reverend Alabaster had never actually taught us *how* to pray. He had only really told us *to* pray and had only taught us how to say the Lord's Prayer, by rote (which I had known anyway as my mother had already taught me it, by rote).

I did not know then of the grim news waiting for me at home in England. If I had I may never have allowed myself to believe in God.

Roderick promised to show me 'the lights and the darks' of Africa. Hyacinth would come along with us. She would be Roderick's *eyes* whilst he showed us the *sights*. Hyacinth, he reminded me, had been to Africa before – he didn't go into specifics, but he did say that the red casket was not the first box of ashes that she had brought home. And so, together with Hyacinth and the blind Roderick I began to discover the very place my father had always talked about.

'Africa,' Roderick said, 'is full of light and clarity. It is full of movement and sound and dance and the spiritworld is never far away.' He chewed on his sugarcane as he spoke and Hyacinth sucked on a raspberry boiled sweet as she stood next to him.

'But it is also a land full of darkness,' he continued. 'There is too much killing here; too much disrespect for life. You see darkness so much more when you're blind, Fitzgerald. You can almost smell it.'

We visited the National Museum and the Jankara Market, both on Lagos Island. We took a crowded bus to the National Theatre Complex at Ebute Metta. We sat together at various roadside restaurants in downtown Lagos and sampled the local dishes; pepper soup (Roderick would allow me to have only a little), *gari*, cowfoot (probably the nastiest thing I have ever eaten) and, of course, *egusi* soup, *moin moin* and *jollof* rice. Eating the *moin moin* and *jollof* rice made me realise just how different my mother's version was from the real thing. It was like meeting a distant cousin; you knew you were related but you were aware you had so little in common. The meat was so hard to chew that I nearly lost a filling and the chillies left me gasping for water and made my eyes weep (as Roderick had said they would). He and Hyacinth laughed as tears streaked my face. We also had different kinds of bottled drink – Fanta, Sprite, Coca-Cola – which I loved (we could rarely afford such drinks at home and until then I had existed on orange-and-lemon squash and Dandelion and Burdock at Christmas and lemon barley water when any of us was ill). Roderick paid for the drinks and sat back, chuckling as I struggled with the chillies and rock-hard meat. In between chuckles he drank from a bottle of beer, his cloudy eyes rolling in their sockets.

We sat on a tour boat in the Blight of Benin and, as water lapped around us, we looked back at the port of Lagos; at Yaba, the district where our hotel was situated (teeming with life) and Ikoyi Island. We took an overnight bus across red and bumpy land to the eastern city of Onitsha. Twice the bus almost veered off the road to avoid enormous pot-holes and at one stop-off point the driver, a man with dried snot around his nose and eyes like honey pots, lumbered up the aisle, grabbed hold of a large, sweaty woman and dragged her down to the front of the bus. When he reached the door he pushed her out, head first. She screamed as her weighty body bounced off the stairs and she landed on the dirty road wailing like a hysterical child. The driver cursed – 'Fucking robber woman! Fucking whore woman! Fuck you, you shit-bag!' – and then he slammed the door shut and we continued our journey. No one came to her aid.

'What did she do?' I asked Roderick nervously.

'She didn't pay her fare,' he replied. 'But don't worry, there'll be another bus along soon, maybe she'll have the fare by then.' His eyes sparkled momentarily and I could hear loose change tinkling in his pocket as if it was moving about of its own volition.

When we arrived in Onitsha, Roderick took us to a museum; the Beatific Museum, a small family-run business on the outskirts of the town that was usually, Roderick said, missed by tourists.

It was not like any place I had ever visited, certainly nothing like the museums we visited in London. It was really nothing more than a large house. The walls were supposed to be white but the sun had cracked the paintwork and veins of red dirt streaked them, like a map of the London Underground. The floors were marble but were so covered in dirt it was very difficult to distinguish where the outside ended and the inside began. A small girl with crusty, bare feet and a smile that began and ended in full view of her ears sat on a rusty tricycle a few yards away from the main doors. She eased the trike slowly back and forth and it creaked just like little Lily Drinkwater's. She watched me as we neared the entrance and I could almost hear little Lily's voice calling out to her brother. The smell of urine that I had noticed outside the airport was present again, lingering around the entrance like a vagrant with nowhere to go. The doors were heavy and creaked as Hyacinth eased them open. A man with flaky skin, shabby clothes and a cowboy hat was sitting by the door, a rusted tin bowl at his feet.

'Kobo, kobo, kobo,' he chanted in a strangely fake American accent. 'Naira, naira, naira.'

Roderick leaned down and sprinkled coins into his bowl and Hyacinth followed suit. The man touched his hat in thanks and continued to chant, 'Kobo, kobo, kobo. Naira, naira, naira.' A row of red soldier ants came out from behind his bowl and walked in line towards his feet like a group of orderly children on a school outing. 'Urghh! Ants! Ants! Ants!' he shouted kicking out at them. 'Damn you! Damn you! Damn you!' He still swore with the American accent and apart from the 'urghh' everything came in threes.

Inside the museum light shone through several windows and the smell of urine receded. Hyacinth shuffled over to a little kiosk and exchanged some money for three tickets with a man who was so broad that the kiosk seemed to be struggling to contain him. The kiosk reminded me of the one at the Picture House just off Passover Crescent and I felt a momentary pang of homesickness. The museum was all on one floor, no escalators, no ushers, no signs saying 'Quiet Please'. Aside from the three of us there were several other visitors and the unmistakable sound of the whirring fans. Black and white photographs lined the walls in the foyer. As Hyacinth came back over I began to walk towards the photographs.

'Wait,' Hyacinth said, 'take Roderick with you. Let him show you around the museum.'

I stopped and turned back towards Roderick. He held his arm out and I took it.

'Let's look at the photographs first,' he said and Hyacinth slipped away to the other side of the room. I guided Roderick towards the mounted photos. Several shocking pictures awaited us; a picture of a young man lying on the ground holding an ancient rifle, his frightened eyes staring up at me; a group of skinny children sitting by a bombed-out classroom, their bellies distended, flies sitting on their faces as if *they* owned the faces and not the children. In another, a row of young men (perhaps only boys) standing to attention in raggedy uniforms, each one clutching a rifle. In still another, and most disturbing of all, a pile of semi-naked bodies in the back of a battered truck, two soldiers standing nearby, cigarettes wedged into the corners of their mouths, staring at me with the same frightened, lost eyes.

'The Biafra War,' Roderick said, seemingly knowing what I was looking at. 'The Biafra War was a civil war, Africans killing Africans. See what I mean about the darkness. Look into their eyes and you can clearly see it.'

I nodded and then, realising that Roderick could not see me, I said, 'Yes.'

'What did your father tell you about Africa?' Roderick asked, breaking the silence.

'To be proud,' I replied, looking up at Roderick's swirling eyes, glad to look away from the photographs.

'Why, my friend?' he said, his eyes looking toward the light streaming in through the window. 'Why would he want you to be proud of this?'

I looked again at the man with the staring eyes, clutching the rifle.

'Because he said I am part African. That's what I should be proud of.'

'Did he ever tell you *about* Africa?'

'No, he never did.'

'Do you know why?'

'No, I don't. Perhaps he didn't know very much about it. But he was African, wasn't he?'

'Yes, Fitzgerald,' he said, 'of course he was. Of that there can be no doubt. Come, let's move away from these pictures.' We moved away and I wasn't sure who was guiding whom. We stopped at a neat row of carved wooden masks hanging from a wall. I noticed the prominent features of one mask in particular.

'What do you see?' Roderick asked.

'A face mask,' I said. 'A wooden carving.'

'Let me feel it,' Roderick said and he reached out a hand. I guided it to the mask. He felt carefully, exploring every nook and cranny of the mask with his knobbly fingers. 'Touch it, my friend,' he moved my hand towards the mask. 'Feel the features.'

I did as I was told, feeling the nose and the cheeks and the bulge of the eyes.

'Now feel your own face,' Roderick said. 'That's how you really get to know a face. By feeling it. You can know good faces and bad faces just by feeling them.' I did as Roderick said and felt my own face. I had never really felt it before. I felt the slight bulge of my cheeks, the hardness of my cheekbone, the soft putty of my nostrils and the firmness of my forehead.

'How does it feel?' Roderick asked.

'Like the mask,' I said. 'Like the mask only softer. And the colour is almost the same as my skin; the colour is the same as afrormosia wood.'

'An African face,' Roderick said. 'A good face just like your father's. Your father was and always will be an African, you must hold on to that truth, Fitzgerald; you'll need it.'

'Even though he never actually came here?' I said.

'Yes, Fitzgerald, he always will be. Does a man have to remember being a baby to know he was once a baby?'

I frowned, puzzled.

'Do you have to have seen death to know that you, yourself, will die one day? That it is all of our destinies to one day die?'

I shook my head. A gecko ran out from behind the mask and scurried up the wall, disappearing behind a larger wooden carving.

'Then so it is with your father. Even though he knew very little about Africa, he knew enough to know that he *was* African. His spirit was African, Africa was inside of him.'

I stood still, watching the carving, waiting for the gecko to reappear. It didn't.

'It's inside of you too, Fitzgerald. You don't always have to *see* things to know they are there, that it's inside of you. Can you *see* the air that you breathe?'

I looked at Roderick's eyes, their whiteness swirled in his sockets like creamy coffee being stirred. I looked at his hands and at the walking stick so in need of repair.

'My mother once told me my father didn't really know where he was from,' I said. 'And I don't think he did. He used to go to his room and lay down for hours in the dark; I think he must have been thinking about where he was from when he did that. All he really knew was that he was part English and part African. And a little bit Irish too.'

'Nobody is part anything, Fitzgerald,' Roderick said. 'The sea is part salt but that doesn't stop it from being wholly the sea. Because a tree is part bark and part leaf is it any less a tree when its leaves fall off? No, it is still a tree. Is the sun any less the sun when part of it is hidden by a cloud?'

I looked over Roderick's head and at the window behind him. Shafts of sunlight poured in. Two birds swooped past the window outside, singing merrily as if discussing good news.

'He belonged here as much as anyone does and so do you, Fitzgerald.' Roderick smiled, his strong, white teeth contrasting Hyacinth's dental despair. I looked at my feet, the red dust sprinkled over my trainers, and I knew then that Roderick was right. Now that they had trodden on African soil I knew that I need never worry about the *Hinterland* again.

'Your father never came here,' Roderick continued, his eyes moving wildly in their sockets, 'but his spirit yearned for Africa. He was so troubled, so afraid of losing his Africanness. But he never did, Fitzgerald. It's not something that can be lost. Good or bad, dark or light, you can never lose it.'

The gecko reappeared and, seeking refuge from the light, scurried back behind the mask that looked like me.

Later I stood in another part of the museum, whilst Roderick and Hyacinth chose to sit down to rest, and I studied the many wooden carvings around me. There were hundreds of masks; carvings of men (with protruding belly buttons) and women (with hanging breasts). One piece in particular, a delicately crafted wooden walking stick, held me spellbound. I was fascinated by the intricacies of the carving. I thought of Roderick and the white tape hanging off his feeble stick. And I thought of his namesake Saint Roderick and how he had helped disabled people. As I looked at the carvings, a man crept up beside me. He was a small man with flat feet and an arched back. His hair was matted tightly to his head and his fingers didn't stop moving, as if he was being electrocuted. His hands were tiny, almost like a child's. He smelled of too much *Hai Karate* aftershave; I recognised it as the same brand that Uncle Albie wore whenever he visited us with one of his 'ladies'. The man coughed and then he swallowed. I could almost hear the phlegm sliding back down his throat. He stood next to me, looking at the carving.

'I wish my own hands were as big as yours,' he said.

'Thank you,' I said.

'Mine are small,' he said, the electrical charges still surging through his fingers. 'I've always wished I had bigger hands. You can get so much more done with large hands.' The man coughed again; this time I could see the ball of phlegm as he rolled it on his tongue before swallowing it. His fingers continued to twitch and he turned and moved away to another carving.

My own hands began to tingle and throb, as if the electric shock had been passed on. As I looked at the intricately carved

walking stick I felt the need to hold some wood; the tiniest flakes
of sawdust fell from my hands. The seed of an idea about what
it was I could create with my new hands began to germinate in
my mind. I looked at my afrormosia skin, and held my hand up
to the light and compared its colour to that of the carvings. Many
of them were so similar to the shade of my skin or darker. But
I noted that one in particular, a carving of a large man with a
child at his feet, looked distinctly out of place, its shade and the
grain altogether different from those around it. I knew the wood;
I knew the wood that the carver had used. I knew it was European
beech. And yet here it was comfortably positioned amongst a
multitude of carvings that were much darker in shade.

'Such a lovely carving, isn't it?' It was Hyacinth's voice. I hadn't
noticed them return.

'Yes, it is,' I said. 'It's European beech. The wood, it's European
beech.'

'What colour is that?' Roderick asked.

'It was the colour of my father's skin,' I said.

'And it looks so at home amongst all the other carvings, doesn't
it, Fitzgerald?' Hyacinth said.

'Yes,' I said. 'I suppose it does.'

We stood silently and looked at the carving. The man's hand
was resting on the child's head and the boy was playing with what
looked like a small toy. I heard a familiar rustling of paper behind
me. Hyacinth coughed and pulled out her crumpled bag of boiled
sweets. 'Does anyone fancy a sweet?' she said.

Little was said on our return to Lagos. The bus rattled over pot-
holes and rickety dirt tracks and the smell of stale sweat lingered
in the air around us like a bad idea. The heat had overwhelmed
Hyacinth and she quickly fell into a deep sleep, her teeth rattling
in her mouth each time we hit a pot-hole. Roderick sat beside her
fanning her face gently with a handkerchief until he too succumbed
to sleep. I spent most of the journey looking out of the window,
trying to take it all in; the teeming children trying to sell their
wares to every car that was at a standstill; the burnt-out lorries in

the bush on almost every bend we took; the scrawny goats tethered by the roadside and the green and yellow taxis driving as if the drivers were on some chaotic suicide mission.

After several humid hours, as we eventually began to near Lagos, Roderick awoke. Speaking quietly and without waking Hyacinth he told me what we would do on our return. We would, he said, take the red casket, the ashes, out to a little island he knew in the Blight of Benin, the bay surrounding Lagos.

'It's a small island,' Roderick said. 'So small it doesn't even have a name. It isn't included on any maps and most people don't even know that it exists.'

'Are you sure it does?' I said.

'Oh yes, my young friend,' Roderick said. 'I've learned in life that just because something does not have a name that does not mean it does not exist. Now, when you go be sure to take the unbroken piece of wood with you.'

I was not sure how Roderick knew of the unbroken piece of wood but it did not surprise me that he did. It didn't surprise me either that we were to take it with us.

To this day I am not wholly sure if I actually went to the island or if I only really dreamt of going there. Or perhaps I did both, the waking and the dream worlds merging together for a moment in time.

The little wooden boat pulled up on the sandy shore and the wiry Thomas jumped out, his webbed feet squelching in the wet sand. He grabbed hold of the helm of the boat and dragged it a few feet up the shore until it could move no further. It wedged firmly in the sand. I hopped out and held my hand out for Hyacinth who carefully stepped over the side, one hand holding mine, the other the red casket. The boat rocked slightly as she climbed out. I reached back into the boat and took out the unbroken piece of wood, still slightly damp. The wood was light and it was glowing again, slightly. I was struck also by the brightness of the colours around me. The sky was so blue that it looked more than blue, almost purple. The moon was still hanging in the sky like a white splodge of paint. The yellow of the sand was a hue that I had never seen before. All around me the colours seemed *more* than colours. Iridescent. I felt as if I could almost taste the colours. It was that *vividness* that may have led me to believe that I was perhaps dreaming.

'I will wait here for you,' Thomas said as he stood by his boat, eyes sparkling, droplets of clear water glistening on his skin. The sun shone brightly above his head.

'Nobody lives on the island,' Roderick had informed us. 'There's very little to actually live on. Unless you count the coconuts and fish from the sea.' As he spoke I was reminded of one of Mrs Freemantle's favourite records, one we often played at our house when she was feeling lonely or sad. When she was missing her Henry.

'Put this on the record player for Mrs Freemantle,' my mother would say to me, pulling a familiar LP out of our record rack. 'She's feeling lonely. We need to cheer her up.' And I would go over to our record player and put on the record. It was the *Best of Guy Mitchell* and Mrs Freemantle's favourite track was 'She Wears Red Feathers'. The album cover shows Guy Mitchell grinning from ear to ear. On 'She Wears Red Feathers' he sings about his island love who wears red feathers and a huly-huly skirt and lives on only coconuts and fish from the sea. My mother said that you could almost hear Guy Mitchell's grin through the record. 'He grins a lot,' she said, 'especially on that track.'

We would play the track through several times until Mrs Freemantle no longer felt sad and then she would return to her home and to her cats and to her memories of Henry. As she departed she would always take with her our copy of the record wedged firmly under her arm, Guy's face smiling happily out from the cover, the corners of his lips almost falling off the sides of his face. Yet again his singing had brought joy to the world. Joy to Mrs Freemantle. 'I'll just borrow it for a few days,' she would say, bringing it back a few days later, thanking my mother and giving Guy a quick peck on his cheek before my mother returned him to the record rack.

In the boat, as it crossed the bay, Thomas told us that the only people who came over to the island were the occasional fisherman and bereaved relatives who, like us, had come to scatter the ashes of their loved ones. Displaced Africans. It was, he said, a holy burial ground.

We left Thomas standing by his boat and walked up a steady incline. There was little on the island other than sand, lots of sand, littered with rocks and, in the centre, a thick area of forest. From within the forest I could hear the sounds of hundreds of birds, singing together like an orchestra rehearsing for a concert. The green of the trees glimmered in the sun and the slight breeze caused their leaves to shimmer and the smaller branches to bend slightly. I could smell a heady mixture of perfumes coming from within the forest.

I followed Hyacinth as she climbed, her head held firm, her scraggy neck muscles taut, her hands clasping the red casket. I wedged the unbroken piece of wood into the sand in front of me, using it as a walking stick. On reaching the top we stopped, Hyacinth breathing heavily, both of us sweating freely. We could see out across the bay, on the horizon stood the tall white skyscrapers of Lagos cloaked in smog. The sun caused the buildings to shimmer and shake, like a mirage in the desert.

'It's time, Fitzgerald,' Hyacinth said, handing me the red casket.

I nodded and took the casket from Hyacinth. It felt heavy, like a burden.

'Where shall I sprinkle him?' I asked, swallowing hard and looking at the rocky sand around my feet.

'Just here will be fine,' Hyacinth said. 'Open the casket and just throw the ashes out into the wind. The wind will take them to wherever they can rest. That's what the wind is for, my dear.'

'But there is no wind,' I said as the slight breeze circled my head. 'Only a slight breeze.'

'Then that's all you will need. Trust me.' Hyacinth then turned her back on me. I knew that I needed to do this on my own. I could hear the rustling of a boiled sweet being unwrapped and the sound of Hyacinth's teeth moving in her mouth.

I opened the red casket and looked in at my father's ashes. It was the first time that I had actually seen them. I was sure I caught a faint whiff of his baccy balls but I could have imagined it. I thought of his giant frame, of his baggy grey clothes, of his tight brown curls, of his freckles, of his large hands (the oars) and of his bright blue eyes and his light brown skin (the European beech). I looked at the meagre pile of ashes in the casket and I was shocked that a man of such vast proportions could be reduced to such a small pile.

I held the red casket at arm's length and tilted it slightly. 'I made it, Dad,' I said. 'We made it, Dad.' I hesitated, not sure I really wanted to let the ashes go and then I tilted the casket completely and allowed the ashes to fall. They fell slowly and gently; the first few ashes looked like the first flakes of snow in winter. As they descended towards the rocky sand, the breeze increased in force and began to disperse each tiny fragment across the island. I watched in wonder as every last piece was sprinkled by the wind in different directions, quickly disappearing. Soon it seemed as if the ashes had never been there at all, as if my father's huge frame had never existed and that now he lived only in my and other people's memories. His brief visitation; the vision, and my confidence in his place in paradise gave me some comfort, some hope, as his ashes disappeared, that I would see him again, but I knew for sure it would not be in the same form that I remembered him (that others remembered him). And I knew with an utmost certainty that I would never smell his baccy balls again. I would look at photographs of him in days to come (as would others) but no photograph could truly capture his vastness. Pictures of him as an adult would always have parts of his body cut off; the top of his head perhaps, or the edge of his arms or maybe his huge feet; the whole of his body could never be squeezed into the frame of any picture.

'Was he really that big?' some would ask.

'BIGGER!' I would reply, desperately trying to remember just how big he really was. People, I felt sure, would, as I grew up, comment on how much I reminded them of my father and that in some way he lived through me – 'Isn't he just like his father,' I knew they would say and I knew I would reply, 'But my father was much bigger than me.' And I knew they would nod in agreement when they acknowledged the truth of what I was saying.

The slight breeze died down, the ashes had now all gone. I stood on the steady incline with the empty red casket. I closed the lid, becoming aware of how hot it was, my shirt sticking to my back. I looked out over the sea and watched the birds swoop and dive through the sky. Down at the shoreline I could just make out Thomas waiting patiently, his lean body resting against his boat, his webbed feet splayed out in front of him. I felt Hyacinth's knobbly hand rest on my shoulder and I jumped; she had remained quiet throughout my ceremony and I had forgotten she was there.

'I'll leave you here for a while,' she whispered in my ear and I could hear the rattle of her stumps against the insides of her mouth as she spoke. 'I'll go and wait with Thomas. You'd better pick up the unbroken piece of wood. You don't want those hands of yours to become idle.'

I bent down to pick up the unbroken piece of wood; it was no longer damp.

'Here, take this, it'll get you started,' Hyacinth whispered, slipping a small frayed and dirty bag of tools into my palm. She then squeezed my hand, turned and slipped away quietly. I sat down on the dry sand and opened the bag. Inside was a small carving blade, an adze, a carver's mallet and several carving chisels. I removed my shirt and laid it beside me, allowing the sun to scorch my back and then I picked up the unbroken piece of wood and caressed it. Then, using the small blade, the African sun beating down on me, I began to carve.

XV

The Note

Our street looked desolate as Uncle Albie's Opel Kadett turned into it from North Cross Hill. It looked extremely grey. We had arrived back from the airport; Uncle Albie had been faithfully waiting there to meet us. The flight landed at Heathrow (an hour late) in the pre-dawn hours and we drove back through the waking streets of west and south London in almost total silence, speaking only to answer a few of Uncle Albie's questions about our trip. We went into London and back out again because Uncle Albie said he needed to collect some tools from a job he had been working on whilst we were away. I gazed out of the window at the mosaic of waking shops, newsagents and launderettes and the early morning streetwise London pigeons cooing as they bobbed about searching for breakfast on the litter-strewn streets. Uncle Albie always said that London pigeons carried knives to protect themselves.

When we reached the countryside and began travelling the few miles to Wistful, the sun was beginning an attempt to rise from behind a blanket of misty clouds. As we came over the Great Green Hills and the road rolled down into Wistful, to the northern arcs, I was struck by the contrast between the vibrant, dancing colours of Africa and the film of grey across the Wistful sky, even the trees were grey; as if the artist had run out of paints and decided to mix the black and white together and paint everything the same colour. By the time we reached our road a sheet of drizzle had begun to descend from the clouds, completing the desolate picture. I closed my eyes and tried to picture Africa but I couldn't find it.

Something was wrong. Uncle Albie's demeanour was wrong; he wasn't himself. He appeared to be trying too hard to be jolly, to be normal. I had the feeling that grim news was in the air. Hyacinth knew, I could tell she knew something was wrong, she'd stopped sucking her boiled sweets and her teeth were too quiet in her mouth. I asked Uncle Albie what was troubling him but he shook his head and said nothing.

As the Opel Kadett crept up our street I wound down the rear window and breathed in the smells. I loved the smells of our street. Despite the wonderful fragrances of my brief African visit I had missed the smells of my street. It was the smell of growing up. The dampness of the morning only added to my delight. A damp day in Wistful always woke my senses. The street was almost empty, the massed choir had long since departed, not even an echo of Mr Parker's trumpet could be heard. I could still picture in my head the people rocking from side to side, clapping and only Mrs Braithwaite clapping on the off-beat. A few of the children in our street were beginning to surface. It was a school holiday so many would be in bed for several hours yet. The Granite children came out of their door (they were always up early) and, turning on their heels, they strode purposefully together down the street whistling a tune in duet, I think it was 'All Things Bright and Beautiful', but I couldn't be sure. They were on their way to the newsagent. They always went together, early in the morning, to buy a copy of *The Times* for their father. Wayne Haynes hurtled down the street on his skateboard. It was a new skateboard he had bought just before we left for Africa.

'I've got a new skateboard,' he told Michael Sawyer and me as we sat on the wall together at Parson's Park (Wayne Haynes had been standing below looking up).

'What's wrong with the old one?' I asked (looking down).

'Nothing,' he replied. 'There wasn't an old one. I've never had one before.'

'Then why didn't you just say, "I've got a skateboard"?'

'I don't know.'

'Did you buy it from the shop?' Michael Sawyer asked.

'No. But my mother did.'

'Was it new?' I asked.

'Yes.'

'Brand new?' Michael Sawyer queried.

'Yes,' Wayne Haynes replied and he picked up the skateboard and walked away, disappearing behind the trees. We then heard the sound of his new wheels rolling over the gravel path as he hurtled off down the hill.

Neither Wayne Haynes nor the Granite children saw me as the Opel Kadett pulled up outside our house. Uncle Albie applied the handbrake, which was very loud and in need of some of his oil. I looked at our front door and noticed that it was slightly ajar. I could hear voices coming down the hallway and squeezing out through the slight gap in the door. I thought I could hear sobbing too. Or rather wailing. I climbed out of the back seat of the car and closed the door behind me. Hyacinth, who had been sitting in the front seat, also got out. She stood and looked at the open door. She too could hear the sobbing. The wailing. Uncle Albie turned off the engine and climbed out. He stood next to Hyacinth fiddling with the car keys. By now it was plain that the sobbing that came from within was indeed wailing. Uncle Albie looked uncomfortable. A crow cawed above our heads. We looked up. Its black body balanced precariously on a telephone wire (the wire that ran to our house). Its gaze was directed at us and for a few fleeting moments its eyes stared directly into mine. I shivered. Then the crow lifted its mighty black wings and flew off over the terraced rooftops screeching. I suddenly felt cold and my hands felt clammy. Hyacinth coughed.

'You'd better go in, Fitzgerald,' she said. 'I'll help Albie with the cases.'

I nodded, stepped up to the front door and pushed it open. The wailing was amplified, echoing frighteningly down the hallway. I knew it was my mother. I could hear two other voices, one male and one female. The female voice was cooing but her coos were drowned out by the ferocity of the wailing. I recognised the voices; Mr Plucker and Mrs Freemantle.

I eased open the front-room door reluctantly, a smell of anguish mixed with Rose Petal air freshener forced its way up my nostrils; the wailing penetrated my eardrums. Mr Plucker sat on the Wonky Stool of New Cross. The wonk of the stool forcing it to lean to one side, his wonky hip snaking out in the other direction as if trying to offset the stool's wonk – he struggled to keep his balance. He looked like a disfigured trapeze artist; an odder, less alluring version perhaps of Karina the Flighty who had run away with his precious gemstone of a wife. I saw then why my mother had never wanted him to sit on the wonky stool. It was frightening to behold. Mr Plucker looked up at me and nodded. The effort of nodding forced him to wobble on the stool slightly and I noticed a flush of panic spread across his cheeks when, for a moment, he thought he might fall.

Opposite Mr Plucker sat Mrs Freemantle. She was sitting on one of the threadbare chairs. The purple, pink and red of her floral-print dress highlighted the drabness of the chair, which looked even more threadbare than usual. The purples, pinks and reds were also the only real colour I had seen all morning. Mrs Freemantle was cooing and her own eyes were red from crying. She was rubbing my mother's back with an outstretched hand. My mother sat between Mrs Freemantle and Mr Plucker on one of the stools from my father's shed. Her body heaved with the force of her wailing. Her head was bowed but I could see that her face was wet with tears and flushed red. Snot dripped from her nose and hung suspended from the tip, pleading to be wiped off. I had not seen anyone cry quite so much or as loudly before, not even when my mother's grief had poured out like the rain outside the timberyard. In her trembling hands my mother held a piece of paper. It was damp from her tears and I could make out handwritten black ink on it, scrawled across the paper in large letters. The black ink had smudged in places. The paper shook as my mother held it.

Aware that I had entered the room, Mrs Freemantle looked up at me and smiled pathetically. 'Welcome back,' Mr Plucker mouthed silently but he couldn't sustain eye contact and let his woeful eyes drop to the carpet. Mrs Freemantle managed to keep looking at me but her eyes were vacant and a little fearful.

'What is it? What's wrong?' The unexpected boom of my voice shook my mother like a minor earthquake. A tremor. Her body trembled. The wailing ceased and, looking up at me, she tried to regain her breath, her usual breathing pattern, like a baby when it tries to stop itself from crying after having had a tantrum. My mother stared at me, her face puffy, wet and red. Her eyes were even more fearful than Mrs Freemantle's; they were like the eyes of a frightened child watching lightning from behind a curtain. Mr Plucker shuffled his slippered feet nervously and leaned further to one side. Mrs Freemantle continued to rub my mother's back with one hand and with the other she picked at a loose thread on the threadbare chair. The room was deathly quiet, the only sounds my mother's stifled breaths and the distant sound of a plane overhead on its way from the local airfield. I wished I were on it.

'What is it, Mother?' I pleaded. 'What's wrong?'

My mother looked at me, her eyes desperate. 'It wasn't an accident, Fitzgerald,' she spoke. 'It wasn't an accident! Grim news has caught me by surprise again!' She thrust the smudged note into my hands and my shoulders heaved as I held it. I felt somehow that its contents could change everything for me. I opened out the note and tried to focus on the smudged words, the handwritten words. My hand shook and I had to steady it with my other hand. The clock ticked behind me. It was too loud. A milk float pulled up in the street outside and I heard the pleasant and neighbourly clinking of milk bottles as our milkman, Mr Harper, withdrew a couple of bottles from his crates and placed them outside

Mr Plucker's door; Mr Plucker always had one gold top and one silver. I could hear Hyacinth and Uncle Albie outside chattering quietly and was surprised they had not yet come in.

Gradually, as my eyes adjusted to the words (unmistakably written in my father's large, sloping scrawl) the horror of what was written began to dawn on me. I felt a churning in my stomach as if someone was letting off fireworks in my belly.

Dearest Pauline (my LOVE),

I'm sorry but I feel I need to go away. I need to go far away. I've thought this through long and hard and it is, most definitely, the only way.

I love you very much (even more than my wood) but I can't go on.

I never knew my father and I never knew me. I am lost.

I feel I've got lost somewhere.

I think I've been affected by the HINTERLAND.

I feel I am lost in this world and need to return to a place where I can rest. I'm hoping someone will carry me HOME.

I wish my mother had told me who my father was, then maybe I could have found myself. I shall buy one more piece of wood and then I shall be gone. Don't look for me in Wistful, maybe you'll be able to see me in the wind or the rain (you know how much I love the rain in Wistful) or if I'm really lucky maybe you'll see me in the trees (the Beech or the Silver Birches). I hope that Fitzgerald (my beloved SON) will perhaps get the piece of wood. Let it be my final gift to him.

Tell him I love him. Tell him he should always be proud to be African. Tell him I'm sorry that I found it too hard. I will see you all again one day, I'm sure it will be in a better place. One day you'll understand.

Your loving husband.

p.s. Your jollof rice and moin moin are just great.

I felt like crying, I willed the tears to flow but none came. My hand continued to shake so much that the paper sounded like a kite flying in the wind (Clive Barrington would have been pleased). Mrs Freemantle prised the note out of my hand, allowing it to shake freely without the added distraction of the flapping sound. My mother looked at me forlornly, recognising the anguish in my eyes.

'It wasn't an accident, Fitzgerald,' Mr Plucker spoke and Mrs Freemantle nodded.

My mother dropped her head. 'He wasn't killed?' I said.

'He killed himself,' Mrs Freemantle said and she looked as if she was about to be sick.

My mother raised her head and forced the words out of her mouth: 'He must have taken his own life. I found the note in his favourite jacket pocket when I was clearing out the wardrobe. He knew I'd find it eventually. He must have planned it. He knew when they took deliveries at the grocer's store, God knows he went past it often enough whenever he went to the timberyard. He must have stepped under the wheels of the lorry on purpose.'

'But why?' I asked. 'Didn't you say that it was the wood that wooed him?'

'He was addicted to the wood all right,' my mother conceded. 'Even in his own death plans he had to be with his beloved wood.'

'But why would he want to kill himself?' I looked at the three faces before me and searched for answers. They stared blankly back at me, each trying to comprehend the tragedy before them. My mother dabbed at her wet face with a balled and damp handkerchief. Mrs Freemantle placed her hand on my mother's back again and kneaded it. I knew that in her head she would be reliving that fateful day outside the grocer's store, seeing the sickening angle of my father's broken neck and that also thoughts of her own beloved, Henry, would be resurfacing; his Dean Martin face shimmering in the corners of her memory. Mr Plucker, still teetering on the edge of the stool, would on the one hand be trying to fathom the mind of my father as he stepped into the path of the oncoming lorry and on the other would be reminded of his own lost love, Edith's disappearance with the well-balanced Karina the Flighty. I knew that Melancholia was whispering in his ears again.

'But you don't know that he killed himself,' I said, 'not from this letter. You don't know for sure.' I snatched the note back and shook it in front of their faces, trying to make sense of it all.

'He made it quite clear,' Mrs Freemantle said. 'He wanted to end it all. He wanted to go away. He took his own life, Fitzgerald! God rest his soul, he'll be damned for ever!' And Mrs Freemantle crossed herself several times.

'But you don't know that he killed himself. He could have meant that he was just going away,' I said.

'Then he would have told me,' my mother said. 'We talked about everything.'

'He said in the note that the pain was too much,' Mr Plucker said. 'That's not the talk of someone just going away for a break. I know about pain, Fitzgerald.'

'And where he would have gone?' my mother said. 'He had nowhere to go.'

'He'll be damned,' Mrs Freemantle said. 'He shouldn't have killed himself.'

'No he won't,' I said. 'He's safe, I know he is. And you don't know he took his own life, not from this note.'

'How do you know he's safe, Fitzgerald?' my mother said.

'Beacause I saw him. He told me. And I've scattered his ashes. Hyacinth told me he would be at rest now.'

'But he killed himself!' Mrs Freemantle shouted and again she looked as if she was about to throw up, as if the very thought of suicide was making her sick. 'You don't talk about being carried home and coming back in the trees unless you plan to end it all.'

'Maybe he was planning to go to Africa, maybe that was it. Perhaps he should have gone instead of me.'

'He would have told me,' my mother wailed. 'He would have wanted you to go with him.'

'Maybe he just knew he was going to die,' I said. 'Maybe he just had a premonition or something. Maybe that's what he meant by going far away. Maybe he knew his time was up.'

'No, *I* would have known,' my mother said. 'I could have warned him. I *always* know when grim news is in the air. I should have warned him.'

'Could you have stopped him buying his wood?' I said. 'Could you have stopped the lorry from being on Drummond Street? Maybe the note is just to warn you that *he* knew he was going to die. Maybe *he* knew that grim news was in the air.'

'Or maybe it's a suicide note, plain and simple,' Mrs Freemantle said and for the first time in my life I felt totally helpless and again my hands felt heavy.

'Or maybe he was planning to take his own life but the lorry hit him first,' I said but no one said a word.

The reality that my father could have taken his own life dawned on me. I'd seen the signs. I was in shock but I knew. I knew that he had so dearly wished that he could have known his own history or have had some contact with any of his unknown African relatives. I knew that he tried so hard to be proud to be African but in truth knew so little about it. But would that be reason enough for him to kill himself? His mother had never told him who his father was and even on her deathbed had never revealed his identity. I was in the kitchen eating toast and boiled eggs on the night my father came home from the hospice when Granna had died. He spoke to my mother in the front room. I couldn't see them but I could hear them. I knew that my mother was sitting in the threadbare chair picking at the threads and, from the way my father's voice kept moving around the room, I knew that he was standing. In fact he was almost wandering and pondering in the front room, pondering aloud.

'She's dead,' my father said.

'I realised that, love,' my mother said. 'What was it like?'

'Awful,' my father said.

'Death is awful, love.'

'I know, but I didn't feel anything, not for her. I still don't.'

'But you will, love. In time.'

'Will I, Pauline?'

'You will, love. Death is like that, it helps you forget the bad things about people.'

'I hope so, Pauline. I really hope so. She coughed so much, Pauline, I thought she was going to cough her lungs right up there in front of me.' My father's voice sounded weaker than I could ever remember hearing it before, like he had borrowed someone else's voice for the night. 'And she smelled, Pauline, she smelled so bad, of death. It was like death had already been visiting her over the last few weeks.'

'It probably had, love. It had probably been waiting in the shadows for her,' my mother said and I could hear her shift on the threadbare chair. I put a spoonful of egg in my mouth but it tasted hard and dry like I was eating cardboard.

'Did she tell you which one was your father?' my mother asked.

'No,' my father said. 'She told me about a dispute she was having with her neighbour about a wall. She told me about that instead.'

'A wall?'

'Yes, a wall. She said, when she had the extension added to her kitchen, her neighbour had complained that the wall was too high.'

'Too high?'

'Yes. He said it, the wall, cut out his light.'

'His light?'

'Yes. But Mother said that she needed her privacy. She didn't want him looking in whilst she cooked, whilst she dillied and dallied in the kitchen, that's why she wanted the wall to be so high.'

'And what did the neighbour say?'

'She didn't tell me what he said but she did say that, in her opinion, privacy was more important than light. She said privacy always won over light.'

'But that's not right, surely?' my mother said. 'And besides Granna's not been at her own house for months now.'

'I think it was an old dispute,' my father said. 'Nothing she said was in sequence. But she said that's why she wouldn't tell me who my father was. She said it was her life and her life is private to her.'

'But what about your life? What about your right to know, your right for some light to be thrown on your life!' My mother's voice was angry.

'Privacy is more important than light is what she said. She said that that part of her life is a closed book and she would never open it, not even for me,' my father said. 'She said she *really* didn't know which one it was and she really didn't care.'

I had swallowed the last piece of my toast quietly, I didn't want them to hear me in the kitchen. The toast tasted like cardboard too.

'She must have known,' my mother said. 'She was a woman, she would have known all right. She could have told you more.'

I knew, looking back, that my father had tried too hard to compensate for his loss but he'd had nothing tangible with which to hang it on. He was very much an African alone. A fatherless African. His arguments with my mother over food were perhaps the nearest he ever got to feeling he belonged to something identifiable; the buying of plantain from London perhaps gave him some hope. Telling me, his only child, to be proud to be African and seeing my eagerness must have given him some hope too, but I knew now that it was not enough. Not enough hope. I knew too of his all too frequent dark periods. Even as I remembered them I could recall the two smells; the smell of mental pain and the smell of lemon barley water coming out of his room whenever he had a dark period. God alone knew what thoughts possessed my father as he lay sipping his barley water, oozing dark despair from every pore.

We all loved my father – me, my mother, the nearest and dearest, even some of our neighbours. He knew that. I know he did. But it couldn't replace the loss of himself. He would often say he felt 'different'. Even at our parents' evenings at school I had noticed how shy and clumsy my father would become in Mrs Braithwaite's company, seemingly embarrassed of himself in her presence, fearing perhaps that she would sense what was missing and accuse him of being a fraud.

'I'm different,' he would say to my mother.

'Different than what?' she would reply.

'Than everyone around me, wherever I go.'

'No you're not, you're no different than anyone else.'

'I am, I'm different. I don't really belong here. I'm African.'

'But you're part English too. Besides it doesn't matter how "different" you think you are, I love you and so do lots of other people.'

But I would notice a faraway look in my father's eyes whenever they had that conversation, as if he was searching for something, himself perhaps. Sometimes on his return from one of his London trips I would hear him and my mother having a variation on the 'different' conversation.

'Even in London,' he would say, 'when I'm surrounded by hundreds of other black people, I still feel different.'

'Why?' my mother would ask.

'Because I don't know *how* to be black.'

'But you *are* black, well brown anyway. What are you supposed to *do*?'

'I don't know, that's the problem. I just don't know what to do.'

And my mother would shrug her shoulders; she wouldn't know what to say. They would stand opposite each other, silently, each thinking their own thoughts. I don't think even my mother could have known just how real the pain was that my father was carrying. His addiction to wood seemed to mask the pain. It would have been so much easier, more comforting to know that it was simply carelessness that had led to him falling under the wheels of the lorry as it delivered its rice and milk. It would have been so much easier to come to terms with. The grief would have been long and painful, but it would have dulled over time; a numbness would have set in. I was mature enough to know that now. There would have been no awkward explaining to do, either, to anyone who should ask how my father had died. I had already rehearsed in my head what I would say to anyone.

'Where's your father? Does he live away?' people would be bound to ask.

'No,' I would reply, looking directly at them, into their eyes. 'He was killed.'

'Oh dear,' they'd say, reaching out a consoling arm to me. 'And how did it happen? How did he die?'

'He was killed by a lorry delivering rice . . . and milk. It was an accident. He stepped into the road without looking. No one could have prevented it.'

'Oh no.' They'd make the appropriate facial gestures. 'Such a terrible tragedy.' And I would nod in agreement and wait for the temporary comfort of their soothing words.

Now, if Mrs Freemantle was right, if it was no accident, no tragic twist of fate but rather my father's own choice that he had ended up crushed beneath the wheels of a lorry, all that would have to change. Simple explanations would no longer be enough. I knew now that, if I was to believe Mrs Freemantle, my answer to their heartfelt questions would open up raw wounds for both the enquirer and me.

'Where's your father? Does he live away?'

'No.' I would avoid their eyes, looking instead at their nose or their mouth perhaps. 'He's dead.'

'Oh dear,' they'd say reaching toward me. 'And how did he die?'

'He killed himself. He took his own life. He threw himself under the wheels of a lorry.'

Their hands would shrink back, recoiling in horror.

'Oh no,' they'd say, the awkwardness now registering on their faces. They would not want to hear the answer to the next question but would feel compelled to ask it anyway. 'Why was that? Why did your father kill himself?'

'Because he was ashamed,' I would say.

'Oh,' would come the feeble reply and they would drop their gaze, avoiding my eyes, looking instead at their own feet. No further questions would be asked or words said. The awkwardness of death and shame would hang in the air like two filthy rags hanging out to dry on a washing line and I would think of the *Hinterland* once again and its part in my father's death. But now, after my own visit to Nigeria, I knew that my father had nothing to be ashamed of. I knew that he was as African as the most African of Africans. I knew that he didn't have to prove it. He just *was*. I wished I could have told him that. Before he had died. Telling him that I was very much proud to be African and that it wasn't just part of me that was but all of me and all of him too but I also realised that if my father hadn't died then I would never have known that. It was his death that gave new life to me. I wished I could have told him that it didn't matter if I ate *jollof* rice or fish fingers, that Mr Josiah and little Bobby needn't have taken our freezer away. I could have eaten them both, on the same plate!

I wished I could have told him that it was more than what I ate or what I did, more than the colour of my skin even, more than afrormosia, more than European beech. I knew now that since I had released his ashes his spirit would be free. Something in me knew, as soon as I released his ashes, that my father was home.

'But he's all right, Mother,' the words sprang forth from my quivering lips.

My mother raised her head, her face still puffy and red.

'He's all right,' I repeated. 'When I saw him he looked well enough. Now that his ashes are free, he'll be all right; the pain will have gone. He'll be stronger when we see him again, I know he will.'

My mother tried to stand, to come closer towards me, but she couldn't, her spirit crushed, her feet gave way. She sat back down heavily.

'How do you know?' she bleated. 'How do you know it was him you saw?'

'People see people after they're dead,' Mr Plucker said, 'but usually only in their head. It's a known fact, when they're grieving. I should know, I still see Edith every night when the lights go out.'

'I saw him. He spoke to me here in this room. It had to be him. Trust me. Hyacinth knows. Ask her.'

'Don't frighten your mother, Fitzgerald,' Mrs Freemantle said, rubbing my mother's back. 'She's delicate, can't you see? Stop all that talk about your father, about visions. Stuff and nonsense that's what it is. Now's not the time for that.

'And you can't be sure it was your father you saw, you could have been dreaming. It could have been your imagination.' And then she crossed herself again and muttered a prayer.

'I'm not trying to frighten you, Mother. I wasn't dreaming, it *was* him. He spoke to me, I told you,' I said. 'I'm just trying to make you feel better, to make you strong again. My father is with his Maker, I'm sure of it. Hyacinth knows. Ask her.'

As I spoke, the front-room door shunted open and Uncle Albie appeared, wheezing. He was holding my suitcase in one hand and the unbroken piece of wood, which I had now carved into the beginnings of a walking stick, in the other. He looked at us all, his eyes taking in the scene before him. We waited for Hyacinth to come in behind him but she wasn't there.

'Where's Hyacinth?' I asked, looking over Uncle Albie's shoulder and down the murky hallway.

'She's gone,' he replied and he loosened his grip on the suitcase and wiped the back of his palm across his nose. He had a slight cold. I could see the snot on his hand like a snail trail. 'She said she had important business to attend to, places to go. She said to say "goodbye" to you Fitzgerald and to you, Pauline. She asked me to tell you, Fitzgerald, to be sure you finish that walking stick. She said to tell you that it was only the beginning of your work. She also said that you should never be ashamed of your father. She said to say that he loved us all very much, *all* of us. She said to say that you should always be proud of him, Fitzgerald, and that you should always remember him whenever you feel the wind on your face or hear the rain tapping at your window. She said to say that whenever you look at a tree, remember your father.'

Mrs Freemantle looked up. 'How did she know?' she said. 'How did that woman know?' And she crossed herself again, several times.

Uncle Albie's words stung my face like fiery darts. I knew that I would never see Hyacinth again. She was gone. I turned to face my mother. She looked at Uncle Albie, her eyes misting over and then, dramatically, she fell from her stool, crashing to the floor. As she fell she clipped Mr Plucker, causing him finally to lose his battle with the Wonky Stool of New Cross. He too crashed to the floor. They converged together in a strange, tangled heap, Mr Plucker's legs wrapped around my mother's legs, causing them to look as if they were attached at the hip; Siamese twins. The Wonky Stool of New Cross had collapsed in the fall, the wonky leg itself having come completely away. As I looked at the strange heap my first thought was not to worry about my mother or even Mr Plucker but rather that I could easily mend the stool, maybe even make it better than it was before, take the wonk away entirely. Mrs Freemantle began to cry, her tears rolling on to her floral-print dress, and Uncle Albie dropped the walking stick and rushed to the aid of those caught up in the strange, tangled heap. Mrs Freemantle was still mumbling 'How did that woman know?' to herself.

Uncle Albie lifted my mother on to the orange sofa, loosening her collar and checking her for injuries as she came around. Mr Plucker, only slightly bruised, got himself up and sat down in the threadbare chair, his spindly hands shaking, his chest heaving, his hair sweeping across his face as if he was caught in a storm. 'We need something wet and warm,' Mrs Freemantle said as she slipped out into the kitchen to make a pot of tea. 'It will help to soften the shock.' She returned a few minutes later with the huge pot and enough cups and saucers for us all.

'There's some carrot cake in the tin by the cooker,' my mother managed to say as Uncle Albie puffed cushions around her making her comfortable, 'I made it this morning.'

Picking up the beginnings of the walking stick (the unbroken piece of wood) and the (broken) Wonky Stool of New Cross, I walked to the kitchen and opened the back door. A morning chill rushed into the room, pleased to get in from the cold, followed by the sounds of people beginning to wake up in the houses that backed on to our street. I could hear the shrill cry of a kettle boiling and what sounded like a large dog barking. I also caught the faintest whiff of frying bacon and thought of my mother's own morning bacon. I felt a slight pang of hunger but knew that food could wait and I let the pang pass.

'Where are you going?' my mother asked, easing herself into a more comfortable position.

'To the shed; to my father's shed,' I said and looked at my mother, deep into her eyes. She seemed to know that I had to go, and so did the others. 'No, I'm going to *my* shed. I need to get to work on this walking stick and the stool.'

235

'Do you want a piece of carrot cake, before you go? You've not had breakfast,' my mother whispered.

'No thanks, Mother, we ate on the plane. Besides, I've told you before, I don't like carrots.'

My mother and I looked at each other. She reached out and touched my arm and then pushed me gently out of the door. I smiled at her, seeing my reflection in her eyes smiling back at me and then I turned and closed the door firmly, leaving my mother, my nearest and dearest and the carrot cake behind me. I walked slowly towards the shed, the unbroken piece of wood wedged firmly under my arm.

XVI
Drummond Street

I read and re-read the note several times in the shed at the bottom
of the garden, trying to work out what my father had meant.
Then I folded it neatly and put it away in one of the drawers. I
picked up the unbroken piece of wood and continued to carve.
I used a combination of my father's tools (which were many) and
the bag of tools that Hyacinth had given me on the island (which
were few, and included the adze). It was still the school summer
holidays and I had several weeks left to be alone, learning new
skills. Sometimes my mother appeared outside the door of the
shed (which I kept closed) with either a plate of food or a cup
of milky tea or both. Usually she would be alone but occasionally Mr Plucker or Mrs Freemantle or my friend Michael Sawyer
would be with her.

'Fitzgerald!' she said once, rapping gently on the wooden door,
'Are you all right?'

'I'm fine, Mother!' I shouted back. 'It's going well! It's all just
fine!'

'Oh, all right!' my mother hollered, raising her voice to overcome the sounds of my carving. 'I've brought you food.' she
shouted. 'There's some meat-paste sandwiches, some tea and a
bowl of *jollof* rice!'

'Thank you, Mother!' I shouted back. 'Just leave it there and I'll get it in a minute!'

Another time, when Michael Sawyer was with her, he shouted, 'Hello, Fitzgerald! It's me, Michael Sawyer! Would you like to come out to go to Parson's Park or up to the bus garage?'

'No, Michael!' I replied, continuing my carving. 'I've got to finish my work! And besides don't you think we're a little too old now? For Parson's Park . . . and the garage? Next you'll be saying you've still got the wicker hats!'

'I suppose so,' he reluctantly replied. 'And no, I haven't got the hats! Aren't you going to let me in?'

'I can't, Michael!' I said. 'There's so much I need to be doing. I've got to be on my own!' And I heard him and my mother shuffle away. Michael's feet, in particular, sounded sad as they padded away up the path.

I enjoyed my time in the shed. It went some way towards helping me to overcome the pain of my father's death. I consumed the woody fragrances, the sweet, nutty smell of the oak, the ebony that smelled not unlike my mother's fried bacon. I caressed the pieces of wood with my hands and enjoyed sliding my feet through the piles of sawdust on the floor. At first, I just sat on the floor with the tools, working out their various uses. The tools that Hyacinth had given me; the adze, the small knife, the carver's mallet and the selection of carving chisels. They always felt particularly warm to the touch and were my favourite of all the tools. Sometimes I would feel my father's presence and was sure that he was guiding me and teaching me his craft. I never saw a vision of him again but I could *feel* him there with me. I wasn't addicted to wood either, not then, but I guess I was as close to being addicted to the wood as any boy of my age could be.

I began with the unbroken piece of wood. I sat in the middle of the floor with the wood between my legs, holding it in place with one foot and I continued to carve the wood into a walking stick that was beginning to resemble an African staff. I was barefoot, sitting on an old rug to protect me from the splinters. My trainers were discarded by the door, next to my father's weighty copy of *The Official Rules of Sports and Games*. When I wanted a break from the stick I worked on the Wonky Stool of New Cross. I completely removed the last shards of the splintered leg and discarded them and the broken leg itself in the large metal bin by the door. Then I smoothed the splintered edges, planing them down and set to work on creating a new leg, a wonkless leg. The wonk would be gone. From now on it would be known simply as the Stool of New Cross.

When I had corrected the wonk I returned to my carving, to shaping the walking stick. The stick was solid, hence its developing resemblance to a staff. I thought of the blind Roderick as I carved and knew that people like him would be able to *feel* the intricate carvings. There would be no need for any more feeble walking sticks with flaps of white tape hanging off them, like the one Roderick had been forced to use.

All the walking sticks I created were beautiful and all carved from a teak similar to the unbroken piece of wood. The teak was a tough, gritty wood and my tools would become blunt easily; I made sure to keep my chisels as sharp as possible, taking frequent breaks to sharpen them. I would grind the blades to remove the nicks and get them down to the correct bevel. I sharpened the tools on my father's sandstone wheel; I'd watched him do it many times so I knew how to use it. After the grinding I would hone the tools. It was hard work but it felt good. When the tools were sharp the wood felt like butter to carve. On each stick I carved images into the body and on the handles. I took the images from those that I had seen on my visit to the Beatific Museum; women with large, hanging breasts and prominent nipples; boys with protruding belly buttons; women with pots balanced perfectly on their heads and men with firm shoulders and full lips. I had some pictures too that I'd photocopied from magazines at the library and I had the pictures spread out on the floor around me and stuck to the walls; pictures of African carvings, faces from front and side angles for me to copy from. I carved proud, beautiful, solid Africans.

I began to carve the beginnings of a family, an African

family. A family to replace the family my father had never known. I carved two or three family members into each stick, surrounded by intricate patterns, and I named them all using names I had picked up from my visit to Nigeria. I also gave them status in relation to my father. They were his missing relatives: Achike, my father's uncle, a dreamer of dreams, extremely tall and with round cheeks and misty eyes (a man who loved my father with a passion and would ruffle his hand through his hair just like my father used to do to me); Nnamdi, my father's cousin, broad shouldered and bald (who was, like my father had been, and I was becoming, good with his hands and excelled at sport); Obiamaka, my father's sister, stunningly beautiful with dimples in her cheeks (who was the spitting image of my father but much more delicate and sensitive); Benedicta, my father's niece, a tiny, beautiful girl who had the largest, sparkliest eyes you had ever seen (and she could play the harp like an angel and sing like the birds in the trees); Chinwe, my father's other sister, who was very tall and looked nothing like my father (but was still as beautiful as a rainbow in a leafy glade); and Azikiwe, another uncle, square-jawed and with perfect teeth (a carver and a teller of tales who had travelled the world and back again).

When I'd finished carving, I stood back and looked at my work. It dawned on me that the actual work was in the chippings on the floor; what was left was everything I hadn't removed. It was as if I had found what I was looking for by removing all the wood that wasn't needed. That's what creating was, searching hard to find the very best. It was as if in my carving I had been searching for the family who could only be revealed as I carved. The carved family wasn't real. I knew that. I knew they only existed in my head and in my carvings. But in some strange way I needed them to be real, for my father. I needed the hope that if he had known them and been loved by them then perhaps he wouldn't have been so ashamed and would not have felt he had lost himself. I also needed them to be real for me. I needed them to exist to cement my new-found confidence in my own identity.

I needed them to guide me. And perhaps they *were* real, as real as any memory anyway; as real as any thought in my head.

I knew how much my mother, Uncle Albie, Auntie Nerys, Mr Plucker, Mrs Freemantle and my school friends loved me. And I knew that their love would be with me all the days of my life. They were my family but, with the exception perhaps of my mother, I knew that their love would not be enough. I knew that they would not know how to fully understand, and in some cases accept, all of me. I hoped that as I grew older I would gain the courage to return to Africa on my own. There would be no Hyacinth, no blind Roderick. I was sure I would never see either of them again. There would be no red casket either and no ashes.

If Mrs Freemantle was right, the shadow of my father's suicide would hang, like a hot-air balloon, over our tiny house. Visitors to our street, our neighbourhood, would see it hanging there and whisper about it in hushed, secretive tones and be shocked by the size of it and the amount of light it cut out from our house. Very few people know much about the mechanics of something so huge, so very few would cope with its awesome presence. Their conversations would be brief, their glances furtive, and then they would look away and hurry on to go about their business.

'Why did he kill himself? The carpenter?' a visitor would ask, gazing in horror at the looming shadow.

'It was something to do with being coloured; with being black,' would come the inevitable, misinformed reply. 'He didn't like it. He was ashamed, although to me he didn't look that black at all. Not black enough to want to kill yourself anyway.'

Several days after I finished the third walking stick, I gathered them up and took myself and the sticks to the top of the Great Green Hills, to the north of Wistful. I laid the walking sticks out on the grass in front of me and sat down. It was a sunny day and the sun burned brightly above my head. One or two of the trees around me were just beginning to shed their leaves in preparation for autumn and the occasional crispy leaf fell, tapping me on my shoulder and tumbling down my shirt before landing, gently, on the green grass. Clouds bobbed by in the sky and a flock of starlings weaved in between them. I took off my shoes and socks and let the air get to my feet. My toes wiggled, enjoying their release from captivity. I looked at my wiggling toes and was reminded of my father's own big, brown toes stretched out in front of the two-bar heater in our tiny front room.

My hands felt for the walking sticks and I began to caress them, my fingers wandering through the grooves of my newly carved family; a nose, an eyelid, an ear, tight wooden curls. The firm feel of the wood, the teak, pleased me. As I felt the wood, I was startled by my own ability to create such wonderful and elaborate designs. I was surprised too by the ease with which I had picked up my carving skills, by my own comfort in using wood. I looked up at the sky; the bright blue, the wispy clouds, and I thanked my Creator for my newly discovered skills. I thanked my father too. I picked up a small piece of bark from a tree and held it to the sky in thanks.

I sat and gazed out across Wistful. My eyes scanning the length and breadth of the town spread out before me, like a picture book, open at my feet. The northern arcs were just below me at the foot of the hills on the road that led into the town and I could just make out the southern arcs slightly obscured by the looming gas station to the south of the town. I could see the postal sorting depot on Frenarby Grove, completed now and in frequent use. As I had told Michael Sawyer, the days were long gone when we could jump from the heady heights, with our wicker hats strapped to our heads, into the damp sand below. A part of me wished they weren't. Beyond Frenarby Grove, I could just make out the bus garage on Franklin Street, the heavy green and cream buses spewing their fumes into the air. I thought of Timothy Drinkwater and his little sister, Lily. I could almost hear the creaks of her rusting tricycle. On the corner of Passover Crescent stood St Roderick's, stark and imposing, the red bricks glowing in the sunlight.

Further down the hill from St Roderick's stood Our Gracious Lady of the Morning Dew, nestling between Mrs Poetaster's and the Bingo Hall. I could see a matchstick figure coming out of the huge, oak-panelled doors at the front and I knew it would be Father Ferdinand holding his rosary beads in one oak-panelled hand, the eyebrow dancing wildly above his flickering eye. The sun bathed the stained-glass windows and the Blessed Virgin and her rainbow colours were reflected across the façade of the church, bright colours, beautiful colours, multi-colours. Starlings circled above the church, tiny specks on the skyline. I looked up at the sun, a burning ball, and knew that it was the same sun that had shone over Africa. Sweat sprang from my brow and my hands felt moist. I stood up and stretched my legs. I bent forward and picked up the walking sticks, tucked them under my arm and, taking one last glance over Wistful, began the long climb back down the hills.

When I reached the bottom I weaved my way back home through the brooding streets. On reaching Drummond Street, I walked up past the timberyard, the smell of the wood causing me to stop briefly just to breathe it in. As I passed the grocery store a lorry slowly drove up the road and turned into the cul-de-sac so it could pull up just outside to deliver its load. It wasn't going fast at all, only about thirty miles an hour or so. I stopped to look at the lorry just as Mrs Freemantle came out of the store. We didn't see each other, I was watching the turning lorry and she was looking the other way. We bumped into each other and my carvings fell to the ground next to her. She dropped a small package that landed by my foot.

'Oh, Fitzgerald,' she said. 'I'm so sorry.' She bent down, her tidy hair not moving and she began to pick up the carvings. I kneeled down too and reached for her package.

'Luncheon meat,' she said, looking at the package, 'for the cats. They've been so good this week it's their treat.'

The lorry pulled up, the brakes wheezing as if it was tired of driving and was grateful for the rest. The driver jumped out, his hands were small and his eyes were like little marbles. He saw

Mrs Freemantle struggling with the carvings and bent down to help. 'Thank you,' Mrs Freemantle said.

'It's a pleasure,' the man said and his eyes rolled in his head as if he was actually using them in a game of marbles. He looked at me holding the package.

'Luncheon meat,' I said and he nodded. Then he got up, wiped the dust from his knees and slipped into the grocery store.

'Let me take those, Mrs Freemantle,' I said reaching out for my carvings.

'No, no, Fitzgerald,' Mrs Freemantle said. 'It's no bother.'

'Well let me a least take some of them,' I said.

'All right then,' Mrs Freemantle said and she gave me two of the walking sticks and held on to the third. I gave her back her luncheon meat. 'Are you going home?' she said.

'Yes,' I said.

'Then I'll walk with you,' Mrs Freemantle said and we set off together, Mrs Freemantle holding the one walking stick and her luncheon meat, me holding the other two. The delivery lorry purred behind us as we walked away up Drummond Street. The driver had left the engine running.

When we neared my house, I was aware of the tinny jangle of a big band and a jiving beat coming from within my house. The front door throbbed and the house appeared to be shaking. I put the key in the lock and let myself into the hallway. The music enveloped us and I recognised the tune, it was Bix Beiderbecke's 'Baby Won't You Please Come Home', the distinct sound of the cornet so real it could have actually been in the house. I hurried down the hallway, clutching the sticks under my arm and pushed open the front-room door. Mrs Freemantle was close behind. The music pounded from the tiny speakers almost knocking me off my feet, Mrs Freemantle put her stick and the package down and held on to her hair as if worried that the music might blast it away or at the very least unsettle its tidiness.

In front of us, dancing all alone, her sandy hair twirling above her head, her ample breasts swaying pendulously, was my mother whirling and twisting to Bix's insistent beat. And as she jived, my